EDINBUR

Aga **blue** eyes were as brilliant as sapphires.

'Is it beyond your imagination that some actresses might *not* want a coronet? I am one of them. I answer to the stage, not to any duke.'

'Come, come,' he said. 'You're indulging in playacting now.'

Her eyes snapped blue fire. 'You seem to think a titled wife is such a prize. Why, I'd rather be a mistress than a wife to an aristocrat like you.'

'My mistress?' He raised a brow. 'At least you've made your price clear.'

'You're twisting my words,' she said through pinched lips. 'I merely mean to say that being a duke's wife is not what *every* actress wants.'

Author Note

I've always applauded the daring of great actresses of the past. Historically, ladies of the stage were considered not much better than ladies of the night. For centuries being an actress was a scandalous if not dangerous profession, and the most an actress might expect was to become a wealthy man's mistress. But in the nineteenth century this began to change. My interest was piqued when I discovered that a so-called 'epidemic' of actresses married into the aristocracy. The theatre became a marriage market as well as a playhouse.

Playing the Duke's Mistress is set in the theatrical world of Victorian London in the mid-nineteenth century. At that time many actresses were labelled title-hunters or worse—as Darius Carlyle, Duke of Albury, initially suspects actress Calista Fairmont to be. Yet not *every* actress wants a coronet…

Happy reading!

PLAYING THE DUKE'S MISTRESS

Eliza Redgold

MILLS & BOON

All rights reserved including the right of reproduction in whole
or in part in any form. This edition is published by arrangement with
Harlequin Books S.A.

This is a work of fiction. Names, characters, places, locations and
incidents are purely fictional and bear no relationship to any real
life individuals, living or dead, or to any actual places, business
establishments, locations, events or incidents. Any resemblance is
entirely coincidental.

This book is sold subject to the condition that it shall not, by way of
trade or otherwise, be lent, resold, hired out or otherwise circulated
without the prior consent of the publisher in any form of binding or
cover other than that in which it is published and without a similar
condition including this condition being imposed on the subsequent
purchaser.

® and TM are trademarks owned and used by the trademark owner
and/or its licensee. Trademarks marked with ® are registered with the
United Kingdom Patent Office and/or the Office for Harmonisation in
the Internal Market and in other countries.

Published in Great Britain 2016
by Mills & Boon, an imprint of HarperCollins*Publishers*
1 London Bridge Street, London, SE1 9GF

© 2016 Eliza Redgold

ISBN: 978-0-263-91697-3

Our policy is to use papers that are natural, renewable and
recyclable products and made from wood grown in sustainable
forests. The logging and manufacturing processes conform to the
legal environmental regulations of the country of origin.

Printed and bound in Spain
by CPI, Barcelona

Eliza Redgold is an author, academic and unashamed romantic. She was born in Scotland, is married to an Englishman, and currently lives in Australia. She loves to share stories with readers! Get in touch with Eliza via Twitter: @ElizaRedgold, on Facebook: facebook.com/ElizaRedgoldAuthor and Pinterest: pinterest.com/elizaredgold. Or visit her at goodreads.com/author/show/7086012.Eliza_Redgold and elizaredgold.com.

Books by Eliza Redgold

Mills & Boon Historical Romance

Enticing Benedict Cole
Playing the Duke's Mistress

Visit the Author Profile page at millsandboon.co.uk.

EDINBURGH LIBRARIES	
C0047131896	
Bertrams	18/05/2016
	£4.99
NT	DO NOT USE

For my muse, Nell Gwynne.
If she'd learnt to write she'd have penned a witty play.

And for my long-time friend Erika Jacobson,
playwright and fellow PhD finisher, who loves Nell too.

Acknowledgements

My thanks go first to my fabulous editor, Nicola Caws
at Harlequin Mills & Boon in London, who brought this
book into being. Thank you, Nicola, for your patience,
tact, insight and for your brilliant editing skills.
You are amazing!

Thanks to the Wordwrights critique group
for their comments on early chapters and to my critique
partner Jenny Schwartz, who calls a plot a plot—
writing would be no fun without our beachside
café meetings. I'd also like to express my gratitude to
the romance writing community, at home and abroad,
for their warmth and generosity.

Thanks also to my academic colleagues, including
those in the emerging field of 'Love Studies'.

Finally, thank you to all the romance readers worldwide
who keep the dream alive. Long live love!

*Who writes, should still let nature be his
    care,
Mix shades with lights, and not paint all
    things fair,
But shew you men and women as they are.
With def'rence to the fair, he bade me say,
Few to perfection ever found the way:
Many in many parts are known t' excel,
But 'twere too hard for one to act all well;
Whom justly life would through each scene
    commend,
The maid, the wife, the mistress, and the
    friend.*

Nicholas Rowe: *The Fair Penitent* (1703)

Chapter One

What! shall I sell my innocence and youth,
For wealth or titles, to perfidious man!
To man, who makes his mirth of our un-
      doing!
The base, profest betrayer of our sex!
Let me grow old in all misfortunes else,
Rather than know the sorrows of Calista!
Nicholas Rowe: *The Fair Penitent* (1703)

Covent Garden, London—1852

'No dinners with dukes,' said Calista firmly as she wriggled out of her costume and stepped into her petticoats, one lacy layer after another. 'You know my rule.'

'Please, Calista,' Mabel entreated from the other side of the painted screen. 'It's a private supper party.'

Calista's fingers trembled as she adjusted the

waistband of her top petticoat. She forced herself to keep a steady hand. She'd lost more weight and had to pull it tighter than usual. 'A private supper is even worse.'

She tossed a light cotton wrapper over her bare shoulders and tied the ruffled edges loosely across her corset. She knew she ought to put on her dress or even a woollen shawl, but her skin was still warm from the glare of the gas footlights.

Mabel's voice became a whine. 'I can't attend if you don't come with me. It's at the Coach and Horses, upstairs in one of those dining rooms. I'm longing to see it. Do you intend to keep me apart from Sir Herbert?'

Calista stepped out from behind the screen and sat down at the dressing table, resting her elbows among the pots and jars of creams and powders.

'Last month you were besotted with a marquis,' she reminded her friend, who was slouched on the *chaise longue* in a pink silk dressing gown. 'Now it's a baronet. It's actresses like you who give us all a bad name.'

She softened her reproving words with a smile. Mabel had a good nature, even if she did care more for flirtation than learning her lines.

Mabel giggled. 'A bad name has turned many an actress into a lady or a duchess.'

Calista sighed. Ever since a flurry of actresses

had married into the aristocracy, many young women had come to consider the theatre as no more than a marriage market. It made it very difficult for those who aimed to become the best at their craft, as she did. Gentlemen from the audience hung around by the stage door, making advances, which Calista was forced to fend off, sometimes politely, sometimes by calling the doorkeeper to hasten the men away. The members of the aristocracy, she'd discovered, the more time she'd spent in the theatre, were the worst. They seemed to think they had offstage rights to an actress, in some form of *noblesse oblige*. A few so-called gentlemen behaved as if she were no more than a lady of the night. Indeed, some seemed to think actresses and courtesans were one and the same thing.

Calista shuddered inwardly. She'd determined to stick to her rule more firmly than ever before since that awful incident that had occurred a few weeks ago. She'd told no one about it, not even Mabel. It still shook her to think of it, but she had to carry on coming here, carry on performing. She had no choice.

'I know you have your rule, Cally, but perhaps I'll be doing you a favour if you come to the supper party,' Mabel wheedled. 'It's true my dearest Herbie is only a baronet, but his cousin is a duke with an enormous fortune. Why, he's the Duke of Albury!'

'I've never heard of him.'

Mabel made a faint moan. 'He sounds terrifying. Herbie told me to bring along another actress to keep him company tonight. I thought of you immediately. You can cope with anyone.'

Calista picked up a pot of *crème celeste*, her favourite cold cream. It could remove the thickest powder and paint. She wanted to help Mabel. Beneath her friend's brazen exterior, Mabel's heart had been bruised more than once. Still she hesitated. 'Can't you ask someone from the chorus?'

'I could,' Mabel said doubtfully, 'but you're the leading lady. Herbie said the duke is frightfully intelligent and to pick someone who would keep him entertained.'

'I have no desire to entertain a duke,' Calista said crisply. 'He can pay to see my performance, like everyone else.'

'Please,' Mabel begged, her blonde curls falling over her dressing gown and her big blue eyes widening in the fashion that had brought her so many admirers. 'I'm scared to face the duke without you. You'll know the right things to say. Do come to supper, Cally. Herbie is the man for me. I know it!'

'I'm sorry, Mabel—' Calista started. With her

finger hovering above the pot, about to daub in the cold cream, she stopped halfway.

The rouge on her cheeks would come away, like her costume, like the part she played. It was always the same after the tumult of applause at the end of a play when the curtain went down. When she curtsied to the audience there was a moment when she came back, when she stopped playing a role and became her own self again. It was the strangest sensation, as though she was dropped back into her body from the flies above the stage. If that feeling ever disappeared she would give up acting, she'd vowed. It was a kind of vainglory to seek applause for Calista Fairmont. The claps and shouts were for the character she created on the stage, the other person she inhabited the moment she stepped out of the wings.

Tonight, she'd played Rosalind in Shakespeare's *As You Like It*. From the first until the final act she became the daughter of a duke, forced to pretend to be a boy and hide in the woods of Arden. It was a role that suited her well, the theatre critics agreed, not merely for her more-than-average height and slim figure, but because of her portrayal of Rosalind's intelligence and wit. She'd made the role her own.

Yet recently, coming back to herself at the end of the play had felt like a jolt. Tonight in particular she'd experienced a horrid sense of deflation as she had come off stage to become once more Miss Calista Fairmont, with all her troubles. It was as if a dark cloud had edged across the painted backdrop of a perfect blue sky.

In the looking glass, she studied her reflection and saw her fingers now clenching the pot of cold cream. Her hair had been pinned up while she'd played the part of a boy. Laying down the pot, one by one she released the hairpins.

Her black locks rippled over her shoulders, but the curls were limper than they ought to have been. They shone with less gloss than before. Once they had glinted as blue-black as damson plums, or so her father had declared. Columbine had asked if they tasted like plums, too, and their father had picked the girl up in his arms and laughed, declaring that surely his daughters were sweeter than any fruit, his Calista and his Columbine.

Columbine. Her young sister had caught a chill recently and it had given her a high fever. All day she had been red-cheeked, as she had continued to cough and wheeze.

Calista stared again at her own scarlet cheeks. At least the rouge disguised her pallor, and beneath her eyes the dark circles of fatigue were hidden by the layers of powder. If only she could sleep better. Lately all she could do was toss and turn all night. One worry would turn her one way.

Then when she flung herself over, yet another would grip her.

Somehow, she must carry on. It might be better to try to keep her spirits high. A supper party would be a diversion from the constant cares that gnawed at her, and Columbine would be asleep at home; her sister and Martha didn't wait up for her, not any more. In happier days there had been supper by the fire, a chance to talk and to share the play's successes and failures. But now she walked alone.

Alone.

Her breath squeezed through her lungs. Fear had entered into her body, ever since…

No. She refused to think about it.

She put her hand to her chest and tried to breathe. This choking grasping of air must be what Columbine experienced when she had one of her terrifying attacks. Perhaps it would be good to be with company tonight and she could go part of the way home with Mabel after the supper party.

It might be safer to walk a different way.

There was no reason to hurry home. It was best to let her sister sleep peacefully, even if she could not do the same any more, and she was hungry, too. She might be the leading lady of the Prince's Theatre and earn wages that were higher than those she had got for playing bit parts, only speaking a line or two, but the pounds weren't stretching nearly far enough. The cost of warm lodgings, food, the doctor's bills…all now had to be covered by her income alone. She often pretended to have eaten supper before going home, in order to save the price of a meal. No wonder that beneath the rouge her cheeks were hollowed and fitting her slim body into a boyish costume was easier than ever.

Another long walk alone followed by a restless night full of worry suddenly seemed more than she could bear. Doing Mabel a good turn might take her mind off her cares.

Calista laid down her hairbrush. 'All right.'

Her friend, who had slumped miserably on the *chaise longue*, stopped twirling a long golden ringlet in her hand and sat up eagerly. 'What?'

'I'll come and have supper with the Duke of Albury, but I can't promise to entertain him.'

'You'll come?' A waft of rose enveloped Calista as Mabel leapt up and hugged her. 'Oh, I'm so grateful, Cally, and my Herbie will be, too. You won't regret it!'

Calista sighed as she put the lid back on the unused cold cream. Already she suspected she would.

Darius Carlyle, the Duke of Albury, stretched out his long legs and waited for the actresses to enter the private dining room of the Coach and

Horses Inn. The small wood-panelled room, where the oak was scratched and rubbed worn in some places, was safely upstairs, away from the crowd at the tables and bar, yet noise drifted up through an open, lead-paned window from the street below. The fog had crept in earlier in the evening, but it barely muffled the sounds of raucous voices and laughter that rang out all night in this part of London.

Inwardly he groaned. He could be in his comfortable club right now, or at home in his bed in his Mayfair town house, the thick curtains drawn. Why had he allowed himself to get caught up in his younger cousin's affairs yet again? It wasn't the first time he'd been forced to rescue Herbert from some kind of scrape. Darius had been rescuing him ever since their childhood, when they had attended the same boarding school, and it seemed he was still forced to do so. Herbert was a fool, but he was a Carlyle. As head of the Carlyle family it was up to Darius to sort things out, as usual. No Carlyle would get into this particular mess ever again.

Actresses. His cousin could always pick them. They were like showy birds, fine feathered, their cheap clothes brightly coloured, with too much paint on their faces.

And they always had claws.

Now one of them had got her talons into Herbert and it didn't sound as if she was going to let go.

She would be made to let go, if he had anything to do with it.

He picked up his whisky glass and tossed back the remnants. He'd use the supper party as an opportunity to assess how far the situation had gone. It would be better to be cruel than to be kind and nip the affair in the bud. He was fonder of his cousin than he cared to admit, always had been. But it was his duty to ensure the Carlyle name wasn't dragged once more through the mud of scandal. It wouldn't be pleasant, but it had to be done, and Darius never shirked his duty.

Herbert fancied himself in love, but he hadn't yet made the mistake of proposing to the girl—not that it would make any difference if he had. Proposing marriage to an actress could always be hushed up as long as there was enough money thrown about to muffle the gossip. Actresses could always be bought off. He knew that much.

Darius drummed his fingers on the table. The only question was how much money it would take. Tonight he would find out how greedy and ambitious the actress who'd hooked Herbert was.

Tonight he would put an end to Herbert's infatuation.

The Carlyle curse must be broken.

The door of the private dining room opened.

In came the actresses, two of them, followed by Herbert.

Darius's lip curled.

The woman with whom Herbert was currently besotted entered the wood-panelled room first. He'd caught a glimpse of her with his cousin before. She wore a purple feather in her improbably golden hair and a low-cut dress that displayed her ample bosom to full effect.

Beaming with pride, Herbert stepped forward. Beneath his sandy hair he'd never lost the plump round face of his childhood. He looked like an excited schoolboy holding an iced bun. 'Darius, may I introduce Miss Mabel Coop.'

'Your Grace,' she said in an accent that made him wince. She swept low into a curtsy, displaying even more of her deep cleavage.

Herbert's eyes popped.

'Charmed.' For a moment Darius wondered if his cousin had gone mad. Could any man willingly contemplate a lifetime of listening to that voice?

He turned to the other, taller woman who had entered the room.

Darius frowned. The young woman's face was simply covered in paint. Her cheeks were a bright red and she wore thick powder over what appeared to be a fresh complexion. Why did actresses get themselves up in such a fashion? He loathed such artifice.

However, her garments were less showy than her friend's. She wore a grey woollen cape and beneath it a dress of dark blue that only revealed the upper part of her *décolletage*. She was thin, too thin for his taste, although her collarbones, he noted, were particularly delicate.

His eyes returned to her face. To his surprise she met his gaze with deep-blue eyes fringed with dark lashes. Her expression held a hint of humour, as though she was aware of his rapid assessment.

Unexpectedly he experienced a flare of physical attraction. He suppressed it instantly.

'I'm Miss Fairmont,' she said after a moment, when it appeared Herbert was unable to wrest his attention from the charms of Miss Coop for long enough to perform introductions. Her voice was low and husky, with no discernible accent.

'Eh, what?' Herbert stammered. 'So sorry, allow me to introduce you properly, Miss Fairmont, to my cousin, the Duke of Albury.'

Darius inclined his head. 'Delighted.'

In reply she made a sketch of a curtsy.

He frowned again. The young woman appeared to be well schooled in manners. Her curtsy held unexpected dignity. There was no flash of cleavage from her, but a dip with a straight back that would present well even at court. Yet the gesture held a challenge. It was not insolent, but showed a certain self-possession that spoke of independence.

He watched as she removed her cloak and laid it on a chest by the door. Yes, much too thin, he thought, as she moved towards the table in the middle of the room, but her walk was elegant, almost mesmerising. She was nowhere near as obviously pretty as Miss Coop, yet it was she who held his attention.

'Do sit,' Herbert urged. 'Supper will be brought momentarily.'

Like a butler, he pulled out a chair for Miss Coop, who rewarded him with another flash of cleavage.

Darius returned to his place at the head of the table, already set with a white cloth, plates and cutlery. Miss Fairmont sat at his right, Miss Coop at his left. From the left he smelled a floral fragrance, so strong it could spoil the bouquet of a good wine. From the right, to his relief, it was clear that Miss Fairmont seemed not to have doused herself in cheap scent. She sat with her back straight, her hands in her lap.

'Would you care for some champagne, ladies?' Herbert asked. He brandished a bottle from a melting bucket of ice.

'Ooh, yes,' said Miss Coop.

Miss Fairmont shook her head. Darius also declined. Instead he poured a little more whisky into his glass from the bottle he'd ordered up earlier. He'd need it tonight, even if drinking whisky at dinner wasn't the done thing. In such company he supposed it barely mattered, although he noticed Miss Fairmont gave his glass a perceptive glance.

'I've ordered lobster,' Herbert told Miss Coop as he shook out his napkin.

She clapped her hands. 'Oh, that's my favourite, Herbie!'

Pet name terms already, Darius thought grimly. Mentally he'd already estimated an amount to offer Miss Coop. He nudged the price up a few hundred pounds.

'Do you care for lobster, too, Miss Fairmont?' he asked the young woman seated to his right.

'Yes, thank you,' she replied.

'We're always starving when we come off stage, aren't we, Cally?' Miss Coop giggled.

'Well, it is hard work,' Herbert said admiringly. 'I say, you were very good tonight.'

'I spoke two lines,' Miss Coop said proudly.

'You were marvellous. And so were you, Miss Fairmont,' Herbert added hastily.

Miss Fairmont smiled. It was an unaffected smile with no vanity in it, which was unexpected from an actress. 'Thank you.'

Darius gave her a sideways glance. Again she coolly met his gaze.

'Did you have a speaking part, too?' he enquired.

Miss Coop squealed. 'A speaking part? Calista has the main part!'

Darius raised an eyebrow. 'You do?'

She nodded.

'Miss Fairmont is quite famous,' Herbert explained. 'I thought you knew.'

'My apologies,' said Darius.

'It's quite all right.' The corners of her mouth curved. 'I wasn't familiar with your name either.'

He drew back.

'I take it you're not a theatregoer.' She seemed unconcerned that he hadn't heard of her. She didn't pout or exclaim at his ignorance. Instead she reached for her glass of water and sipped. Her lips were pink and full.

Darius shook his head. 'I don't care for playacting, Miss Fairmont.'

He became aware of her studying him as she replaced her glass on the table. Her head was lowered, but he sensed the acuteness of her dark-blue stare.

'Miss Fairmont has played many roles of note,' Herbert went on. 'Juliet, Rosalind, Ophelia…'

'And the fair penitent?' Darius asked.

Her head jerked up. 'You recognise the source of my name. I thought you said you disliked the theatre.'

'Not the theatre, Miss Fairmont.' He glanced towards Miss Coop. 'Play-acting is what I despise.'

When she spoke, Miss Fairmont's voice held a sharpness that brought him back to look at her. Her lips had tightened. 'I understand.'

Now he could sense her fragrance as heat reached her cheeks, making them even redder. The scent of her warm body reached him, too, along with the faintest waft of lavender from her hair.

'I don't understand!' Miss Coop exclaimed. 'What on earth are you two talking about?'

'My name, Mabel,' Miss Fairmont replied swiftly. 'It comes from a play by Rowe, called *The Fair Penitent*.'

'The main male part is Lothario, I believe,' Darius drawled.

'The seducer of women, yes,' she flashed back in reply. 'The kind of man who sees all women in one light.'

'I told you my cousin was clever,' Herbert said proudly to Mabel.

'You did, Herbie.' She beamed at him.

'Perhaps he isn't as clever as he thinks,' said Miss Fairmont.

Her head was held high, revealing the bird-like shape of her collarbones and her long neck. Darius was reminded, suddenly, of a swan that glided on the lake at his country home. It had bitten him, once.

Herbert looked from one to the other. 'I say, what's the matter?'

'Is something wrong, Cally?' Miss Coop asked.

'We're here under false pretences, Mabel,' the actress said with scorn. 'For all his contempt of play-acting, the duke has turned in a fine performance.'

Mabel Coop's hand went to her bosom. 'Herbie, what does she mean?'

'I've not the faintest notion,' Herbert replied, slack-jawed.

'Ask your cousin to explain,' Miss Fairmont said.

There was a scratch at the door and suddenly two of the inn's servants entered, bearing aloft silver-domed platters. They laid them on the table.

'Leave the lids,' Darius ordered when one of them made to begin serving.

He waited until the servants had left the room. No doubt they would hover outside the door to listen to the conversation between two gentlemen and a couple of actresses. It made it all the more pressing to end this affair immediately. Herbert clearly had no idea what he was getting himself into.

Beside him he noted Miss Fairmont's slender fingers were gripped together.

'I suppose we can get straight down to it, Miss Coop. I had hoped to handle this with some finesse, but since Miss Fairmont presses the point…' A glare in her direction was met with an answering flash of her eyes. With effort he wrenched his attention from her to focus on the blonde actress. 'You're a young woman of obvious charms, Miss Coop, but if you have ideas about marrying my cousin Herbert I'm afraid I must put them to rest.'

Her big eyes instantly brimmed with tears. 'What? Oh!'

'I say, Darius,' Herbert protested. 'We're here for a pleasant supper. Steady on.'

Darius ignored him. 'I'm the head of the Carlyle family. My cousin will under no circumstances marry an actress.'

'What do you have against actresses?' Miss Fairmont demanded from his right.

He twisted to face her. 'Must you force me to be blunt?'

Her chin tilted higher. 'Please. Let's not playact.'

Darius shrugged. 'Actresses are no more than title-hunters.'

Miss Coop gave a shriek.

'That's an outrageous thing to say.' Miss Fairmont hardly raised her voice, yet the anger in it reached him. 'Women have been on the stage since the days of King Charles the Second. How long will it take for us to be granted respect for our craft?'

'Acting isn't a craft,' he said scathingly. 'For women, it's merely a version of the oldest profession, at which they are well versed.'

'Men are actors, too,' said Calista.

'Male actors act,' Darius conceded, with a derisive look at Mabel's *décolletage*. 'Females of the species merely display their wares.'

'Now, Darius,' Herbert blustered from the other end of the table. 'That's a bit much.'

Darius took up his glass of whisky. 'Miss Fairmont is correct about my motivations. My desire is not to spend time in the company of actresses. It is to discover the price of avoiding such company in future. Let's get down to business. How much money will it take to ensure you leave my cousin alone, Miss Coop?'

Now tears trickled down the blonde woman's chin into the crevice of her cleavage. Her bosom heaved.

Miss Fairmont leapt to her feet. Except for the two spots of redness in her cheeks her complexion appeared pale, almost waxy. 'You're being extraordinarily rude. Don't speak to my friend in such a manner. You have no right. You don't know her.'

Darius banged his glass down and stood. Miss Fairmont came to just above his shoulder.

'I know of actresses. Every actress in Covent Garden wants to marry a lord or a duke. It's become an epidemic. Perhaps you're the same. Are you angling for a title, too?'

'How dare you!'

'Lady Calista. Countess Calista. Duchess Calista,' he mocked. 'Is that why you're here tonight? Is that your secret hope, like all actresses?'

Against her white skin Miss Fairmont's blue eyes were as brilliant as sapphires. 'Is it beyond your imagination that some actresses might not want a coronet? I am one of them. I answer to the stage, not to a duke.'

'Come, come,' he sneered. 'You're indulging in play-acting now.'

'Not at all,' she said. 'My family goes back four generations on the stage. I have a lineage as proud as yours. My mother and grandmother were actresses, and my father...' her voice wavered '...my father was a playwright. You'll never understand what the stage means to me. You talk of the actresses who left the stage to marry into the aristocracy. I'm sure many of them regretted it and longed for the stage when their husbands refused to allow them to act again.'

'As I'm sure many aristocrats regret their marriages to actresses,' he shot back. 'I've seen it myself in the circles of my acquaintance. It never works. It leads to ruination. As head of the family it's my duty to ensure no Carlyle becomes embroiled in such a disastrous match again.'

Her eyes snapped blue fire. 'You seem to think being a titled wife is such a prize. Why, I'd rather be a mistress than a wife to an aristocrat like you.'

'My mistress?' He raised a brow. 'At least you've made your price clear.'

'You're twisting my words,' she said through pinched lips. 'I merely mean to say that being a duke's wife is not what every actress wants.'

'Every actress has a price.' He spun on his heel and faced the sobbing Miss Coop. 'Well? What's yours, Miss Coop?'

The actress's lower lip wobbled. 'I just wanted some lobster.'

Darius released a stab of a laugh.

Miss Fairmont moved swiftly around the table. Even in anger her walk maintained that elegant glide. 'Come along, Mabel. We're going home.'

'Herbie…'

Herbert's napkin fell to the floor as he stood. 'I'll call on you tomorrow, Mabel,' he said nervously. 'I promise.'

'Come now,' Miss Fairmont urged, helping her friend up and pressing a white handkerchief into her hand. 'Please. Don't stay here for such insults.'

Over her shoulder she cast Darius a look of

scorn. 'I only hope no actress ever has the misfortune to become your wife.'

'What a performance.' Darius lifted his glass to her. 'You're almost convincing, Miss Fairmont. Bravo.'

Miss Calista Fairmont slammed the door behind them.

Outside on the street Calista pulled her cloak around herself. Beside her Mabel still sobbed.

Never before had Calista been quite so furious.

Title-hunters! How dare he!

The way the Duke of Albury had treated her, as if she were beneath contempt, as if the craft she poured her life and soul into was nothing. To accuse her of only wanting a title, when she went to such lengths to avoid exactly such entanglements!

If he only knew…

Tears stung her eyes. Her fatigue, an exhaustion that went deep into her bones from weeks of worry and lack of sleep, combined with the aftershocks of rage, left her trembling. To have to defend her profession against such aspersions was intolerable.

No dinners with dukes, Calista resolved anew. Never, ever again.

Chapter Two

*When that great man I loved, thy noble
   father,
Bequeathed thy gentle sister to my arms.*

Nicholas Rowe: *The Fair Penitent* (1703)

'Cally? Are you awake?'

Calista's eyes were open before the second word was out. 'Columbine. What time is it? Are you all right?'

Columbine snuggled into her arms. Even from beneath the bedcovers Calista could feel how thin and frail her sister was. She was much lighter than an eight-year-old should be. She hardly made a dent in the mattress.

'It's nine o'clock and I'm very well today,' Columbine said brightly. 'I feel much better.'

Calista laid her hand on Columbine's forehead. It was true, her temperature had dropped and the hectic flush had gone from her cheeks.

'I didn't hear you come in last night,' her sister said. She slept in the other larger room with their maid, Martha. By day it served as their sitting room, kept warm by the fire. Her own room was little more than a cupboard and a chill one at that.

'I was later than usual,' Calista explained. 'I went out to supper with Mabel.'

'I like Mabel,' said Columbine, burrowing deeper into the bed. 'She always gives me sweets when I come to the theatre.'

Calista sighed, thinking of her friend. Mabel was kind-hearted, and she insisted she was in love with Sir Herbert Carlyle, or so she had declared all the way home after the disastrous supper party. Her infatuations didn't usually last too long, but that didn't excuse the behaviour of the Duke of Albury.

The memory flashed in her mind, followed by a blast of anger.

Actresses are title-hunters.

Calista winced. Over and over the phrase rang in her head. It had stung more than the duke might guess. It was galling to think in what contempt he held her profession. She'd never had such sentiment spoken to her face although she knew what people said behind her back. It hurt.

She raised her chin. The opinion of the Duke of Albury wouldn't put her off her life's vocation. She would continue to hone her craft until actresses had the respect they deserved, no matter what men like him believed.

At dinner the night before—not that they'd actually eaten anything—she'd studied him. She always studied new acquaintances carefully, for she'd learnt they might have a manner or trick of speech she could later bring to life in a character on stage. Yet, to be honest, it hadn't been for her craft that she'd watched him. He was a man who compelled attention.

Tall. Broad shouldered. Immaculately dressed in a dark evening jacket, a claret-coloured velvet waistcoat and pristine shirt so white it rivalled new-fallen snow. His evening trousers had been pressed, his shoes polished. She'd noted he wore a crested gold signet ring on the small finger of his right hand. It was a strong, large hand, a whip hand. It was clear he was a man who expected to be obeyed instantly. He could have been a performer himself, having that rare presence a great actor must possess in order to maintain the interest of the audience. His height, his deep voice and his dark good looks would make him a perfect stage hero.

No.

Not a hero.

A villain.

Scraps of dialogue Calista wished had come to her before had kept her awake until nearly dawn.

She'd jotted down a few of the lines in the loose-leaf folio she kept on the table by the bed. Her father had always told her that the best play-wrights wrote constantly, not just when they were working on a play.

'Use all your emotions to write,' he'd told her. 'The same as when you're on stage.'

She had no trouble conjuring up emotions when she considered the Duke of Albury, she thought as she gritted her teeth. She could still taste her fury.

Yet for an odd moment, when their eyes had first met, after his almost insulting survey of her face and figure, she'd felt a connection spring to life between them. Something tentative and hope-ful that had evaporated in the blast of his arro-gant rudeness.

Calista pushed the thought of the duke away and focused on her sister snuggled beside her. When she'd found her father's half-finished play in his papers she'd determined to finish it. The play was an adaptation of a story, so it was pos-sible for her to pick up where her father had left it. Somehow, continuing his work kept his presence alive. Today, she had planned to write more, but it was Columbine who mattered most. 'I don't have a matinee performance this afternoon. Would you like to go to Hyde Park?'

'Oh, yes, please!' Columbine leapt up, sending

her long black braids flying. 'It's hard to be indoors all day with only Martha for company, not that she isn't very kind to me,' she added hastily. 'But I love to spend time with you best, Cally. Can we take a picnic luncheon?'

'If you like. Go and ask Martha if she will cut us some sandwiches.'

'She might even put in some seed cake.'

'I'm sure she will.'

Columbine scampered from the bedroom.

Calista lay back against the pillows. From the window opposite, pale sunshine beamed into the small room. The April showers had passed, and now it was Maytime, her favourite season. Summer was at last coming to bring some warmth to the London streets. The cold winter had been terrible for Columbine's health and Calista had wished she had the money to send her young sister to a warmer climate for those long, cold months. But she couldn't leave the theatre and take Columbine to Italy or France, where the air might clear her lungs. Nor could she afford to send her abroad with only Martha, loyal maidservant that she was. She was more than a maid, really. Martha had nursed Columbine since their mother had died, and had cared for them both as best she could in the cramped rooms Calista rented. Ever since their father had gone Martha had always tried to refuse the few coins Calista gave her each week.

Calista bit her lip. Last night when she'd told the duke that her father was a playwright, as she'd said it, she realised she had used the past tense.

Had she given up hope?

Perhaps it was time to face the brutal truth.

Her fingers gripped the edge of the linen sheet. She couldn't. Not yet. She would continue his work and care for Columbine until their father came home.

Yet day by day it became harder.

And more frightening.

She pulled up air through another of those painful, chest-tightening breaths. The tiredness from the night before hadn't disappeared, and she almost wished she might snatch a few more hours sleep. But it would do her more good to see Columbine play in Hyde Park. Perhaps there would be a Punch and Judy show on such a fine day, or even a brass band playing.

A sunny day in the park would drive the horrible words of the Duke of Albury from her mind.

Darius awoke.

A vision flashed before his eyes.

Dark hair.

A long neck.

A bite.

The same face had appeared when he had
fallen into bed the night before. He'd sent his
valet, Hammond, away with a quick word and
stripped off his garments to lie awake for longer
than the amount of whisky he'd consumed had
promised.

At the Coach and Horses Inn, when he'd seen
off the actresses, he had expected to feel satisfaction. Instead, as Miss Fairmont had slammed
the door of the private dining room, he'd experienced a quick surge of emotion he couldn't put
his finger on.

Compunction?

Regret?

Surely not remorse?

He ran his hand through his hair. He'd had to
come down hard on silly little Miss Coop, with
her obvious designs on his cousin Herbert.

But he wasn't entirely sure Miss Calista Fairmont was quite the same type of young woman.

He'd been more harsh towards Miss Fairmont
than he meant to be. She'd been caught in the fir-
ing line. The Carlyle name meant everything to
him and he didn't intend to let anyone ruin it. But
he'd come at her with pistols blazing and though
she had fought back with a few fine shots of her
own, he hadn't intended to treat her in quite that
manner.

Had he come on too strong? No, he decided. It

had been necessary. Cruelty was often kindness in the end. Herbert had to be protected from himself and Miss Fairmont had unfortunately been caught up in it all. Normally he would never have spoken to a woman in such a manner, but drastic action had been called for.

She was only an actress. Yet he had to admit, she wasn't what he expected from an actress.

Again the vision came.

Dark hair.

A long neck.

And an air of dignity that would have befitted a duchess as she defended her friend.

There it was again. The damnedest thing.

Remorse.

That was it. Remorse.

It wasn't an emotion with which Darius was overly familiar, and it was damned uncomfortable.

He shrugged it off along with the eiderdown and seized a dressing gown before he rang for Hammond to arrange his morning shave and breakfast.

It couldn't be helped. The situation had called for speedy action on his part. No actress was going to marry into his family and Herbert did appear to be particularly attached to Miss Coop.

His cousin's reaction after the actresses left the

dining room had only reinforced Darius's view that he had needed to act, and act decisively.

'How dare you speak to Mabel that way,' Herbert had stammered, red-faced. 'You've gone too far this time, Darius.'

'I've done you a favour,' Darius told him curtly.

Herbert would see it his way in time.

His cousin would probably be at their club that afternoon. Darius would talk to him again and convince him a quick cut to break the attachment would be better for all concerned. He'd always been able to guide Herbert. After all, it was his duty to keep him out of trouble, and his affection for his cousin meant he would do whatever was needed to ensure Herbert's future happiness.

Darius looked out the window. The day was fine, too fine to spend entirely indoors. This morning there were business matters and correspondence to attend to, but in the afternoon he decided he'd go for a walk in Hyde Park.

Darius ran his hand through his hair again.

He possessed a strange urge to see the swans on the lake.

Calista breathed in the fresh air.

Already she felt like a different person. The air and sunshine was like a tonic. Her fatigue seemed to melt away like ice cream in the sun. Even though she'd lost writing time, she had needed the outing and Columbine needed it even more.

She pushed back her bonnet and lifted her face to the warm rays. May had arrived at last. The garden beds were bursting with bright flowers, including daffodils and the first of the bluebells. Squirrels darted among the trees and one delighted Columbine by peeping out from behind a tree near their picnic blanket. They'd spent a good few hours in the park and as every minute passed Calista felt her spirits lifting.

The park was full of people enjoying the weather. Riders clip-clopped past. Couples strolled together arm in arm or sat on the benches. There were children playing with hoops and balls, and feeding the ducks. Swans glided elegantly across the lake.

With a much lighter picnic basket in hand, Calista was making her way to the Punch and Judy stand where Columbine was watching the puppet show when a man spoke from behind her. 'Miss Fairmont.'

She turned. 'Yes?'

The owner of the voice, a portly man wearing a red-spotted cravat, beamed at her. 'I thought it must be. You are Miss Fairmont, are you not, who has charmed us all lately with your performance of Rosalind in Shakespeare's masterpiece at the Prince's Theatre?'

Calista smiled. It was impossible not to smile at the man. 'I am.'

'My dear!' he exclaimed. 'You were quite marvellous.'

'Thank you,' she said. 'You're very kind.'

'It's not kindness, Miss Fairmont,' he protested. 'You're an ornament to the stage!'

He bowed and gave a cheery wave. 'Good luck to you, my dear!'

Calista watched him disappear down the path. At least someone appreciated what she was trying to achieve. The man's praise almost took the sting from the duke's cruel words about actresses merely showing their wares.

Almost, but not quite.

Darius strolled through Hyde Park, glancing idly at the assortment of groups dotted over the lawns. On the grass, children played under the supervision of nannies who were clustered together chatting. He spotted one or two courting couples. Others were families. All of whom appeared happy and smiling as they took their picnics in the park.

Darius felt the familiar pang before he supressed it instantly. Surely the contented family tableaux he witnessed were a farce. They couldn't all be as happy as they seemed: these mothers fussing over their offspring, fathers trying to hide their beams of pride behind their moustaches. Two boys were being instructed by their father how to fly a kite while a laughing mother rescued her toddler whose face was smeared with jam from almost falling into the lake. A small crowd of children were gathered by a Punch and Judy puppet-show booth.

Darius stopped in his tracks.

Standing at the back of the crowd was the actress, Miss Calista Fairmont.

There could be no doubt it was her, although she didn't look like an actress today. In the fresh afternoon air she wore no powder and paint, no garish or florid colours. Her plain grey bonnet was pushed back from her head, revealing her dark hair that shone almost blue-black, like the sky at midnight. In a grey cloak and simple frock with white lace at the collar she looked more like a governess than a star of the London stage. Yet to him it seemed as if she were lit up by footlights.

She had a young girl beside her, who had hair the same colour as Miss Fairmont's, worn in two long braids that hung over a shabby tweed coat. The two were clearly related. They were watching the show and the girl was laughing.

Then Miss Fairmont laughed, too.

She had barely smiled the night before at the supper party and so he hadn't realised: Miss Calista Fairmont was beautiful.

Her warm laughter lit up her face. She glowed. Like a candle in a darkened room. Like a light one was drawn to, as if it could make you warm inside.

Darius stepped closer. Intent on the puppet show, she didn't notice him.

Her cheeks were pale today, though there was pinkness in her face, no doubt from the fresh air and her laughter. Her fresh complexion, presented in its natural state, made him realise she was younger than he'd first thought. She must not be much more than twenty years of age.

She wasn't much more than a girl. Yet her dignity made her seem of greater years.

Now he saw that dignity was a permanent part of her posture, bred into her bearing. It hadn't been put on the night before. And there was something else. In spite of her excellent deportment, for such a young woman she appeared to be burdened with care. It didn't cause her shoulders to bow, or that long neck, but it was there in the set of her face and the way she anxiously watched over the child beside her. At her age surely she ought to have appeared light of heart, here at a puppet show in the park.

But Calista Fairmont wasn't light-hearted. Even as she smiled that glowing smile he sensed she was troubled. Beneath those sapphire eyes were dark shadows, too deep for a woman her age, and they told of sleepless nights.

Darius frowned. Perhaps the shadows under her eyes told of a debauched lifestyle. But gazing at the young woman who hovered with such obvious concern over the child at her side, he suspected that wasn't the case.

Again that uncomfortable feeling came over him.

Remorse.

He slammed it away.

No matter how young and unaffected she looked in the park, Miss Fairmont was still an actress.

He turned away. What could he say to her? He had to protect Herbert and he had done what he needed to do, even if he regretted that this woman had suffered his scorn in the process.

Darius pulled his coat tighter. The air had suddenly chilled. As he walked back to his club in St James's he became even more determined. No actress was going to get her claws into a Carlyle again. He would convince Herbert to give up Miss Coop before he got in too deep. Darius knew more than any man that actresses were title-hunters. There was no doubt that Mabel Coop would destroy his cousin, his reputation and his happiness. Darius had to prove it.

* * *

The square was quiet as he approached the club. The doorman bowed as Darius entered. 'Your Grace.'

Darius dragged off his gloves and greatcoat. 'Good afternoon. Is my cousin here?'

'I believe so, Your Grace. In the drawing room.'

The room was packed. Given the excitement in the air, there appeared to be some sort of high-stakes game happening. Occasionally Darius would join a green gaming table, but whilst he usually won at cards, right now he wasn't in the mood.

He nodded the curtest of greetings to one of the players seated at the felt-topped table.

Francis, Lord Merrick. Darius curled his fists. He'd never liked him, not even at school. No, that was an understatement. Lord Merrick was the ringleader of the same group of young pups who had given his cousin Herbert so much trouble in his childhood. Frankly, men like Merrick had given both the school and the club a bad name.

Merrick was the worst of the lot. The man lacked any sense of honour, of *noblesse oblige*. But at least he'd been prevented from making Herbert's life a misery.

Darius had seen to that.

Now, Merrick leaned over the card table. He

wore his sandy-coloured hair too long, an affectation Darius despised, and his pale blue eyes were set too close together as he studied his cards. Nothing was ever pinned on him, but Darius always suspected him of dishonest dealings. There had been a few grumblings of unscrupulous circumstances.

Passing by the players, he spotted Herbert seated at a table by the window overlooking the garden square at the quieter end of the room. Some of the inhabitants were reading, some having tea or a taste of something stronger in the all-male environment, doubtless avoiding the female-dominated ritual at home. Many men used the club as a hiding place.

Herbert stood up. 'Darius. I've been waiting for you.'

Darius raised an eyebrow. Herbert's tone was surprisingly determined. His cousin was also drinking whisky before six o'clock.

'Shall we sit?' he enquired.

'I'd prefer to stand,' Herbert replied obstinately. 'See here, Darius. I've got a few things to say to you about Mabel.'

'You've seen her today.' Darius sighed.

Herbert's eyes boggled. 'How did you know that? Never mind. The thing is, I'm going to ask her to marry me and you're not going to stop me.'

Darius hailed a passing waiter. 'Whisky.'

He faced his cousin. 'Let's sit down. We can't have a conversation like this at paces.' More than one pair of eyes watched them from over the tops of newspapers.

'Now,' he said, when he had a cut-crystal glass of the amber liquid to match Herbert's. He hadn't wanted the drink particularly, but requesting it had given him time to gather his thoughts. It was a useful strategy, making Herbert wait and increasing his tension and uncertainty. His cousin was easily ruffled, easily persuaded—something Mabel Coop had most likely discovered. 'What's all this about? I suppose Miss Coop has spent the afternoon crying prettily on your shoulder, playing on your sympathy.'

Herbert grew red. 'She was most distressed by your callous treatment at supper last night. I spent the afternoon comforting her.'

Darius could just imagine.

'It made me realise it was time to speak up for myself. But it wasn't Mabel who made me decide to stand up to you. It was Miss Fairmont.'

Darius choked on his whisky. 'Miss Fairmont?'

Herbert nodded. 'I've never seen anyone stand up to you like that, Darius. She has inspired me to do the same.'

Darius hid a groan behind his glass. 'For goodness' sake, Herbert. The woman is an actress. It was all part of a play.'

Herbert shook his head obstinately. 'The woman was magnificent. It ought to have been I who stopped you insulting Mabel. I've been a coward, letting you run my whole life.'

'You were grateful enough for my help at school,' Darius reminded him. Besides Merrick, he'd fought more than one bully on Herbert's behalf and had a few scars to show for it. Not that he'd ever begrudged his cousin the effort. He'd defend any Carlyle. 'And I intervened with that barmaid at Oxford…'

Herbert set his chin determinedly. 'I'm not a schoolboy any more, or such a stupid fellow. Mabel makes me feel like a man.'

'Can't you see she's playing you for a fool?' The words exploded from Darius's mouth. In the drawing room, a few heads turned. He lowered his voice. 'Actresses are all alike. You know our family history. They'll say anything, do anything, to marry into the aristocracy.'

'That's not true,' Herbert stammered. 'Why, Miss Fairmont told you last night she'd never marry a duke.'

Darius gave a bark of derision. 'That was acting at its finest! I promise you, she is a title-hunter like every other actress. I tell you, if I paid court to Miss Calista Fairmont, she'd accept my marriage proposal.'

He remembered she had said she would be his

mistress before she'd be his wife. Darius slammed down his glass. A ridiculous assertion. Of course she wanted a coronet. He ought to know.

Herbert shook his head. 'From what Mabel said today Miss Fairmont wouldn't let you make her an apology, let alone a proposal. And you owe her one for what you said last night about actresses, you really do.'

Darius stared at his cousin, amazed. 'What on earth has got into you?'

'I told you. Miss Fairmont is my inspiration.'

He gritted his teeth. This Miss Fairmont was clearly an actress to be reckoned with. No wonder she had the lead role at the Prince's Theatre. She'd certainly managed to hoodwink his cousin.

'Have you proposed to Miss Coop yet?' he demanded.

Herbert shook his head. 'Not yet. I was hoping you'd allow me to choose a suitable ring from the family vault.'

The thought of an actress wearing the family diamonds made Darius drain his glass of whisky in one gulp. He'd seen enough Carlyle jewels on grasping fingers to last a lifetime.

He thought fast. He had to stop Herbert making a hasty decision and a disastrous mistake, falling prey to the Carlyle curse. All he needed was some time. This affair would soon fizzle out, he was certain of it.

Then it came to him.

The vision flashed again before his eyes.

Dark hair.

A long neck.

Darius leaned across the table. 'Listen to me, Herbert. I'm right about these actresses. Let me prove it.'

'How would you do that?'

He smiled with an unexpected sense of anticipation. 'I'll pay court to Miss Calista Fairmont.'

Herbert's jaw fell open. 'What?'

'It will be a sham courtship, of course,' Darius explained quickly. 'She's declared openly that she will never wed a duke, but if I can persuade her to accept a marriage proposal from me, surely you'll have to agree that actresses only want one thing. A title.'

'You can't play fast and loose with Miss Fairmont's affections that way!' Herbert exclaimed.

He shrugged. 'If she's as good an actress as you claim she is, she'll see through my play-acting efforts.'

'Well, that's impossible,' said Herbert. 'You'll have no chance with her. Why, Merrick has been after her for months and even he hasn't had any success. And you know what a way he has with the ladies.'

Darius glanced over towards the card table where the rogue seemed to be engaged in some debate over the winnings. He'd clearly had too much to drink.

'Merrick is after Miss Fairmont?'

Herbert nodded. 'He's very keen on actresses, very keen indeed. He's a regular at the stage door of the Prince's Theatre. And Miss Fairmont's the star of the stage, of course.'

Darius drummed his fingers on the table. So, Merrick had been unsuccessful. He had to admit that only added to her charms.

'Quite the prize,' he murmured. 'Well, well.'

'I tell you, you won't get anywhere with Miss Fairmont,' Herbert said stubbornly.

Darius sought his cousin's gaze and held it. 'Give me some time. If I fail, and you still to want to marry Miss Coop, I'll not stand in your way. But if I persuade Miss Fairmont to marry me, you must promise to think again.'

Herbert averted his eyes. 'Mabel won't like waiting.'

'Some time, that's all I'm asking of you. Surely you owe me that much. I've never steered you wrongly before.'

Herbert's eyes flickered towards the group playing cards. 'I appreciate everything you've done on my behalf in the past.'

'Waiting won't make any difference to Miss Coop's affection for you, surely?'

'I suppose not,' Herbert said a little doubtfully.

Darius raised his glass. 'Miss Fairmont will consent to marry this duke. I'll prove to you what actresses are.'

Chapter Three

Yet mark me well, young lord; I think
  Calista
Too nice, too noble, and too great a soul,
To be the prey of such a thing as thou art.

Nicholas Rowe: *The Fair Penitent* (1703)

'Another fine performance, Miss Fairmont.'

Calista spun around to see a tall shadow emerge from the dark laneway into the light of the stage door. The Duke of Albury.

Tonight, he appeared even taller than he had in the private dining room of the Coach and Horses. He wore a top hat and a coat made of broadcloth with wide lapels that emphasised the breadth of his chest. A paisley-patterned necktie was folded four-in-hand beneath his jaw. But his arrogant face with his winged eyebrows and the hard line of his mouth were the same.

The stage door swung closed behind her. She stepped into the lane, but stayed in the light.

'Your Grace.' She couldn't ignore the man or pretend they had no acquaintance. Instead she inclined her neck as little as politeness could possibly allow. 'I'm surprised to see you again. Particularly at the theatre.'

The duke shrugged. 'Let's say I've become intrigued. I'm ashamed not to have witnessed your talents on the stage before, Miss Fairmont. Your work is something to behold.' He stepped closer. 'I'd like to talk to you, if I may.'

Calista bit her lip. It was never her way to be rude, but she owed this man no politeness and she was exhausted after her performance. She'd got caught up in a discussion about props with the theatre manager and by the time she had removed her costume she had been much later than usual leaving the theatre.

Apart from the duke and the stage doorman, who was a few feet away, busy picking up playbills dropped by the audience to re-use the next day, the alley was empty, thank goodness. Some of the terror that had tightened her chest abated. Usually this area was filled with a crowd waiting for cast members to appear, but the rest of the actors had already gone home or on to further merriment for the night.

She had no time to waste with the duke, nor the

energy to duel with him again. He'd already demanded enough of her attention. The sting of his words from a couple of nights before had hardly subsided. The sight of him only reignited her indignation. 'There's nothing you might say to interest me.'

He raised an eyebrow. 'Not even an apology? Why, Miss Fairmont, don't you owe it to common courtesy to listen?'

'It was you, not I who forgot common courtesy the other night,' she retorted.

'Then I must prevail upon you to allow me to make up for it now.' He took another step towards her, closing the gap between them. She could see him more clearly now, even in the dim light from the door. Around his mouth were two brackets that suggested the hard line of his mouth could break into laughter. She found that difficult to imagine.

'I believe I owe you not one but two apologies, in fact,' he said smoothly. 'The first is an apology for not having seen you perform on stage before. It was my loss. You played an exceptional Rosalind. You were—remarkable.'

'Thank you.' She inclined her bonnet an inch. If he thought she was going to be appeased by flattery for her performance, he was very much mistaken, and she couldn't help feeling suspicious.

The line of his mouth curved. 'You're the first actress I've ever met who doesn't appreciate praise.'

'I thought you avoided actresses,' she replied swiftly.

He released a dry chuckle. '*Touché*, Miss Fairmont. It's true I have limited acquaintance with ladies of your profession.'

She raised an eyebrow of her own. 'Yet you seem to have such set opinions about them. Perhaps you ought to learn more before you make such outrageous allegations in the future.'

'That's precisely why I'm here,' he said to her surprise. 'But let me make my second apology. I ought not to have made such comments about your profession and offered money to your friend.'

Heat surged thought her body just recalling the incident. 'It was an insult. Not just to Mabel, but to all actresses.'

He bowed. 'Allow me to express my regret.'

Calista stiffened and tugged her cloak more tightly around her. Something about the way the duke spoke was unconvincing. She could always tell. Her ear was attuned to insincerity, for a line spoken without conviction would never ring true on stage. Was he mocking her?

'Thank you for the apology. But it doesn't sufficiently excuse your behaviour, especially as a member of the aristocracy. You have only made me more determined to avoid your kind in future.' She sketched a curtsy. 'Good evening, Your Grace.'

Her skirts swirled as she made to move past him.

'Miss Fairmont. Wait.'

Slowly she pivoted.

His coat billowed behind him and in a single stride he was once more beside her.

'Yes?'

'It seems I need to be more honest with you.' He paused. 'I'm the head of the Carlyle family. I told you that last night. But my cousin Herbert is my personal responsibility.'

'In what way?'

'Herbert had some trouble when he was younger.' He appeared to choose his words with care. 'I took it upon myself to look out for him.'

She studied him. 'And you still do.'

He inclined his head.

'Your cousin is a grown man,' she said.

'So I've been reminded by him. But old habits die hard.'

Once again she studied his face. This time in his dark eyes she saw honesty and more. 'You're fond of him.'

He nodded. 'He's a foolish fellow at times. But I must own it. I am fond of him.'

'I have a younger sister. She means everything

to me. If she was in trouble, I know I'd intervene on her behalf,' Calista admitted.

'Then you understand family duty,' he said.

'Yes. I do.'

Silence filled the misty air between them.

'Herbert is easily influenced,' the duke said after a moment. 'I'd hate to see him duped.'

Calista stepped back. 'That may be so, but it still doesn't give you the right to speak to anyone in such a manner. And it doesn't excuse what you said about actresses.'

'Perhaps all actresses aren't the same,' he conceded.

Was he sincere? Doubt wavered inside her, but she knew it would be ungracious not to accept his apology. After all, he'd come to the theatre to watch her performance, then waited for her in the cold night air.

Calista held out her gloved hand. 'I accept your apology. I'm not one to hold a grudge.'

He took a step backward. For a moment she thought he wasn't going to take her proffered hand. Then he reached out his own. His leather-clad fingers enclosed her own. His hand was large, his grip firm.

'Thank you for being so understanding,' he said. 'It's most gracious of you.'

His fingers trailed across the woollen palm

of her glove. Even through the fabric she felt the heat of his touch.

Rapidly she withdrew her hand. 'I'd defend my sister, Columbine, and Mabel, too, so I understand your impulse to protect Herbert. And you're wrong about actresses, you know.'

He raised a sardonic brow. 'Am I wrong about Miss Coop?'

He seemed to discern her inner struggle to find an honest reply. Mabel could be flighty; there was no doubt about that. Calista had witnessed enough of her flirtations, and there had been many, and they often ended in tearful disaster. Whether this affair would last with Sir Herbert was difficult to predict. Yet surely the two of them deserved a chance at happiness, without the interference of the Duke of Albury.

'Mabel has a good heart,' she said at last. 'She believes herself to be in love with your cousin.'

A smile darted at the corner of the duke's mouth. 'A most diplomatic answer.'

Calista felt her own mouth turn upward. His gaze followed the curve of her lips.

She felt a flicker, deep inside her, followed by instant wariness.

Calista pulled her cloak over her body. 'Well, goodbye. Thank you for coming to the play and for your apology.'

'I hoped you might take supper with me,' he said suddenly, to her surprise.

No dinners with dukes. She'd broken her rule once in this past week and she wasn't going to make that mistake again. She ignored an unexpected shaft of disappointment at the thought. 'Thank you, but I can't accept your invitation.'

'I can promise you might actually eat some lobster this time.'

A laugh burst from her lips. The supper two nights before had held some comic elements, she realised now. 'Lobster is more to Mabel's taste than mine. But it's late and I must go home.'

If he was disappointed by her refusal, he made no sign of it. With his hand raised he moved towards the street. 'Allow me to call you a hansom.'

How she longed for a hansom cab to carry her home safely, but the money could never be spared. Every shilling she spent on herself was money she would be unable to save for Columbine's care.

Quickly she shook her head. 'I prefer to walk.'

His eyes narrowed. He lowered his raised hand.

'Then perhaps you will allow me to accompany you to your lodging,' he said smoothly.

'What?'

'Do you think dukes don't walk? The streets of London are open to everyone.'

'But…but my home is a good distance away.

The walk does me good after performing,' she added as an explanation. 'Fresh air, you see.'

'There's fresh air in London? Then I'm sure it will also do me good.'

Was that slight curve of the duke's lips another half-smile? In the dim gaslight Calista couldn't be sure.

The burly doorman returned to his post. 'All right there, Miss Fairmont?'

'Yes, thank you, Fred.'

The man settled back against the doorframe, his arms folded.

The duke raised an eyebrow.

'There are sometimes gentlemen who won't take no for an answer when they ask an actress to dinner,' Calista told him quietly.

'Indeed?' He frowned. 'I will accept your refusal, but I hope you won't give me one. You will come to no harm in my company. You've already encountered my more undesirable characteristics. I may bark, but I don't bite. Not often at least.'

Calista bit her lip. Her instinct was to trust the duke. How could that be, after his behaviour the other night? Yet she couldn't deny it would be good to have company on the way home, especially in the current circumstances.

She couldn't risk it.

She inclined her head. 'Thank you for the offer. But I prefer to walk alone.'

Ignoring his amazed expression and the renewed band of terror that tightened around her chest, she raised her chin and walked away.

Darius drummed his fingers on the table as he waited for his whisky to arrive. It had only just passed six o'clock in the evening, which was the polite hour to start drinking, but he'd nearly started earlier in the day, consumed by thoughts of his encounter with Miss Fairmont the previous evening.

At a table by the long window he noticed an acquaintance with whom he often played cards having a quiet drink with his father. The two of them looked relaxed together, comfortable.

For a brief moment Darius wondered what it must be like to have such a companionable relationship with one's father. He couldn't recall having a drink with his own papa that hadn't ended in a quarrel. They'd certainly never chosen to spend time together. Family occasions especially had always been avoided.

No wonder he was so cynical about happy families these days. He'd developed a reluctance—no, an aversion—to ever marrying. He'd seen enough of the so-called happy state to put him off for a lifetime.

When his drink was delivered, Darius gripped the crystal glass harder than usual. He never let his thoughts stray to thoughts of marriage or family life. He possessed too much discipline for that.

He knocked back a gulp of whisky and pulled out his list.

Courting Calista Fairmont.

The words were written in black ink and underlined twice.

He surveyed the list.

He'd planned carefully how to prove that she was just the same as any other title-hunting actress. He had anticipated it would be an easy task. He of all people knew all too well what was required to tempt such women.

To drown any further memories he took another sip of drink.

The previous night he'd gone home and had lain restless in bed for hours. Miss Fairmont's company had been more stimulating than he'd expected. He couldn't quite countenance that she'd refused his offer to walk her home.

For a moment, he'd thought she had wanted to accept. There had been a strange flicker in her eyes as she'd looked over his shoulder into the shroud of fog—had it been fear? He could have sworn just for a moment that she was almost terrified, before she'd covered it up with a lift of her chin and a determined step into the dark.

Her dignified acceptance of his apology had surprised him, too. He realised she'd known it to be a sham at first, had sensed it with her woman's intuition, perhaps, yet when she'd offered him her hand, his own honour had kicked in. He couldn't shake her hand in mockery. His apology, at the moment their fingers touched, had become real. Even through their gloves the memory of her fine-boned hand in his seemed imprinted in his mind.

Yet he wasn't going to be fooled by this woman. He'd awoken this morning with a renewed determination to stick to his plan. He wouldn't allow the Carlyle curse to ruin another generation. But he had to admit the previous evening had been something of a revelation. Above all else, there had been Miss Fairmont's extraordinary performance on the stage as Rosalind. He'd seen the play before, of course, but never like that. She *was* Rosalind. She had been utterly believable, completely compelling, as if Shakespeare had created the part especially for her.

And those breeches had revealed a stunning pair of legs.

Of course, it hadn't merely been Miss Fairmont's legs that had convinced Darius he must be watching one of the best actresses of her generation. It was her husky, melodious voice that had carried across the audience. Her gliding movements across the stage. The entrances that captured instant attention, the graceful exits. Her timing, both comic and dramatic. Every element had come together into a perfect performance. She was generous, too, allowing the other actors and actresses to shine, appearing to bring out the best in them. He knew enough of the arts to recognise true greatness.

She possessed it.

A waiter appeared, hovering at his table. 'Another drink, Your Grace?'

Darius shook his head. He tossed back the last of his whisky and folded the list.

Tonight's performance was about to start.

Calista stood in the wings and stared.

In the royal box to the left of the stage she spotted an unmistakable figure. Dark hair. Broad shoulders. Even in the light of the footlights she swore she could see the gleam of those dark, impenetrable eyes.

The Duke of Albury.

It simply made no sense. She couldn't fathom it. What was he doing back in the Prince's Theatre?

'Calista!' a stagehand hissed. 'Calista! You're going to miss your cue!'

'What? Oh!' As she rushed on to the stage she faltered momentarily in her line, but no one else in the cast appeared to notice.

She cast a sideways glance at the box.

It was him. There could be no doubt.

The duke had come to watch the play again.

* * *

'Hello, Herbert.'

Darius's cousin jumped nearly a foot high in the air, sending his top hat wobbling. 'Darius!'

'I don't suppose I need to ask what you're doing here.'

Herbert's eyes darted away. 'I, um…'

'It's all right,' Darius said drily. 'I spotted you inside the theatre. I know you've been watching the play. I saw it myself.'

Miss Fairmont had performed even better tonight, if that were possible.

'So you're going ahead with your plan to court Miss Fairmont?' Herbert asked. 'That's fast work. Oh, I say, there's Mabel. Must dash.'

He scuttled away towards the stage door.

Darius frowned as he backed into the shadows in the alleyway. For some reason Herbert's comment rankled.

Miss Coop appeared from the door encased in yellow fur. The sound of her voice as she greeted his cousin grated on Darius's ears.

His frown became a scowl. In his worst moments, the sound of a similar whining tone still haunted him. He had taken up the title. It was now up to him alone to ensure the family name suffered no further blackening. The Carlyle curse must be broken. And no matter what else she turned out to be, he must not forget that Miss Calista Fairmont was an actress.

As he watched a group of men in top hats jostle by the stage door his lip curled. Merrick wasn't among them, although he'd spotted him earlier, in the playhouse. What was the fuss about actresses? The crowd of admirers in the alleyway looked pathetic, waiting like dogs to be thrown scraps by their mistresses.

How he despised that kind of behaviour. Now for his cousin's sake he was being forced to play along.

A few of the gentlemen were buying flowers from a street vendor. With a flick of his glove he summoned the vendor to his side and passed over a few silver coins. The blooms were scraggy, well past their best, but he bought a bunch of bronze chrysanthemums. No doubt they would appeal to Miss Fairmont's sensibilities. Surely all women, and especially actresses, liked bouquets.

It was some time before she came out of the theatre.

He stepped out of the fog and lightly touched her shoulder. 'Miss Fairmont.'

She spun on her heel, her lips pressed together as if she had barely suppressed a shriek.

Darius frowned. There it was again, that look of fear. He could see in the dim gaslight that she was fatigued, too, from her performance. Two faint shadows lay beneath her eyes. Once again she'd put her heart and soul into the part. No matter his reservations about women of her profession, he had to admire her talent. It was extraordinary.

Her shoulders dropped. 'Oh! It's you again.'

'Indeed,' he drawled. 'Were you expecting someone else?'

'I saw you from the stage. I was most surprised.'

'Were you?' He made the question suggestive.

She didn't respond to his tone. 'I didn't expect you to watch it again.'

'It's you I enjoyed watching, Miss Fairmont.'

She drew back. 'Oh.'

Darius cursed beneath his breath. He never seduced women in such a manner. Hiding his discomfort, he bowed. 'I was hoping to have the privilege of offering you a lift home in my carriage tonight.'

She shook her head. 'Thank you for the offer, but I thought I had made it clear last night. I prefer to walk.'

'I hope I can convince you to change your mind.'

Her expression was frank. 'Why?'

He raised an eyebrow. 'Would you believe I've taken a fancy to nightly exercise?'

She laughed, an attractive low chuckle. 'I'm not sure I believe you.'

'Perhaps I've taken a fancy to your company.'

He was startled to find that wasn't quite a lie. Now that she stood in front of him again he realised just how charming a woman she was. Watching the play night after night hadn't been the trial he'd expected. In fact, it was becoming quite the reverse. 'I'd enjoy more of your company, if you will do me the honour.'

Her next words surprised him even more.

She stepped closer, and spoke quietly, but with a firmness that was unmistakable. 'Your Grace. I appreciated your apology last night. But as a rule, I don't consort with gentlemen from the audience. It gives rise to…' She stopped and bit her lip. 'Unfortunate impressions. Thank you, but, no.'

This time it was he who took a step back. 'No?'

'No,' she said firmly. Then she curtsied. 'I'm glad you enjoyed the play. I hope you'll continue to enjoy the theatre.'

Pulling the hood of her cloak over her head, she made for the street.

'Miss Fairmont. Wait.'

She swirled back, sending the fabric of her cloak flying.

'Will you at least take these?' He pushed the clump of chrysanthemums towards her. Suddenly their yellow seemed brassy and brash.

She inclined her head and took them in one hand. 'Thank you. Goodnight.'

Leaving Darius standing in the alley, she disappeared into the fog.

* * *

Calista chuckled as she dipped her pen in the ink, poised over her folio.

The night before, when she'd refused the company of the Duke of Albury, she'd wanted to laugh, his expression had been so comical. She still couldn't understand why he'd been there a second time.

When he'd touched her shoulder he'd given her a fright. It had been a relief to see it was him and not—

The pen slipped from her fingers. She put her hand to her tight chest. Her senses were still on high alert. Once again, she'd almost been tempted to accept the duke's offer to walk her home. Her instincts made her yearn to trust the duke, but she knew she had to suppress the feeling. She couldn't afford to trust anyone.

Calista picked up her pen and tried to breathe.

Darius studied the tumble of gems that lay in open boxes in front of him.

He couldn't believe Miss Fairmont had refused to let him accompany her home a second time. At the stage door the night before he'd watched, stunned, as she stepped briskly away. It had been so unexpected that he hadn't had the wits to make a rejoinder and convince her otherwise. It had been a most unusual, indeed, disconcerting experience.

After her rebuff, he'd gone home to study his list. It was time for the next item.

Glistening on black velvet, the jewels formed a rainbow of colours. White diamond. Green emerald. Red ruby. Blue sapphire.

There it was. The sapphire engagement ring surrounded by seed pearls that his father had possessed the decency not to use again. He clamped it in his fist. He could still recall how the ring had become looser on that thin finger, until one day it had slipped off. He wouldn't have been able to have borne seeing it on another plump, grasping hand. It would have been the ultimate insult.

He unclenched his palm to study the ring. The sapphire blue was so deep. It reminded him of Miss Fairmont's eyes. He put the ring away in its box and snapped down the lid.

He slid it into his pocket. It didn't belong in the vault.

He paused, surveying the remaining jewels. Now, what would tempt an actress? He'd seen enough to know. The brighter, brassier and more vulgar the better surely.

He passed over the strings of pearls, imagining them around Calista's swan-like neck.

They would suit her, but he needed something more extravagant. Pearls spelt class. To tick this

particular item off his list he needed a bauble that
signalled money. That was what she'd be unable
to resist, he was certain. After all, he'd seen the
strategy work with one particular actress every
time like a shiny charm.

Then he spied it, the perfect item. A gold bracelet, chunky with red ruby hearts. He winced as he
remembered its history. It wasn't one of the family jewels. He held it up and dangled it from his
fingers. The rubies glowed blood red. He weighed
it up and down in his hand. It would be heavy
against Calista's delicate wrist. But it would no
doubt appeal to her.

Darius dropped the bracelet into a velvet
pouch. It would do the trick.

'Please accept this token of my admiration.'
Calista read the note from the Duke of Albury
in amazement.

Why was the duke sending her a gift? Had he
not understood her refusal?

She shook open the velvet pouch. Glimmer-
ing gold and red burst out and snaked on to the
dressing table.

'Did His Grace bring this himself?' she asked
the stagehand coldly, then modulated her voice.
It wasn't this man's fault. He was only the mes-
senger.

The stagehand shook his head. 'No, Miss Fairmont. It was a valet and he's gone. But he said the duke will be in attendance tonight.'

'I see. Thank you.'

He thought she was playing games with him, Calista realised, feeling sick. He had presumed she'd be unable to resist a glittering bribe.

With distaste she picked up the bracelet. The gold chain was thick and five ruby hearts hung from the clasp. She couldn't imagine the kind of person who would wear such an ornament.

Calista's fingers clenched around the metal. A token of his admiration.

She felt a wave of nausea, then anger. For all his dislike of Mabel's affair with his cousin, it seemed the duke was just like all the other aristocrats who hung around the stage door behaving as if actresses were part of the night's entertainment, whether on or off stage. It was disappointing. She'd almost begun to think better of him.

Calista fumed. Tonight, after the show, she would make it clear to the Duke of Albury that the last things she wanted were his bracelet, his flowers or his attention.

She pulled the string of the velvet pouch tight.

Darius took out his watch from his waistcoat pocket and cursed.

He'd missed the performance of *As You Like It*.

The meeting he'd attended earlier had turned

into drinks and then dinner at his club. It was House of Lords' business, and the governing of the country couldn't be stopped for a play, but he was stunned to realise how annoyed he was to have missed seeing Calista Fairmont on stage again. He'd seen her perform two times now, but still a part of him had been eager to see her play the lead role again, and not just for a glimpse of those excellent legs.

Hurrying along the London streets, he pocketed the watch. She usually left the theatre later than the other cast members, so he might still be able to catch her.

Who knew? She might even be waiting for him, the ruby bracelet dangling from her wrist and a coy expression on her face.

Surely no actress could resist such a bauble.

He turned into the alleyway. In the dim light he saw two figures in the fog.

He could just make out Miss Fairmont's slender figure, but it wasn't as upright as usual. She wasn't cowering, her spine was too straight for that, but she was certainly backing away from the taller, male, top-hatted figure who had backed her against the alley wall.

Darius shouted, 'What in hellfire is going on here?'

Chapter Four

What business could he have here, and with her?

Nicholas Rowe: *The Fair Penitent* (1703)

'What's going on?' he shouted again.

The man jerked up his head, sending his top hat spinning to the ground to reveal his too-long, sandy hair. His lips were drawn back, revealing white teeth, and his close-set eyes were narrowed like a weasel.

Lord Merrick. Darius cursed beneath his breath. 'What are you playing at, Merrick?'

'Nothing that concerns you, Albury,' Merrick spat. A drop of spittle clung to the corner of his mouth, he noted with distaste.

'I'm not sure I agree.' Darius shifted closer, his hands clenched, and peered through the fog. Miss Fairmont's face was white and her expression strained. Their eyes met, briefly, before he rounded to face Merrick.

'I'm just asking this lady,' Merrick slurred over the last word, 'to accompany me for a drink.'

'Do you want to have a drink with Lord Merrick, Miss Fairmont?' Darius managed to keep his voice civil. There was no point inflaming the situation.

'Certainly not,' she replied.

Her voice came out a little more high-pitched than usual, but she retained her composure, he was relieved to note.

Darius picked up the top hat that had rolled to his feet, fighting back the urge to put his boot through it.

He held it out. 'I don't think Miss Fairmont appreciates your attentions, Merrick. Your evening at the playhouse is over. I suggest you make your way home.'

Merrick twisted to face Darius. 'That's what you suggest, is it?'

Darius moved another step closer.

'Indeed.' He made the one word a fist.

As if he'd been winded, Merrick stopped in his tracks. With a sneer he flung himself away from Miss Fairmont. 'The wares around here are shabby anyway.'

He grabbed his hat and staggered away down the alley.

Darius rushed to Miss Fairmont's side. 'Are you all right?'

She nodded as she leaned against the wall, breathing heavily.

'Thank you,' she said simply. 'You came just in time.'

'He didn't—harm you?'

'No.' She shuddered. 'But he'd been drinking.'

He frowned. The situation could so easily have got out of hand.

She took another judder of a breath. Then another. 'You know each other.'

'Merrick and I attended the same school and are now members of the same club. We move in similar circles.'

'Oh.'

'He's no friend of mine, Miss Fairmont,' he said drily.

He was relieved to see her smile gleam through the fog. 'I gathered that.'

'I take it he's no friend of yours either.'

She inhaled sharply. 'Certainly not.'

'Does this kind of thing happen often?'

Miss Fairmont bit her lip. 'Leaving from the stage door every night can be somewhat akin to running the gauntlet. Unfortunately, some members of the audience consider it part of their entertainment.'

Darius frowned as he checked the empty lane. 'Where's the doorman?'

'Gone home, I expect. Fred's a good man, but even he can't resist the kind of money that Lord Merrick throws about.'

'A bribe?'

She shrugged her shoulders beneath her cloak, but he noted that the movement still contained a shiver. She was frightened, no matter how hard she tried to cover it up. 'Gentlemen like that are unscrupulous. We actresses know that.'

Merrick hardly deserved to be called a gentleman after the incident Darius had just witnessed. Again, one of these uncomfortable needles of remorse pierced his conscience. Hell. In the circumstances, was he, Darius Carlyle, worthy to be called a gentleman? Was he equally unscrupulous? No, he reasoned with himself rapidly. He'd never force himself on a woman. His reason for pursuing Miss Fairmont in this fashion was unselfish, for the greater good of the Carlyle family. All the same, it made him increasingly uncomfortable. Darius had to admit his course of action was proving to be more complicated than he had ever expected.

In any case, he refused to leave her shivering in a dark alley.

He bowed. 'I've asked permission to accompany you home more than once. On this occasion, I must insist.'

For a moment he thought she was going to argue again, but then it seemed she thought better of it.

'It's a long walk,' she said, still trembling a little. 'Almost an hour.'

He gestured towards the street. 'Then I suggest we get started, Miss Fairmont.'

The fog wrapped Calista and the duke together in a misty, damp cocoon so that they might have been the only people on the street as they made their way east, away from Covent Garden. Calista's boots clicked on the pavement, the duke's making a deeper echo beside her. They walked in time, she realised, as she began to get her breath back. She was still shaking after that awful scene with Lord Merrick. He'd leapt out of the fog at her and heaven only knew what might have happened if the duke hadn't appeared.

She shuddered again.

She took a sideways peep at the man next to her. His jaw was set, hard, his eyes continually scanning around them. There were still other people out, even late at night. Their faces loomed into view like yellow moons in the gaslights that lit each street corner, their voices resounding in the fog. The clatter of horses' hooves and carriage wheels on the road lessened as they walked further from the city centre. Here, the streets became narrower, the gaslight more scant. Only the public houses were open and the blinds were drawn over the shop windows like stage curtains that had gone down.

The shops changed as they walked further, from dress shops, stationers and tea shops to bakers and grocers. The people, too, changed. Fewer top hats were seen as they walked east, and the clothing of some of the women they passed made Mabel's often low-cut gowns look positively prissy. The policemen carrying truncheons also disappeared. Yet if the duke was aware of the difference, he made no sign. His demeanour never changed and his hands stayed in his pockets of his loose coat. His walk remained a casual saunter as they made their way together in silence, yet she sensed his alertness to every sight and sound.

Safety. For the first time in weeks walking home she allowed herself to relax. Silence was just what she needed after the scare from Lord Merrick, giving her a chance to regain her composure.

It was some time before she broke their hush. She didn't want to talk about what had occurred back at the stage door. Instead, she asked a question that had been puzzling her.

'When you first came to the stage door, you

said you wanted to learn more about actresses. What did you mean by that?'

'Exactly what I said. I wish to learn more about your profession.' He seemed to sense that she needed to change the subject from talk of Lord Merrick.

'You do?'

He chuckled drily. 'I suppose I've earned your amazement. But as I told you, I'm intrigued. I can't promise to change my mind overnight, but I'm willing to learn.' He glanced down the street and frowned. 'This is indeed a long walk home, Miss Fairmont, especially after a performance. Do all actresses live so far from the theatre?'

'We used to live closer. It's only been a month or two since we moved this way.'

'We?'

She hesitated before she replied, 'I live with my sister, Columbine, and our maid.'

'So there's no one who might collect you?'

Calista bit her lip. 'I walk alone.'

'Are you not worried by the fog?'

'The fog helps, actually,' she said.

'What on earth do you mean?'

She grinned. 'In the fog I can become another person. Like this.'

She moved ahead of him so that in the vapour he might only make out her shape and shifted her body so that she appeared like an old woman, a hunched, creeping figure in the dim street.

'Or this.' Now she made the shrunken shape of an old woman transform to that of a man with a confident stride.

'That's extraordinary,' he said, when she appeared beside him once again as herself.

'Sometimes we use a method of inhabiting the body of an animal. To become a cat—' momentarily she arched her back '—or a bear, or snake. That sense of the creature helps to shape the character of the part we play.'

'I shall beware,' he said drily as they fell back in step together.

She chuckled. 'Audiences may think it is the costumes or dialogue that make a good actor or actress. But it's movement. It's in the body. That's what my...I was taught.'

'Do you find it difficult to move in and out of character?'

'You're the first person to ever ask me that,' she said. 'It's probably the most important part of the play, when it's finished, I mean. Some actors I know are still in their roles when they go back to their dressing rooms. They might even stay in character for a day or two. But I come back to myself when the curtain goes down.'

'Surely it's safer that way,' he observed. 'Otherwise, you might lose sight of yourself. It could be dangerous.'

She shuddered at that last word.

Another acute glance came from beneath his top hat. 'Is there really no one who might walk you home?'

'Not at present.' She stopped under a gaslight and pointed across the street. 'Those are our rooms over there. Thank you for keeping me company.' She hesitated. 'There's something else. I wanted to return this.'

From her reticule she pulled out the blackvelvet pouch that held the ruby bracelet. It had made her so angry earlier, but after tonight she found she wasn't angry at him any more.

'I ought not to have sent it to you, Miss Fairmont,' he said quietly. 'It was an error of judgement.'

She studied his face as if searching for more clues as to his character. 'That bracelet. It doesn't seem…like you.'

He stiffened. 'Your astuteness surprises me. I'll admit it isn't entirely to my taste.'

Her forehead furrowed. 'But you thought it would be to mine.'

'It was a regrettable error. I thought it the kind of thing actresses like.'

'Do you know many actresses?' she asked curiously.

He dodged her question. 'Please, accept my apology. It seems I'm making a habit of apologising to you. It appears all actresses are not what I expected.'

She smiled as she curtsied. 'I might say the same of dukes.'

At that he laughed. The two brackets she'd noted around his mouth were laughter lines after all. The expression took years off his age. She had thought him to be over thirty, but now she realised he must be eight and twenty, at the most.

'I'm glad to hear it,' he said.

'And thank you,' she added softly, 'for what you did tonight, back at the theatre.'

'That was my pleasure, too,' he said rather grimly. 'Goodnight, Miss Fairmont.'

'Goodnight, Your Grace.'

Calista picked up her skirts and darted away, into the night.

Darius stared across the street at Miss Calista Fairmont's slender, vanishing figure.

He uncurled his fingers. His fists had been clenched for the whole journey, hidden in his coat pockets. He rarely walked so far abroad in the city, especially at night. All his senses had been on alert, his body ready to spring into action. Most of his walks he took across his country acres, with his Labradors at his heels. Yet she covered the long distance at such a late hour and showed remarkable courage on the dangerous London streets. She had made a play of it, but he was sure it must terrify her, even without men like Lord Merrick around. By God, there weren't even adequate gaslights here, they were so far from the better part of the city. Now Darius understood the circles under her eyes. To perform a demanding role like Rosalind and then to walk for an hour without a meal… Her thinness was now also explained.

He frowned and glanced down the street. The poor lighting made it difficult to see too far, but he made out the row of small mean buildings. There was a public house on the corner, and he could hear raised voices, two men having a brawl. Surely it was only a matter of time before some other drunken lout bumped into Calista and saw the beauty that she was.

All she had to protect herself was her extraordinary skill in transforming her body into another shape in the shadows. He had known Miss Fairmont wore skirts, but such was the masculine posture and presence she had emanated that he would have sworn it had been another man coming towards him in the dim cloud of night.

Darius stiffened. She was an actress. It wouldn't do for him to forget that. Yet it horrified him that a woman of her talents lived in such an area. Her posturing in the fog wouldn't fool everyone. Not if they saw that face. And that smile. It lit up the fog, brighter than a gas lamp.

He took a closer look at the brick-fronted, two-storeyed building into which she'd disappeared. She'd referred to rooms. That must mean she didn't even have a house to herself and her sister. It seemed the sole income for the small family was being provided by Calista's skills on the stage and that wasn't enough pay for decent accommodation.

Under his breath he released an expletive.

Nothing had gone as he intended. Not at all. Like an actor himself, he'd been prepared to play Lothario, had planned what he might say to flatter and perhaps even begin to seduce her. He'd made his list of ways to woo an actress. He'd seen it all before, had learnt the hard way what women like that wanted. Flattery had been at the top, for actresses thrived on attention, or so he'd thought. But Miss Fairmont would have none of it. She despised flattery of her art and loathed the attentions of men like Lord Merrick.

His brow furrowed deeper. Such wholesomeness—could it be feigned? There seemed to be no trace of pretence in her. She played no character when she came off the stage, except herself.

He walked back towards more respectable

streets where a hansom cab might be found, still brooding.

Her sister Columbine must have been the girl with whom he had seen her in the park. The ill child clearly wasn't made up, an imaginary character in a sad story designed to play on his sympathy or his wallet. Unbeknown to her, in Hyde Park he'd already witnessed Miss Fairmont's anxious care of her sister, fussing over her like a mother water bird. He had sensed from what she'd said, or what she hadn't said, that the stress of dealing with her sister's welfare was beginning to break her health, too, if not her spirit. Why was she so alone? Unprotected?

When Merrick had her trapped against the wall... Darius swore. He'd never felt such unaccountable rage. She'd been cornered, yet with her head still held high she'd looked briefly into his own eyes. Hers had been anguished, inky as indigo, full of unshed tears. He had been torn between giving Merrick what he deserved and wanting to take Miss Fairmont into his arms. He'd wanted to comfort her. To promise it would be all right, that he would make it so.

An ironic laugh escaped him.

It was the damnedest thing.

Darius pulled off his top hat and ran his hand through his hair.

If he were to hold an audition for the Duchess of Albury, the actress he'd just accompanied home would surely win the part.

Brave. Intelligent. Loyal.

Miss Calista Fairmont was exactly the kind of woman Darius would want for a wife.

Chapter Five

Shew every tender, every grateful thought,
This wondrous goodness stirs.

Nicholas Rowe: *The Fair Penitent* (1703)

Calista stared out of the window and groaned.

Rain spattered on the sill, dripped down the pipes and fell into the puddle below with a pitiful splash. The May sunshine of the previous couple of weeks had vanished as if it had never been, as if it had all been a dream. And before long she would have to make her way to Covent Garden. It would be harder than ever through this dreary weather, and today she had a matinee as well as an evening performance.

She laid her forehead against the cold glass. To her surprise, she'd slept through the night before without waking once. She thought she'd have nightmares after what had happened with Merrick, but her sleep had been untroubled. It was as if the comfort of the duke's presence had stayed with her ever since that night. Walking home before she'd often felt frightened, but she'd never been lonely. There was a difference between loneliness and being alone. Yet with the duke at her side, for the first time in so long, she had felt safe in his companionship. Even the roughest men at the corner pubs had taken one look at the man and had moved aside.

Companionship.

Protection.

And more.

The duke was a witty and charming man. Dangerously charming. They'd shared a companionship on that long walk, which she'd rarely enjoyed with a man before. She'd revealed things to him she hardly ever spoke of to others. Talking about her life and her craft wasn't something she often indulged in. It seemed vain or conceited to discuss her acting methods and not many people understood, yet she had found herself confiding in him, even demonstrating the way she could change herself into another character with a simple word or step.

Beneath the duke's brusque exterior, she intuited a more sensitive man, and their conversations, or even their companionable silence, told her that intuition was true. She'd allowed herself to enjoy the challenge of matching his long stride beside her and had given herself up to the unexpected pleasure of his company.

Calista put her hand to her chest as a pang in her chest surprised her. It wasn't a pang of fear, but a strange kind of desolation. She'd had to resume her lone pilgrimages to and from the theatre.

Yes, it had been so good not to walk alone, and not only because it meant she hadn't had to worry about Lord Merrick. The other cares she carried had also lightened for an hour.

But there was even more to it than that.

Was that what it would be like to be married? She thought it must be wonderful to have the man you loved by your side, to have someone to turn to in woe or in happiness. To have a companion, a friend and a lover. Three in one. Was it possible to find such a husband, who could be all these things? She would have to enjoy his company, like him, and love him, too…

But it wasn't likely she would find out.

Calista straightened her back. Self-pity hovered over her shoulders for a moment, almost causing her to stoop. She had a different path in life and she refused to complain. She'd told Darius at their first meeting that she would never marry a duke. But there was more to it than that. It wasn't just witnessing the way so many men treated actresses that had made her determined to stick to her declaration not to seek a man. She'd vowed to care for Columbine and no man would want such burdens. Her sister was Calista's responsibility now, and she wouldn't shirk that duty.

Yet how strange it was to be disappointed that she would never see the duke again. Now that she'd made it clear she did not desire his attentions, or his jewels, their paths would doubtless not cross another time.

'Cally!' Columbine rushed into the bedroom. 'There's a gentleman—a *duke*—at the front door!'

'What?' Calista's petticoats brushed the floor as she hurried from her bedroom into the front room. 'Oh!'

The Duke of Albury stood framed in the doorway. He bowed. 'Miss Fairmont.'

Calista made a quick curtsy, casting her eyes around the room as she did so. Thank goodness for Martha who kept their humble abode so tidy. Although there was no option to do anything else, for there was barely room to move in any case and disorder would make it impossible to function in the space. Even now, Martha, open-mouthed as she stared at the duke, her cap atilt, was hastily smoothing the counterpane of the bed in the corner where she slept with Columbine. 'This is unexpected.'

What would have passed for a grin from anyone else flashed across the duke's face.

'Forgive me for calling unannounced,' he said. 'When I saw the rain it crossed my mind to enquire whether you would be travelling by foot to the theatre today in spite of the weather.'

He'd read her mind.

'I'll be walking to the theatre, yes,' she replied. 'But a few raindrops never hurt anyone.'

'That's not what you said last week, Cally,' Columbine interjected. Her face was alight with interest as she stared at the duke. 'You said you were a drowned rat by the time you got to the theatre and that you were surprised you didn't leave a puddle of water on the stage.'

Calista gritted her teeth.

'Is that so?' The duke sounded amused as he addressed Columbine.

The girl's long braids bounced as she nodded. 'Yes. And once Cally said the wind blew so hard she almost flew to the theatre.'

Calista yanked Columbine back to her side.

'It's not quite as terrible as all that,' she said lightly. 'My sister has a flair for the dramatic.'

The duke raised a brow. 'A resemblance you share.'

'I don't want to be an actress,' said Columbine.

'No?' replied the duke.

'I'd like to be an acrobat,' Columbine confided. 'I saw one in a circus once. Riding on horseback.'

'Really?'

Calista pushed Columbine behind her skirt in an attempt to stop her talking. 'Please come in.'

The duke entered the room, dominating it with his presence. Instantly the space seemed even smaller than usual. He glanced about idly as he took off his hat and drew off his gloves.

'This is my sister, Columbine,' she said, allowing Columbine to peep out from behind her for a moment. 'And this is Martha, who helps us here at home.'

She knew it probably wasn't the done thing to introduce servants to aristocrats, but she wasn't going to leave Martha out.

To her astonishment the duke bowed towards the maid. 'How do you do?'

His smile was so charming that she blushed beetroot-red. 'Pleasure to meet you, my lord.'

'You say "Your Grace", Martha.' Columbine pushed past the bell of Calista's skirt. 'That's right, isn't it? You said you were a duke.'

'Columbine!' exclaimed Calista. 'Please allow me to apologise for my sister on her behalf.'

'There's no need for any apology. I've become accustomed to the frankness of the Fairmont sisters,' the duke said. 'I suppose you're wondering why I'm here. I know you've refused my offer before, Miss Fairmont. But when I saw the abominable weather I deduced you might need transport by carriage to the theatre this afternoon.'

'How did you know to come at this time?' she asked, mystified. Many people didn't realise how much earlier she had to arrive at the theatre in order to prepare. Costumes, paints, powders—all took time, as well as conversation with the other actors, to get into the role. She needed an hour before she went on stage to stop being Calista and to become Rosalind.

'I made the further acquaintance of your door-keeper at the theatre,' he said smoothly. 'Fred, I believe? He informed me of your habits.'

'I see.' She got the feeling he'd said something else to Fred, too.

Columbine rushed to the window. 'Is that your carriage? The one with the four black horses? Oh, Cally, look!'

Calista followed her across the room and peered out of the steamed-up window. She rubbed at the glass with her finger. Outside on the street was one of the most magnificent carriages she had ever seen. It was painted black and gold, a crest on the door. A driver held the reins of four horses and steam was rising from their damp, glistening backs.

'Have you ever seen your sister perform her role as Rosalind?' the duke asked Columbine.

The girl shook her head wistfully. 'No. I used to go to the theatre with Papa, of course. We saw the very first time Cally was ever on stage. I can still remember it. But now it's not possible for me to go. It's too much for me to stay out and there's a long walk home.'

She sighed.

The duke bowed. 'Allow me to be of service. Perhaps I can offer a lift to the theatre to both the Misses Fairmont.'

Columbine clasped her hands together. 'Oh, do you mean it? I would be able to ride in that beautiful carriage?'

'Columbine!' Calista turned to the duke. 'Thank you, but as I've already told you, I prefer to make my own way, even if it is on foot.'

'Come now, Miss Fairmont.' His voice was mild, but his eyes had darkened. 'Must you prize your independence even at the price of your own discomfort? Can't you take advantage of my offer?'

Calista lifted her chin. 'It's very kind of you. But, no.'

'Cally,' Columbine said reproachfully. 'Do you really mean it? You know I've always longed to see you perform as Rosalind. And look at those horses!'

The duke turned to address Martha. 'Have you ever seen Miss Fairmont in a play, Martha?'

Martha ducked, holding on to her apron. 'No, my lord, I mean, My Grace'

'Then we could make a party of it,' he said,

making no reference to Martha's stumble. 'If Miss Fairmont will consent.'

'Please,' Columbine begged. Her eyes were alight in a way Calista hadn't seen for months. 'Please let us come with you.'

'I promise to bring your sister home the moment the curtain goes down after the matinee performance,' the duke said. 'She'll be tucked up in bed in no time.'

'But you'd have to wait a long time for the play to start,' Calista demurred.

'I could always take your sister out to tea at Gunter's,' he said, as if it were the most natural thing in the world.

'Gunter's Tea Shop!' exclaimed Columbine. 'Do you mean you've actually eaten one of their ices?'

'Indeed.' Again the duke sounded amused. 'It's near my London home, in Berkeley Square. I can recommend the pistachio nut.'

Columbine had turned pale with excitement. 'Oh, Cally, please! Ices!'

Calista felt herself wavering. Martha would go with them. Unexpectedly, her instinct was to trust the duke, and she always relied on her instincts. So far she hadn't been proved wrong. Yet surely it was irresponsible to allow her young sister to be alone in company with a gentleman she hardly knew.

The duke moved a pace nearer. 'Miss Fairmont. We've not spent much time together, only an evening walk. But I hope you will do me the honour of trusting me on this occasion.'

He glanced out at the rain, bucketing down on to the street. 'I didn't ask the servants to perform a rain dance, but surely you must admit the weather is on my side.'

'It's always raining in England,' Calista said, a curve to her lips.

'And we Englishmen know how to make the best of it.' His answering smile was that same brief grin as before. 'Allow me the honour of escorting you and your sister in the carriage.'

They exchanged glances. They both knew the rain wasn't the only reason he didn't want her to walk alone.

As she continued to hesitate he shifted even closer. She caught the clean scent of his clothing. 'It's unconventional, Miss Fairmont, but not improper. You need have no fear. Your sister will come to no harm in my care. I promise you that.'

Once again he'd guessed her thoughts correctly.

Columbine's hands were still clasped as if in prayer. 'Cally! Please say we can go in the carriage. Please!'

With a laugh Calista raised own her hands in surrender. 'We'd be delighted to accept your invitation. Thank you for your kind offer, Your Grace.'

As he bowed once again, she saw that close up the duke's dark eyes weren't brown as she'd assumed, but a very deep blue. 'Believe me. The pleasure is all mine.'

In the darkened theatre Darius ran his fingers through his hair. When he'd first started court-ing Miss Fairmont, he hadn't expected to end up seated beside an eight-year-old girl watching a matinee performance.

It wasn't on his list.

Somehow, too, during the performance, his fingers had become entwined with Columbine's small hand. The girl had seized his hand and gripped it tightly throughout the entire second act of the play, so involved had she become in the plot. Only now, as the play came to an end, did she release her childish grip. On the girl's other side sat stolid Martha, open-mouthed as she watched Calista on the stage.

Darius, too, had watched closely once again. By now, it wasn't simply the clever plot that held his attention, masterful though the Bard's work was. One figure alone captured his gaze. It seemed as if he was speaking every line with Miss Calista Fairmont, willing her to perform to the height of her skill. He seemed to feel some kind of connection to that slim, elegant figure, as if she were lit by a spotlight, the other players fading away to form a mere backdrop.

That morning, when he'd awoken to the sound of rain pounding on the luxurious cocoon that was his London town house, his first thought had been of Miss Fairmont, as it had been every morning since that night when he'd accompanied her to her lodgings.

His next thought had been that if he saw Lord Merrick at the stage door again this evening he'd make excellent use of every puddle in the alleyway.

She must never walk alone again, he had vowed then. The terrible weather would only make it harder for her. He'd envisioned her hurrying along the slippery London streets beneath an umbrella. Why, he had thought, she would arrive at the theatre with wet feet, something that one should never do, a fact his old nanny had impressed upon him in the nursery.

Now his lip quirked in amusement at himself. Worrying about Miss Fairmont's feet had surely been taking things too far. Perhaps it was because of her feet's connection to her excellent legs that had been on display in her boy's guise on the stage.

For a moment that morning he had allowed himself to imagine her feet, always hidden by the leather boots she wore. Her feet would be slender and narrow, he had decided, pale and white, her toes as pink as the inside of sea shells. A vision of her naked legs and feet and his lips upon them had had him springing from his bed and sending Hammond to the Prince's Theatre to make a proposal to the doorkeeper, who, guineas in hand, had apparently become most obliging. The doorman's information, combined with what he'd learned from her, meant Darius now knew a great deal about Calista's habits.

What he hadn't been prepared for was the realisation that her situation appalled him.

When he had entered her lodgings that afternoon he'd managed to hide his dismay at her surroundings. That she was forced to live in such a place came as a shock, even though the exterior did nothing to recommend the dwelling. The paint peeled from the damp walls and a meagre fire only warmed a foot or two in front of it. The room was a sitting room—though only one shabby armchair had been in sight—as well as a dining room, for there was a table with four chairs, one broken, as well as a scullery and bedroom, too. But it had been scrupulously clean. The way Calista had lifted her chin at the sight of him had told Darius any pity or sign of repulsion at their obvious poverty must be disguised. But it was no place for a young woman, let alone an actress of her calibre, to bring up a child.

He glanced at Columbine. Never had he imagined himself seated at Gunter's Tea Rooms with a young girl as she scooped up spoonsful of ices, expounding to him the various merits of vanilla, chocolate and pistachio. Nor had he expected to take the horses multiple times around Berkeley Square to please that same girl before accompanying her and her nursemaid to the theatre.

He generally avoided children. He didn't dislike them, exactly, but they were just not part of his world. He'd grown up without the company of brothers and sisters, so his school friends and cousin had been his companions. But at Gunter's, Columbine had kept up a steady stream of chatter in between bites and exclamations over various delicacies, and Darius had gleaned even more information about Calista.

He shook his head. Why in the blazes did he care about Calista Fairmont's situation? It wasn't as if he was courting her in earnest. Of course she wasn't suitable as a wife to an aristocrat. He didn't know what had come over him to have even entertained such a thought that night. It had been ridiculous to think it, even for a moment.

Applause broke around him, jolting him out of his reverie.

'Oh, thank you so much for bringing me.' Beside him Columbine was clapping wildly, sending her braids bobbing. 'I forgot Cally was my sister during the play. It was such a good story, wasn't it, even if it is confusing with how they all dress up and pretend?'

'Indeed.' The duke smiled as he joined in with the applause. The statement was no pretence. Watching Miss Fairmont was a pleasure. He knew how she became Rosalind now; she'd shown him on the street. She'd claimed it to be a skill, but he knew it to be a rare talent.

Columbine giggled as they watched Calista accept a huge bouquet as she took another curtsy. 'People from the audience are always giving her flowers. Cally gives them all to Mrs Nesbit down the street. She can't get out because of her rheumatics.'

Darius hid a smile. That had no doubt been the fate of the bronze chrysanthemums. They had probably deserved it.

Columbine was still clapping. 'Cally is marvellous, isn't she?'

'She's made to be an actress,' he replied.

'Oh, Cally never wanted to be an actress!' the little girl exclaimed. 'She wants to write plays. That's her dream, to be a playwright like our father.'

The duke turned back to stare at the dark-haired, slender figure bowing on stage, sweeping her hand to the audience, her wide mouth set in a beaming smile.

'Indeed,' he murmured.

Calista Fairmont was acting a greater part than he had ever suspected.

'Goodnight, Miss Fairmont.'

Fred nodded as Calista passed him. He appeared to be glued to his post by the door tonight and there was no sign of Lord Merrick.

Nonetheless, her legs still felt shaky as she made her way down the alleyway. But she wouldn't allow thoughts of Lord Merrick to spoil what had been a special day. Between performances she had managed to snatch a few precious minutes with a thoroughly over-excited Columbine in her dressing room, although she hadn't seen the duke. He'd waited in the theatre lobby.

A wave of unanticipated disappointment washed over her. It was an impropriety, of course, for the duke to come to her private dressing room, but unaccountably her heart had dropped when she'd realised he wasn't accompanying Columbine.

The ride to the theatre had been fun, more fun than they'd had for months. It had taken away some of the tension in her body that had formed from weeks of worry. It had been wonderful to see Columbine so excited and it had made Calista determined to perform well. She'd put her heart and soul into the matinee performance, knowing Columbine was in the audience.

More than once she'd thought of the Duke of Albury, too.

She frowned. There was a matter regarding the duke she still had to attend to.

'Miss Fairmont.'

Calista spun around. 'Oh! I was just thinking about you.'

The duke flashed her a grin. 'How flattering. Or perhaps not. Dare I ask precisely what you were thinking?'

'I was wondering how to thank you for your attentions to Columbine today,' she said simply. 'She longs to get out. It was extraordinarily kind of you.'

His chuckle in reply surprised her. 'Not what you expected from a duke?'

'No,' she said honestly. 'But I wanted to thank you all the same.'

He raised a brow once more before indicating the carriage by the side of the road. 'The weather has improved, but I thought you may like to travel by coach tonight rather than walk home. After two performances you must be exhausted.'

This time she didn't hesitate. 'Thank you very much.'

He smiled. 'What a relief. I was afraid you

were going to insist upon walking for the fresh air and exercise. After an afternoon with your sister, delightful though she is, I wasn't sure I could manage it.'

Calista smiled back. 'Children are exhausting, aren't they?'

'I never knew,' he said solemnly, but there was a glint in his eye.

She noticed he quickly surveyed the street before he opened the carriage door. 'After you, Miss Fairmont.'

A wave of heat passed through his glove to her bare skin as he helped her into the carriage.

The duke frowned. 'You're not wearing gloves tonight.'

She couldn't tell him that her only pair sat waiting in the darning basket. She'd found a hole in them that morning. 'It's not that cold.'

Inside the carriage, Calista leaned back against the leather seat and took a deep breath. The touch of his hand remained as a shudder through her.

After a word to the driver Darius took the seat next to hers. His knees brushed her skirt as he settled back .

He frowned. 'Are you all right?'

'Oh, yes!' Calista took another breath and used all of her skill as an actress to steady her voice. 'I'm weary after two performances, that's all.'

'Perhaps these will help.' He passed her a box made of card with a pink ribbon tied on top.

Calista lifted the lid and stared at the duke in amazement.

'Your sister told me they were your favourite.'

The pale pastel-shaded sweets shimmered with sugar dusting. 'Thank you.'

'I hope they won't make their way to Mrs Nesbit,' he said drily.

'How did you…?' She laughed. 'Oh. Columbine. I promise that Mrs Nesbit won't be given these. I'm tempted to try one now, but…'

'You're too tired to eat,' he finished for her. 'You often are when you've had both a matinee and an evening show. That's what Columbine also told me.'

'I might make an exception for *macarons*.' She smiled. 'I hope Columbine's chatter didn't bore you.'

'Not at all,' he replied. 'It was most illuminating.'

Calista closed the lid of the box. 'Sometimes after two performances all I want to do is get into bed. I can barely remove my boots.'

His eyes darkened with an emotion she couldn't identify. He rapped on the inside of the carriage and instantly they took off.

For a while they were both silent. It was strangely soothing listening to the carriage wheels turn. But the duke's presence could hardly be called soothing. Her awareness of his presence seemed heightened this evening and she was minutely aware of the inches that lay between their knees.

'Did you enjoy the performance?' she asked him at last.

'You were better this afternoon than ever before. And tonight you were better still.'

'Do you mean you came to the matinee and to the performance this evening, too?'

'It seems I've become a devotee of your work, Miss Fairmont.'

'I find that very strange,' she said frankly. 'You've turned from a hater of the theatre to a theatre lover overnight.'

'Put it down to your charms,' he said smoothly. Much too smoothly for her liking.

Calista stiffened. 'You're flattering me again. I told you I dislike it.'

Amazement showed on his face. 'You really mean what you say, don't you?'

She nodded.

'Then I won't flatter you. But I enjoyed all of your performances immensely.'

'And did you enjoy your tea at Gunter's?' she asked mischievously.

'With the other delightful Miss Fairmont? It

was quite splendid, although I prefer my Miss Fairmonts a little older.'

My Miss Fairmonts. An unexpected ripple of pleasure ran over her skin. To hide it she asked, 'Did Columbine behave?'

'Admirably. She ate all her bread and butter as she promised you and then demolished such an enormous ice I swear I thought it impossible for a young girl to manage it. But somehow she did.'

'That's Columbine.'

'Yes.' He fell silent before asking abruptly, 'What's wrong with her exactly? No, I've put that badly. She seems somehow fragile, in spite of her spirit, which in such a girl is remarkable. What is it that ails her?'

'No one really knows.' Calista found it hard to speak. 'There's no name for it. Sometimes she struggles to breathe so, it's terrifying. I dread those attacks.'

'So you're especially cautious of your sister's health.'

She nodded. 'Her last attack was in the winter.'

'And she hasn't recovered fully yet, has she? I could see that.'

Calista bit her lip. 'It's a constant worry. She hates to be treated as an invalid. Between attacks she feels quite well and I constantly feel like I have to restrain her. I'd like to get her out of London, but with my work at the theatre it's impossible.'

Calista spun on the seat to face him.

'I have to know,' she burst out. 'The walk home. The carriage ride. The tea for Columbine. Your Grace, why are you being so kind to me?'

'Call me Darius.'

'That's precisely what I mean.' She refused to be diverted by the request to call him by his first name. 'You made it perfectly clear when we first met that you despise actresses. So why are you seeking to further our acquaintance?'

Gaslight filtered through the carriage window, lighting his dark eyes. 'Haven't you worked it out by now, Miss Fairmont?'

He pulled her into his arms. The blade of his lips parted hers, opening them to his searching tongue. Beneath her petticoats her legs threatened to send her slipping from the seat. The taste of him, like port wine, made her heady, and she opened her mouth wider, tasting him, wanting more. Her arms went to his neck as he pressed her to him, his hands on the curve of her waist. In that moment, the hardness of his body, the search of his lips, became all she knew. Around them the carriage and the London streets outside vanished.

There was only him. Only his lips, his hands, his tongue.

Calista closed her eyes and gave herself up to

the whirling sensations inside as he teased her, sending her almost sliding down against the seat leather. The carriage seemed to lurch and sway. Somehow she found the strength to pull away.

He drew back with a groan. 'Surely you know why I seek your company. You must realise what's happening between us.'

'I don't know what's happening,' she gasped. 'I've never experienced such feelings before.'

He cupped her chin in his gloved hand. 'Can this be true? Is such innocence possible for a woman of your profession?'

In a flash of fury she pulled free of his fingers. 'Do you mean to kiss me and then insult me?'

'Don't you think I find this situation as strange as you do?' He ran his hand through his hair. 'It's incredible to me that you may be untouched.'

'You seem to make a lot of assumptions about actresses. I'm as you find me,' Calista retorted. 'And how do I find you?'

He exhaled. 'I can't pretend not to be a man of the world. But this…' his breath became a cross between a choke and a laugh '…this is unexpected to say the least.'

Startling her, he ripped off his gloves and gripped her hands, so she could feel the warmth against hers. 'Have dinner with me tomorrow night.'

Calista tried to pull her fingers away. The

burning sensation once again rushed through her body, more powerful and pulsing than before. 'I can't. I have to get home to Columbine.'

'It takes you an hour to walk home. If I take you to dinner and then home in the carriage, I'll return you to your sister not much later.'

'I don't have dinner with dukes,' Calista said, as the pulsing raced through her body.

'If you think I'm going to let you go after a kiss like that, you're mad.' Darius's grip tightened. 'Come, Miss Fairmont. Say yes. I'm prepared to overcome my prejudices against actresses. Surely you will give a duke a chance?'

Chapter Six

Women, I see, can change as well as men.
Nicholas Rowe: *The Fair Penitent* (1703)

The dressing-room door was flung open.

Mabel squealed as she rushed inside. 'Is it true?'

Calista jumped, spilling the pot of powder. 'Is what true?'

'The Duke of Albury picked you up in his carriage last night! I heard all about it from Fred.'

Calista bit her lip. Of course it would have been noticed. 'Yes. It's true.'

Mabel's second squeal was even more piercing. 'Calista! You're being courted by a duke!'

'I most certainly am not,' Calista retorted. 'He did me a kindness. That was all.'

She shivered. She hadn't told Mabel about the problems with Lord Merrick and she wasn't going to worry her now.

'Men like the Duke of Albury don't do kind-nesses without reason,' Mabel said. 'Take the other night, for instance. There must be more to it than that.'

With a flounce of her fur-trimmed cape, Mabel crossed the room and stared over Calista's shoulder at her reflection in the glass. 'You've fallen for a duke!'

'That's ridiculous.' Calista watched in horror as a pink flush stained her cheeks in the glass. 'I hardly know him.'

'You've fallen for him,' her friend insisted. 'I can tell.'

Calista stood up. 'Nonsense. You know my rule.'

'I know your rule, but I know more about men and women.'

'Well, you're wrong in this case. It seems the duke is simply a patron of the arts.'

'A patron of the arts?' Mabel giggled. 'That's a new one.'

Calista's cheeks warmed even more as she re-called the duke's lips on hers. The combination of the heat he had evoked, in stark contrast to his cool demeanour, had sparked a flame deep within her. 'I'll admit there's more to the duke than I expected.'

'After the duke was so rude that night at dinner, Herbie told me a tragedy had happened in his family.'

'What do you mean?'

'He didn't say any more. He got all cagey. It's not like my Herbie. I'll get it out of him somehow.'

Calista frowned. A tragedy? He hadn't told her much about his childhood, only that he was an only child. But it made sense. Something in his past affected him, she was sure of it. Still, she wouldn't press Mabel further to find out. Calista wasn't one to gossip, not like some of the other actresses backstage.

Mabel was studying her with curiosity. 'You really do care for the duke, don't you?'

Speedily she changed the subject. 'What's that wrap you're wearing, Mabel? It looks new.'

Her friend stroked the golden fur on her shoulders as if it were a kitten. It matched the colour of her hair, making her look as though she had a golden mane. 'It is. Dear Herbie gave it to me today.'

'So you're still seeing Sir Herbert?'

'Of course,' Mabel said in surprise. 'You didn't think he'd stop seeing me, did you, because of what the duke said?'

'You seem very certain of him.'

'I am.' Then she pouted. 'I'm surprised he hasn't proposed to me yet. It's rather strange. It's as if something is holding him back.'

Or someone, Calista thought to herself, as a suspicion dawned on her.

Mabel snuggled deeper into her fur. 'But Herbie did give me this lovely gift, I suppose, even if by now I expected an engagement ring.'

'Do you truly want to marry him?'

'Oh, yes,' Mabel said complacently.

'How do you know?' The words tumbled out of Calista's mouth before she could stop them. 'How do you know Herbert is the man for you, that he's the one you want to spend the rest of your life with?'

Mabel's face softened. 'A woman knows. That's all.'

With a final stroke of her fur cape she hung it proudly on the hatstand and began to apply her stage paint.

Calista slipped behind the screen to put on her costume for the first act.

A woman knows.

What did she know about her feelings for the Duke of Albury?

All she knew was that her feelings had been transformed.

By his kindness.

By his kiss.

When she'd first met him at the public house for that disastrous dinner, she had loathed him. When he had walked her home, she had liked him. When he had taken her home in his carriage, she'd been unable to deny the attraction pulsing between them. And when he'd kissed her…

Calista's legs wobbled. She clutched the edge of the screen to steady herself. Was it because it had been her first kiss, swiftly followed by another, then a third, that she had been so overwhelmed by the rush of feelings that had erupted within her, igniting a fire inside? The press of his lips, seducing hers open… It had opened a new world of sensation, one that had taken hold in her body. Now just the thought of the Duke of Albury rekindled that flame.

She'd never had a real kiss, apart from the stage embraces that never felt anything to do with her when the curtain went down. Those embraces belonged to the characters she played, not to her.

Would a kiss from any other man have the same powerful effect?

No.

Only a kiss from Darius.

Her instant, instinctive answer to that question made her tighten her grip on the screen as if she might fall. She put her hand to her bodice and felt her heart quicken.

Darius. She'd called him by his Christian name in the privacy of her mind.

Darius.

A tremor ran through her again, sent her pulse racing faster.

She was going to break her rule. She'd agreed to have dinner with him. All day her thoughts had continued to stray to him. He had hovered in her consciousness as if he had been seated in every room she occupied. He had even appeared in her dreams the night before, vivid, colourful dreams. She forced the memory of what those dreams had contained to the back of her mind.

It hadn't helped that since her outing to Gunter's Tea Room Columbine spoke of little else.

'The Duke of Albury is the nicest duke I ever met,' she'd announced.

'You don't know any other dukes,' Calista had reminded her with a smile.

'He's still the nicest duke in England,' Columbine insisted. 'I'm sure of it.'

Again Calista shook her head in disbelief as she slipped on her dress. That Darius now held Columbine's vote for the title of the nicest duke in England was nothing short of amazing. He certainly possessed no previous claim to that title. The memory of the dinner party made her question everything.

Could Darius have had a hand in his cousin's reluctance to propose to Mabel?

Calista pulled the bodice tight on her costume. Tonight at dinner, she would find out.

* * *

Through the candle flames Calista studied the duke.

The flickering light played upon his face, emphasising his jaw and lips.

After the play Darius had immediately borne her off to a quiet street in St. James's, where they had been ushered into a magnificent dining establishment. The rooms were in the new style, with large tables and comfortable chairs, pristine linen tablecloths and napkins. The forks and spoons were silver plated, as was the candelabra that held six candles flaming between them. The wine and finger glasses glistened. A joint of beef had been wheeled on a trolley to their table, and a waiter wearing a white cap and jacket had carved it to perfection. Mouth-watering puddings, syllabubs and jellies as well as cheeses had also been proffered on another trolley. It had been hard to choose, but she had settled on Eve's pudding made with apples and the lightest of sponges, which had tasted like air on her tongue.

The duke proved to be a charming dinner companion, telling stories about the House of Lords that made her laugh aloud. As they ate and the claret continued to be poured by an assiduous waiter, Calista unfurled in the luxurious dining room like a flower in a hothouse. It was far more relaxing to enjoy a delicious meal in such surroundings after a performance than to walk the dark street alone. Inside the warm, well-lit cocoon of the dining rooms she almost forgot the cold outside.

She loosened the lacy shawl from her shoulders, which was yellow with age as it had been her mother's. Beneath it she wore her favourite evening gown—her only evening gown, to be precise—which was now somewhat worn, but in an unusual wild-rose silk. The colour suited her complexion, she'd noted in the looking glass in her dressing room, made her appear less pale than usual. Tonight, however, she hardly needed the enhancement of her gown's fresh colour. Her whole body was so warm she felt tempted to fan her face with her napkin.

Opposite, Darius swallowed the last of the port that had come with his Stilton. Her eyes were drawn from his lips to his strong throat.

Now those lips smiled. 'You're making a study of my character, Miss Fairmont. Shall I expect to see a version of myself on stage?'

Calista laughed. 'I do tend to stare. I'm sorry. I was just thinking that this dinner is quite different than the first dinner at which we met.'

He raised an eyebrow. 'There's no lobster. Do you feel the lack?'

With a chuckle she shook her head. 'Quite the

contrary. Lobster is a favourite of Mabel's, not mine. This dinner has been perfect. Thank you.'

He swallowed more claret. 'Your fellow actress, Miss Coop. You don't seem alike in disposition. I wonder why you're friends.'

Calista straightened her spine as it tingled with suspicion. It reminded her Darius might well be holding back the relationship between his cousin and Mabel. 'There's much more to Mabel than many people think. There's often a lot of rivalry between actresses, but she isn't like that. I know she appears frivolous, but she's been a good and loyal friend to me, especially when my father... I mean, when Columbine fell ill.' She fell silent, knowing she'd said too much.

Across the table he was also silent for a moment. 'I didn't realise Miss Coop had such attributes.'

'She deserves to be happy. Your cousin is very kind to her and I'm glad of it. Mabel has been badly treated by men in the past.' More than one gentleman had used her as a plaything, in spite of Calista's warnings.

'So that's why you seek to defend her.'

'I certainly don't judge her. Don't you know better than to jump to conclusions about people?'

He lifted his glass towards her. 'If I didn't before, I do now.'

Calista sat back in her chair.

'I'm learning that, too,' she admitted.

His smile glimmered. 'I'm very pleased to hear it.'

He laid down his glass, sending the gold of his signet ring flashing.

'What's that symbol?' she asked curiously. It was a bird, from what she could see.

'It's my family crest. A swan, with its wings flared.'

'That sounds menacing.'

'My family might have been menacing over the years. But I'm sure we're not any longer.'

'I don't know about that. You weren't exactly polite when we first met, Your Grace.'

'I hoped that had been forgiven and forgotten.' He drummed his fingers lightly on the tablecloth, yet his gaze rested on her lips. 'I'm glad you came to dinner tonight. What made you agree?'

'Hunger,' she said lightly. She knew she ought to ask more about his cousin, but suddenly she didn't want to spoil the unexpected pleasure of the warm dining room and Darius's company by peppering him with questions.

He laughed. 'Then I'm glad you enjoyed the beef. Recently I received a leaflet on the street regarding the benefits of giving up meat in the diet. I wonder if it will ever become popular.'

He, too, seemed to seek a light subject for

conversation. It was at odds with the energy that swirled between them across the table.

'I've heard of the vegetable diet,' Calista replied. 'For Columbine's health a light diet has been recommended by some doctors and a heavy diet by others. It makes it difficult to know what to do.'

Darius frowned. 'Surely balance is required. That's what I was taught in the nursery. Moderation in all things.'

Calista raised an eyebrow. 'Is that your motto to go with your crest?'

He laughed. 'No. I take my immoderation moderately.' His face sobered. 'I fear you are immoderate, Miss Fairmont.'

When she opened her mouth ready to protest he raised his hand. 'Not in your eating or drinking habits.' He brushed his eyes over the upper part of her body with appreciation. 'There's no evidence of that.'

'In what way do you accuse me of being immoderate?'

'Do you ever take a holiday?'

'A holiday?'

'It's a strange period of time that people take off from their working lives.'

Calista chuckled. 'I must own I rarely take one. The last time we took a respite was to the seaside at Lyme. My father had sold a play and wanted to celebrate. The sea air did Columbine so much good, but that was four years ago.'

And, alas, that first payment for the play had been all that had transpired. Its performance had never come to fruition.

'That's a long time ago,' he said.

'It is. But it's strange you should ask. The Prince's Theatre is shortly to close for renovations. I'm due to have a week off, as is the rest of the cast. I don't know what I'll do with myself.' Or how they would manage at home with the loss of a week's pay. Not that she would furnish him with that information.

'Is that so?' he asked. 'You're not going away anywhere? To the seaside or to the countryside, or to Europe perhaps?'

She shook her head. 'Not this time.'

It would be a dream to take Columbine to any such destination, but their means were too straitened. She'd only just paid off one of the larger of Columbine's doctor's bills.

Darius leaned across the table. 'Why are you both mother and father to Columbine?'

Calista drew back. 'My mother died when Columbine was born. I remember her, but Columbine doesn't. She was a wonderful actress. And my father is...was a playwright.'

'Was.' He seized at the crucial word.

'I don't know what tense to use.' She took a

deep breath. 'My father's name is William Fairmont. You probably won't have heard of him for we lived in the north for some years, but he's well known in those parts. His plays were performed in York and Leeds and Manchester. A year or two ago we moved to London.'

She stopped. It was difficult to go on. 'Things didn't go as well for us as we hoped here in the capital. The theatres of Covent Garden have their favoured playwrights and my father's hopes were dashed more than once, although he always remained optimistic. He was thrilled when I got my first part, for it had always been his dream to have a play performed at the Prince's Theatre and for me to act in it. We were one step closer. But we still needed money, so my father went back to the north to put on a performance of one of his plays there. He wrote to tell me he'd gone into business partnership with a theatre owner and it all sounded so promising. Papa was convinced his fortune was about to be made. That was a year ago. He never came back.'

'Is he dead?' The duke didn't mince his words.

For a moment she couldn't reply. 'That's just it. We don't know. I pray not. But I must accept that to be the case, I think. I can't believe he'd simply abandon us. He's an honourable man, a good father.' Her chest heaved. 'I…I think he must be gone, just like my mother.'

Darius reached out across the table and seized her hands. His grip was strong. 'Don't, Miss Fairmont. You've got mettle, I saw it on stage. Don't give up hope for your father, until you know for certain. Don't bury him before he's gone.'

Her head drooped. She fought a sudden urge to weep. She'd kept it all inside for so long. She had to be brave, for Columbine, but her courage was sinking and she knew it.

'I've almost given up hope,' she whispered.

'That would be a mistake.' He released her fingers from his grip. 'Have you made enquiries as to what has happened to him?'

Once again her teeth found her lower lip. 'Of course. It's even more puzzling. I contacted my father's business partner. It was he who wrote back and said my father had left the theatre and wouldn't be back. It seems so strange. I've sent more letters and enquired of friends, but no one knows where Papa has gone. And his business partner seems to have disappeared, too.'

She hesitated for a moment before she started speaking again. 'I'd go north myself, but I don't have the means. Not the time, nor the money. Our only income comes from my work on the stage so I can't leave London, especially now that I have a leading role, and I can't leave Columbine or risk her health on the long journey either. Even now she becomes ill far too easily with coughs and fevers. She's worried, too. Worried and frightened we will never see Papa again, though she's a brave girl and tries to hide it. It's been a long winter for us.'

'So that's why you understood my family duty.'

'Yes.' She sighed. 'I'm sorry. I despise self-pity. I don't know why I'm telling you all of this.'

'It doesn't sound like self-pity. Sometimes we simply need to speak of our cares in order to cope with them.'

She peeped across the table at him. His jaw was set hard. 'Have you cares, then?'

'Not like yours. But family duty is family duty. The burden is never light.'

Family clearly meant a great deal to him. Here was the perfect opportunity to question him about his cousin. But before she could ask, the front door of the dining rooms opened and closed with a bang, snapping the thread of their connection.

A flower-seller with a basket wandered inside, bringing a blast of cold air with him, and the man stopped at their table. 'A rose for the pretty lady?'

Darius pointed at a small, half-opened bud. 'That one.'

He passed the man some coins.

'Thanking you kindly, my lord.' He tipped his hat and winked.

Rose in hand, Darius turned back to Calista. 'The shade matches your gown.'

'Thank you,' she managed to reply, as with an incline of his head he passed the bloom across the table. If he, too, experienced the shot of energy that accompanied their touch he gave no sign.

He glanced at her face. 'It matches your cheeks, too.' He gave a light chuckle.

Calista gripped the stem of the rose. Most of the thorns had been stripped off, but a small pointed one remained. 'The colour of my cheeks makes you laugh?'

'Forgive me,' he replied, with another chuckle. 'When we first met, I thought you were the kind of actress who permanently covered yourself in powder and paint.'

'But I never…oh! I remember. I hadn't removed my stage paint.'

'So I realise now. You need no artifice. The natural effect is quite charming, if I may say so.' Darius cast his napkin on to the table. 'It's getting late and I promised to get you home. Unless you would like anything else to eat… A *macaron*, perhaps?'

She still hadn't asked the questions that had burned on her lips all evening. 'Thank you. I've had sufficient.'

'Then I'll take you home. The carriage will be outside.'

He came around the table. As he helped her out of her chair he touched her waist. His fingers seemed to sear through her corset and petticoat, as if he'd branded her. Once again she experienced that strange, powerful connection between them, pulsating through her veins. His lips curved, as he seemed to note her reaction. Stepping aside, he stood by the door while she wrapped her cloak around her shoulders with suddenly clumsy fingers.

Outside on the street Darius helped her into the carriage and then followed her in, slamming the door behind them. He slid across the leather seat and reached for her.

Like a mermaid she slipped out of his grasp. 'I want to ask you a question.'

He took her hand and opened it, pressing his warm mouth to her palm. 'What is it?'

'I can't think when you do that.'

He trailed his lips up her wrist. 'What about this?'

'That's making it even more difficult.' She sighed, as his mouth moved higher.

His lips edged high above her bodice and on to her neck. 'And what about here? Do you want me here?'

She shivered against his lips, feeling the soft graze of his teeth find a sensitive place on her neck.

'Or do you want me here?' He took off his glove and brushed his finger around her mouth.

'You must listen,' she tried to say as his finger teased her. For a moment he continued to play with her lower lip. She fought back her unexpected urge to take his finger inside her mouth. What was happening to her?

She slid away on the carriage seat. It was too dangerous to stay so close beside him when all her senses yearned for him.

His mouth twisted as he took his hand away. 'All right. What is it?'

'It's about my friend Mabel and your cousin.'

Darius looked surprised. 'What about them?'

'Are you stopping their courtship in some way?' she asked bluntly.

His eyes darkened before he glanced away.

So it was as she suspected. 'I knew it! You're opposing their match, aren't you?'

His jaw was set hard as he turned back to face her. 'What did you expect? That I'd applaud and usher them down the aisle?'

'They might be very happy together. Who are you to decide?'

'There are things you don't know.'

'Then tell me, Darius.'

'You're using my name.'

He tugged her towards him and began once more to kiss her neck. 'What is it you want of me? I know what I want. It's to hear you say my name again.'

'Darius.' Half laughing, half serious, she scolded him, 'Listen to me. You ought to not interfere in your cousin's affairs.'

He stared into her eyes, his expression unfathomable. 'You're asking me to encourage my own cousin to court an actress.'

Calista lifted her chin. 'I'm an actress, too.'

'It's not something I'm likely to forget,' Darius ground out, as he pulled her against his body, crushing the rose pinned to her bodice.

His lips crashed down on hers.

Chapter Seven

I know thee, thou art honest;
Nicholas Rowe: *The Fair Penitent* (1703)

Darius knocked back a gulp of whisky and considered yet again the foolish terms he'd set with his cousin. He refocused on his search around the club room. He had hoped to spot Herbert, but he was no doubt spending time with his actress. It was incredible how little Darius had come to care about the whole affair with Miss Mabel Coop. But now Calista was asking questions.

When he'd first made the wager with Herbert he'd planned carefully how to court Miss Fairmont and prove her to be just the same as any other ladder-climbing, title-hunting actress.

Yet so far, nothing had gone according to plan.

Darius reflected on Calista's story. The poignant tale of the loss of her father, missing in the north. Her near hopelessness, the sick young sister. The responsibility she took on herself.

He wondered what had happened to William Fairmont to make him disappear like that, to never come back from the north. Where was he? What had happened to him? Perhaps he had tired of the burden of two daughters to provide for. Yet from Calista's words he hadn't sounded like that kind of man. Could such a man have raised a daughter like Calista?

The recollection of their touch blasted through him, straight to his centre. Sensual fireworks had erupted without warning, burning them both with their flare. She had felt the spark, too. She'd jumped visibly on the street when he had first taken her hand, and that had been through the leather of his glove. Then in the carriage he'd been unable to resist seeing what would happen when their fingers met skin to skin. And then he'd kissed her...

He nearly groaned aloud.

He knew how rarely that extraordinary connection was experienced, that blaze of fire between two people.

There was no mistaking it in those kisses. The sharp bite of passion. That passion was evident in her acting and he knew he ought not to be surprised. But when he had met it lip to lip, combined with the sweet taste of innocence...

This time his groan was audible.

Of course, he didn't know what had come over him when he'd thought that she might be suitable as a wife. It had been ridiculous to think of that, even for a moment.

But when he'd told Herbert that he'd resolved on a sham courtship of the actress, he had assumed it would be fairly straightforward.

Flattery. Flowers. Gifts.

Yet he'd come to realise that Calista Fairmont didn't like flattery and even less so the gifts. Her aversion was no coy actress ploy, but a clear preference. If he complimented her on her art it had to be sincere. She was too discerning for him to do otherwise. He'd planned, originally, simply to wait outside the theatre each night to walk her home, rather than to watch the play over and over again. But still he found himself drawn by some irresistible force to the Prince's Theatre each night. There he sat in his box, unable to take his eyes away from her. His admiration of her art was sincere; there was no need for false flattery.

Now his admiration had extended to her as a woman. She was brave, intelligent and loyal. Passionate and innocent.

His list was exhausted and his plan had been ruined.

Did she know how alluring she was? Dressed in her simple, almost shabby pink gown, with its low ruffles and tiny silvery buttons, the full creamy curve of her breasts rising from it, inviting his lips, his touch.

He wanted more. He had to kiss her again. He had to know if it was true, that her body, pressed against his, had fitted against him in a way that told him instantly that she was made for him alone.

Darius tossed back the last of his drink as the irresistible force pulled him to his feet.

He was on his way to the Prince's Theatre. Again.

When he arrived he took his usual place in the box. He glanced around the space as it began to fill. The theatre had a domed roof, a particularly fine design, plastered in white scrollwork and picked out with gold. On each side of the stage were the boxes, including, next to his, the Royal box, used for years by the theatre-loving prince for whom the building had first been named. There was yet another tier of boxes above in the gallery, but they were less sought after, along with the rest of the cheaper seats.

From his vantage point he had an excellent view of the ornate stage. It had its own gilding above decorated with cupids and flowers. On each side golden pillars held thick candles and lamps swung from the ceiling. To the front was hung the thick red-velvet curtain with gold fringing.

The curtain went up.

Darius leaned forward and gripped the edge of the box.

What in hellfire was going on?

Another actress was playing Calista's part.

Darius paced outside the stage door. The other cast members were beginning to come out, but there was no sign of Calista. To his consternation, Fred the doorkeeper had had no idea why she hadn't performed.

Darius swore beneath his breath.

From out of the corner of his eye he spotted Lord Merrick who had rejoined the crowd of gentlemen waiting outside the stage door. Darius hadn't seen Merrick at the theatre since that incident the other night, when he'd sent him on his way.

'The duke can't hold his harlot. She's gone missing,' Merrick sneered to one of his cronies.

Darius grabbed the man by his cravat and slammed him up against the wall. 'What did you say?'

'I say!' Herbert appeared, putting his hand on Darius's shoulder. 'Steady on.'

Darius only tightened his hold. 'Where's Miss Fairmont? What have you done with her?'

'I wouldn't tell you, Albury,' Merrick choked with a cough. 'But do let me know when you're done with her.'

A squeal came from behind them. 'Calista is at home with her sister!'

Darius twisted his neck to hear who had spoken. Mabel Coop rushed out of the stage door in a flurry of fur. 'What?'

'That's right! That's why she couldn't come to the theatre tonight. Columbine's ill!'

'You're sure?' Lord Merrick was starting to splutter, but Darius kept hold of him, just in case.

'Martha came with a message just before we opened. That's why the understudy went on and the manager is none too happy about it.'

'Mabel would know, Darius,' added Herbert nervously.

He gave Merrick another shake before dropping him like a rat. Then, without another word he turned and strode towards his carriage.

'You'll be sorry for that!' Merrick shouted hoarsely.

Darius spun around. 'Not as sorry as you'll be, Merrick, if you ever go near Miss Fairmont again.'

Calista jumped as a loud rap came at the door. 'Darius!'

The duke stood at the threshold, top hat in his hands.

'I had to come,' he said, his voice low.

'I'm glad you did.' Her relief at seeing him shocked her.

A muscle twitched in his jaw. 'How is Columbine? They told me at the theatre she was ill.'

Calista glanced over her shoulder to where her sister lay in the bed by the fire. 'She had one of her attacks. But she's sleeping now.'

The duke's gaze swept over the room behind her. 'Can you talk with me for a moment? I won't come inside, but perhaps you'll consent to sit in the carriage.'

'You go, Miss Fairmont,' Martha said. 'I'll watch Miss Columbine, don't you worry.'

Calista seized her cloak and threw it over the old cotton frock she'd been wearing all day. Her hair was falling free of her usual chignon and she'd not glanced in the glass all day, but somehow, it didn't matter.

'Just for a few minutes,' she whispered.

Outside on the street he took her in his arms.

She fought back the urge to lean against his broadcloth cloak and sob. She, who was always so strong!

'You're shaking,' he said, tenderly. 'Here, get into the carriage.'

Darius opened the door and, when she was

seated, covered her with a lap blanket before getting in beside her.

'When did the attack happen?' he asked.

'Last night,' she replied, shivering. She wasn't sure if it was the result of the cold air after coming outside, or the after-effects of fatigue. She hadn't slept the night before or left Columbine's side all day.

'You weren't on stage.'

'No.' She bit her lip. 'It won't have put me in favour with the manager, but the theatre closes next week, as I told you. The manager gave me leave tonight, but he won't allow it again. But I couldn't perform. It was impossible. I couldn't bear to leave her.'

'Has the doctor been to see her?'

Calista twisted her hands in her lap. It had cost another vast sum of money that she could barely afford, but she'd had to ensure Columbine got the best care.

'The doctor carried out a thorough examination. It's a childish ailment, he said. All we can hope is that she will outgrow the attacks.' She smiled, briefly. 'He said there's nothing wrong with her spirit, in any case, even though she's been frail for so long. But her chest is so weak. Plenty of fresh air and exercise is what she needs.'

Darius frowned. 'She's hardly going to get that in the city.'

'I'll just have to do my best.' She twisted her hands tighter. 'For the next few days she needs to take it slowly. I'm sure it must be the London air that makes Columbine ill, but next week I can take her to the park every day and...'

Darius reached out and gripped her fingers, encasing them in his, like gloves. 'Calista. You must let me help you.'

'What do you mean?' His strong hands soothed her.

'You must get Columbine out of the city. Might you consider a holiday next week?'

'I'd love to take Columbine away, but we don't have the means.'

'I know a house that is available and excellently suited to your needs. It has woods and fields and a stream bursting with fish. There are stables with horses to suit all abilities, even children, and excellent staff to attend to your every wish. And there's no cost involved.'

'It sounds too good to be true. What manner of place is it?'

'It's called Albury Hall. It's my estate.'

She slipped her fingers free of his hold. 'What?'

He inclined his head. 'If you would care to bring your sister Columbine for a visit, I'm sure it will be of benefit to her health.'

Her jaw dropped open. 'Visit your estate? Forgive me. I'm repeating everything you say. Did I hear you right? Do you mean to invite us to your home?'

'Indeed. It strikes me that an opportunity to play in the fields and to breathe some fresh country air is exactly what your sister needs.' He glanced out of the carriage window. 'A change from London. I can't promise you less rain in Buckinghamshire, but I can offer you less fog.'

Darius raised her palm to his lips, warming it with his breath. 'Come to Albury Hall. Please, Calista, consider my offer.'

Her head spun as Darius's lips lingered on her palm. Once again she experienced that strange, powerful connection between them, throbbing through her blood.

Didn't he know what he asked? To accept such an invitation was beyond the bounds of propriety even for an actress. She knew that. Yet she sensed instantly that his concern for Columbine and for herself was genuine. And she refused to lie to herself. Her relief when he'd appeared at the door... She wanted to be near him. 'I don't know what to say.'

'Say yes.'

'Will you be there?'

'It depends on whether you want me there.'

'Do you often invite actresses to your home?' she asked slowly.

His mouth twisted before he took his lips away, leaving a warm spot on her skin. 'Let me make this perfectly clear. I've never welcomed an actress to Albury Hall.'

But he wanted her. Calista's head whirled.

'Come to my home.' Darius reached out and brushed her hair from her forehead. She felt the strands fall loose. She'd barely scraped it into a bun that morning. All her attention had been on Columbine. 'Bring your sister. Please.'

She shook her head, sent even more curls flying free. 'You're a man of the world. I'm a woman of the theatre. I may not have indulged in the flirtations of my fellow actresses, but I know where they lead. To stay at your country estate is quite out of the question.' She slid away from him on the carriage seat. 'Thank you for your offer, but I must refuse. It would be improper.'

He raised an eyebrow. 'What's this? An actress lecturing a duke on propriety? What of your unconventionality? Don't play coy, I beg you.'

'I've never played coy in my life,' Calista retorted. 'And I don't intend to start now. It's true, I make my own rules, but I have Columbine to think of. I am her example in life and she has no other. How would it appear if I started gadding about the country with a duke?'

His mouth curved upwards. 'I don't believe I mentioned gadding.'

'You understand my meaning very well.' She took a deep breath. 'Thank you for the invitation, but I must decline. We shall be quite all right here in London. My sister is my responsibility and mine alone.'

His jaw clenched. 'You seem to have an aversion to letting anyone help you. Are you determined never to rely upon another person? Is that it? I've already taken your sister to tea and she came to no harm. Surely she won't find it so strange for you at accept an invitation to stay in the country with a friend.'

She met his gaze squarely. 'Is that what we are to each other?'

'That is what we need to find out,' he ground out. 'For goodness' sake, not even an actress of your calibre can counterfeit what we have together. I know you feel it, too.'

Her heart drummed. She couldn't deny it. That was what frightened her most. In his arms, she feared she could deny him nothing. 'This has already gone too far.'

'It hasn't gone far enough.' He paused, frowning. 'Let me think. What if other people were with us?'

'Do you mean my eight-year-old sister? Columbine isn't a chaperone, Your Grace.'

He ran his fingers through his hair in an impatient gesture. It was quite a habit of his, she'd noted.

'What about my cousin Herbert?' he asked after a moment. 'He could come, too—with your friend Miss Coop. Would that do?'

Calista gaped at him. 'You'd invite Mabel to your home? After everything…?'

'Don't you understand, Calista? I'd do anything for you. Say yes to my invitation and I'll ask them both to stay at my estate, along with your sister and your maidservant and whoever else it takes your fancy to have me invite.'

He took her in his arms again. It was taking all her strength to resist him.

'You've been under so much strain,' he said, with that tenderness in his voice again. 'Your father missing. Columbine's illness. The business with Lord Merrick.'

She shuddered. 'Don't remind me.'

'Let me help you,' he urged.

Still she hesitated. For so long she'd carried her cares alone.

'Please, Calista.' Darius held her closer. 'Come to Albury Hall. Come to my home.'

Chapter Eight

~~~~~~~~

Take care my gates be open, bid all welcome:

Nicholas Rowe: *The Fair Penitent* (1703)

'Horses, cows, sheep, pigs, chickens, geese and ducks,' Columbine chanted as the carriage rolled along the country road. 'That's what we're going to see.'

'I certainly hope so after the number of times you've repeated those words all the way to Buckinghamshire.' Calista shook her head with a rueful grin. Columbine's high spirits had come to the fore. Her terrifying lack of breath had abated and the attack had passed, leaving only pallor and not even the faintest wheeze. It seemed to be a pattern. All too often, Columbine went through a kind of honeymoon phase, when it was as if the terrifying breathlessness had never been, but she could then have a severe relapse with even worse symptoms. Now, as usual, Calista's problem would be stopping her young sister from overtaxing herself. At least they were out of the city and the bad air, which she was convinced must be some kind of irritant for Columbine's chest.

She glanced out of the carriage window. Darius had sent the carriage for them. Buckinghamshire was even more rural than she had expected. The summer fields were glossy and green with young wheat and barley and ash. Oak and hazel trees rose beside them in places, sometimes veering off into other wooded copses and lanes. The hedges burst with primroses and some white-and-red flowers she didn't know the name of. Others were shaped like stars, yellow as buttercups. The sky was pale blue, the same shade as Columbine's smock, and dotted here and there with clouds as fluffy as the powder puffs they used in the backstage dressing room.

Never before had she behaved in such an impetuous manner.

She'd opened her mouth to firmly decline his invitation. Instead she heard herself consent. Not once, but twice.

'Yes. Yes.'

Then he'd kissed her again.

His strong, warm embrace had given her the most extraordinary and conflicting sensations of safety and danger. He held her so tight, so safe, and yet there was an edge of current that had ripped through her body so fast she had only wanted to submerge herself in him.

How could a man who had first appeared so austere arouse such a tumult in her? The unexpected kindness she'd found in him warmed her heart. No, the duke wasn't cold. He might have erected a shield made of steel, but behind it…

Calista put a gloved finger to her lips. When he had kissed her that way she'd been unable to resist.

'Come to Albury Hall. Come to my home.' The recollection of that seeking mouth on her lips, her chin, her throat, made her knees weaken again even now. 'Not just for Columbine. For us. Discover what this is between us.'

She had to admit it. She wanted to discover it, too. She refused to play coy or to pretend about these new feelings for the Duke of Albury. He'd awoken something powerful inside her. Calista knew the visit would benefit Columbine and Mabel, too. It might be thought improper to have accepted, but in her life, in her career, she had never fitted the mould expected of her.

And then there was the tragedy in Darius's childhood that Mabel had alluded to. Yes, she wanted to discover more about the duke.

At the news of the invitation Mabel had practically squealed with joy, and already Columbine looked better. The late-May day was warm and they'd opened the carriage windows. The huge breath of clear country air she took into her lungs lifted the lacy frill that covered the threadbare section of her dark-blue foulard gown.

They passed by another stone cottage that had smoke curling from the chimney. Calista wondered what Albury Hall would be like. She guessed it would be a large house with a big garden, and the duke had said there were stables. Beyond that she knew nothing.

When she'd enquired further Darius had merely shrugged. 'It's my home. One stops noticing when one grows up in such a place. You'll be comfortable, I can promise you.'

'Look!' Columbine pointed out the window. 'A-L-B-U-R-Y. That sign spells Albury!'

'Very good, Miss Columbine.' Martha beamed. She, too, looked happy to be out in the country. The maid had grown up on a farm, whereas Calista and Columbine had always lived in cities and towns, wherever their father could find work at the theatres. The countryside was new to them.

'We must be about to see Albury Hall,' Calista said.

Her sister almost fell out of the carriage window. 'Which one is it?'

Calista's brow furrowed as she stared at the cottages lining the road. Why, it was charming, but their surroundings weren't at all what she had anticipated. They appeared to be in a village, a pretty village to be sure, with thatched stone cottages, with a steeple, a public house and a village green, but still, she hadn't expected Darius to live in a village.

Darius.

She rolled the name on her tongue.

'Could that be it?' Calista pointed to the large square, many-windowed house beside the church.

'I think that's the vicarage, Miss Fairmont,' Martha said.

'Oh, yes, of course.'

Columbine wrinkled her brow, perplexed. 'But the sign said Albury.'

'If you don't mind me saying, Miss Columbine, the house might not be in this village. Sometimes a village is named the same as the biggest house in the area. The village belongs to the gentry, if you get my meaning.'

'Do you mean the duke owns this whole village?' Columbine's eyes were like saucers.

Martha shrugged. 'Could be.'

Calista's heart stuttered as the carriage rolled out of the village. She ought to have made further investigations about Albury Hall before they had accepted the duke's invitation. They were definitely going to be town mice in the country, and poor little mice at that. No mere frill on her bodice would disguise their impoverished background.

A-L-B-U-R-Y F-A-R-M.' Columbine pointed down a lane. 'Is that where the duke lives?'

Martha shook her head. 'Don't expect so, miss. In the country there's often a farm that provides for the big house. Gives them eggs, and milk and cheese and such.'

All at once, Calista wanted to rap on the carriage roof, stop the driver and demand he turn around and take them straight back to London. Instead the driver made a sharp turn through a pair of vast stone gates and down an oak-lined lane. The horses sped up as if they knew they were almost home.

Columbine bounced on her seat. 'We're nearly there! I'm sure we are.'

The lane narrowed through a glade of trees. Sunlight dappled through the oak leaves and woodland birds called and fluttered overhead. A tortoiseshell-patterned butterfly darted by the carriage window, and Calista was sure she glimpsed the movement of an animal deeper in the woods off to one side. It looked like a deer, but she must surely have imagined it.

The horses sped up as the carriage made another sharp right-hand turn on to a long drive.

Calista gasped.

Albury Hall was much more than a comfortable country home.

She pushed back her bonnet and stared. A shaft of afternoon sunlight made a beacon flare along the long tree-lined driveway and the carriage continued to roll along. White swans glided on a smooth lake which seemed to stretch on forever.

And then there it was, Albury Hall. Built on an incline of perfectly manicured lawns edged by shrubs and flower beds, the magnificent two-storey building had three rows of long windows on the upper and lower floors that glinted in the sun. Some of the upper-floor windows had balconies leading from them and above was a row of smaller attic windows. The building reminded Calista of an illustration from her old Mother Goose fairy-tale book that she still sometimes read aloud to Columbine. Rendered partly in white plaster, at the front of the building there was a portico and tall proud columns on either side of wide marble steps. At the back were two squat towers in golden stone that looked like turrets.

The Duke of Albury's home was a castle.

On the steps, the wind blowing back his hair from his broad forehead, stood the man himself.

Darius laughed. Miss Fairmont continually surprised him. 'It's not a castle. I swear.'

'It's enormous,' she said in a low voice as he helped her out of the carriage, brushing the footman aside.

'I've never been reproached for the size of my home before,' he said, amused.

'I thought you said it was comfortable.'

This time he laughed even louder. 'It is comfortable. I promise.'

It ought to be. He'd gone for a long horse ride to stop himself from interfering with the servants further, who were quite clearly flummoxed by his unheralded interest in household affairs. He'd never cared much before. He valued the ancient rules of hospitality, but he had to admit his concern for his forthcoming guests wasn't equally spread. His cousin Herbert had visited so often that he was barely a guest, and as for Miss Mabel Coop, he would do his duty as a host, but her comfort wasn't in his cousin's hands. He cared about the little girl Columbine's health with a concern that went deeper than he'd anticipated, yet in truth only one guest's comfort truly concerned Darius.

Since their incredible embraces he'd battled with his conflicting urges: desire and disbelief. Preparing for her arrival, he'd managed to halt himself from making a ridiculous romantic gesture, such as leaving a rose by her bedside in the same shade as the one he had given her that night when they had dined together. He still recalled the rose's scent engulfing him as it had been crushed between them, against her breast. Ever since he had met her full lips with his own and felt the passion of her response that matched his as if she were made for him alone, he had been forced to reconsider his long-held beliefs.

Now with her standing in front of him, desire surged up again.

Her distress at her sister's illness had only made him more certain. He wanted to help her, to protect her. He felt a need to get her out of London and to relieve the burdens of her daily life. He longed to give what was between them room to grow, with no distractions.

He winced. Miss Mabel Coop's arrival later would be a distraction and he would be forced to face Herbert and explain his change of intentions. He knew he could no longer go through with duping Calista. The play was over. He didn't relish having to tell his cousin. He barely knew how to explain it to himself, the force of his feelings resisted words, but for honour's sake it had to be done. It was a price he was willing to pay in order to bring Calista to Albury Hall.

Now she stared up at his home, revealing that long, slender neck. 'Surely calling this a hall is most misleading.'

'It was a hall in Saxon times, though there's

not much left of the original, it's true. It's been added to over the years.'

'How many years?'

'Hundreds. They were keen builders in the Carlyle family back in Tudor times, but it has never been a fortified castle. My Tudor forebears added wood panelling and stonework, and there's still a bit of that black-and-white-striped effect. Then another Carlyle came into some money last century. That was when the classical front and two new wings were added, making the house enormous. They could easily have made a mess of it, but it seems to have come together.'

Calista gazed at the building. It seemed to shimmer in the mellow afternoon light. Albury always shone as the sun lowered in the sky. He was glad she was seeing it at its best.

'It's beautiful,' she said. 'The proportions are perfect.'

'I agree.' He looked straight at her. She appeared even more beautiful than in London in the setting of Albury Hall, and the notion came to him that she was made for it. Even in her shabby grey cloak and the simple blue gown beneath it, as she stood on the steps of the hall she appeared the ideal chatelaine, as if she were poised to welcome arriving guests. Something in the way she stood, her height and willowy figure, and her expression—intelligent, yet kind…

'Hello, Your Grace.' Columbine bounced up the steps and stood beneath the portico. She beamed up at him. 'I like your house. The front looks like it's covered in royal icing.'

He smiled at the girl. She looked in better health than he'd anticipated. 'We'll have to find you some cake with royal icing before you try to break off bits of my home and eat it, like in the story of *Hansel and Gretel*.'

She giggled. 'I won't eat your house. Or huff and puff and try to blow it down like the wolf in *The Three Little Pigs*.'

'Do you like fairy tales?' he asked. 'I believe there are some books upstairs in the nursery if you'd like to look at them.'

'Will you read to me?'

'Columbine...' Calista broke in.

Darius laughed. 'I'm sure we can find someone in my home who will read stories just the way you like.'

'Cally reads them best,' Columbine confided. 'She does all the different little piggy voices.'

'Now that I'd like to hear,' he replied as Calista flushed. 'Please, come inside.'

He led them all into the entrance hall, Jenkins, the butler, hovering at their heels.

The entrance hall was one of the rooms Darius liked the most. It was a room in itself in a fashion, with a black-and-white marble floor and a curving staircase that flowed upwards from the rear.

'That door to the left leads into what was originally the Saxon hall.' He pointed. 'It's now the drawing room and the dining room is beyond it. That way...' he turned on his heel and pointed to the right '...is the long gallery. It leads to the library and some other reception rooms. There's a morning room I've put aside for your special use while you are here. Would you like a tour of the house, or do you care for rest and refreshment after your journey?'

'Oh, please, couldn't we see the horses first?'

'Columbine!' Calista sounded exasperated. 'It's rude to ask that when we've barely arrived.'

'Not at all.' Darius winked, turning to the girl. 'Do you know what you do whilst on holiday?'

Columbine shook her head.

'Whatever you please.'

Columbine clasped her hands together. 'Oh, that sounds wonderful!'

'Columbine hardly needs any encouragement in being headstrong, Darius,' Calista put in.

'Another family similarity.' He leaned close to Calista and added in an undertone, 'I like the sound of my name on your lips. But I'd like to hear you say it when we're alone again. I liked that even more.'

Once again colour suffused her cheeks, darker

than the centre of the rose he'd given her. But she smelled just as sweet. A fresh scent rose from her hair.

Blast. He battled his craving to kiss her, to give her a proper welcome. He was determined to ensure they had some time together without the chaperonage of Columbine, charming as the girl was, or, heaven help him, his cousin Herbert and Miss Coop.

'Do you need any refreshment before we visit the stables?' he asked instead.

'We lunched at Aylesbury,' Calista replied.

'And we've got our walking boots on,' added Columbine. 'Well, they're our only boots, but Cally said they'll do for the country as well as the town.'

Columbine pointed out one booted toe on the end of a darned black-stocking-clad leg. The worn but highly polished boots and the many darns in the stocking made Darius's heart give a surprising clench of something that came far too close to pity.

Calista Fairmont would hate pity as much as she hated flattery.

To eliminate the feeling he spoke teasingly, 'Shall I inspect your boots, too?'

Calista pursed her full lips together. The effect was as powerful as her speaking his name. Desire coursed instantly through his body.

'My boots require no examination,' she said.

'What a pity,' he drawled.

He nodded at Jenkins, who he knew would attend to their luggage. It appeared to consist of a shabby portmanteau and a carpet bag, unless more was to come from the carriage. 'Then we'll go to the stables now.'

'Then you must take a rest, Columbine,' Calista warned.

Columbine seized Darius's hand as they strolled across the ground to the stables. 'I've brought breeches. They used to belong to one of Martha's brothers. Acrobats don't ride side-saddle, even girls.'

Her hand was slightly clammy. With anticipation, he presumed, although he noted Calista giving her sister a worried look.

Darius frowned. Too much excitement was probably bad for the girl. No wonder Calista always appeared so concerned. He'd tell the servants to keep a close watch on Columbine, to give her elder sister a rest.

'Have you had riding lessons?' he asked the girl.

'Not yet.' She puffed out her cheeks, but she didn't seem short of breath, he was relieved to note. 'They're frightfully expensive. Papa used to give me rides on his shoulders, but you're even taller than him. I'd be able to see even more.'

He chuckled. 'My shoulders are at your disposal, but it's probably better if you have some lessons on a horse while you're here, if your sister allows it.' Darius glanced at Calista. 'Did you bring a riding habit?'

'I don't ride, I'm afraid,' she replied.

'Another pity.' She would probably have ridden side-saddle in any case, he supposed, which struck him as a shame. Calista's legs in breeches were worth the price of a trip to the theatre alone.

'Why, these stables are as fine as the house,' Calista exclaimed as they approached the stone building.

'A previous Carlyle had a love of horses.' And cards and women of a certain kind, he thought privately.

Columbine danced with excitement as they entered the vast barn with its stalls of horses.

'There are so many! Black and grey, dappled and bay,' she chanted.

'I have just the horse for you.' Darius nodded to one of the grooms, who'd rushed to attendance. 'Bring out Bluebell.'

'Right away, Your Grace.'

'Oh!' Columbine exclaimed as the groom led out a fat, grey pony. 'Is that the horse I'll ride?'

'Don't you like it?' he asked, amused. 'Here, come and give her a pat.' He stroked the horse's mane. 'Any child is safe on Bluebell,' he added, for Calista's benefit.

With her eyes Miss Fairmont conveyed her gratitude to him. His need to be alone with her grew almost overpowering. He fought back his urge to pull her down into a bale of straw right there in the stables.

'Bluebell is perfect,' Calista said, breaking the tension. 'Don't you think so, Columbine?'

The girl patted the pony's back. 'She's lovely. She just isn't quite what I imagined, that's all.'

'What did you imagine?' asked Darius.

'Why, I imagined a horse like that one.' Columbine pointed to the black stallion pawing the ground in the stall opposite. 'That's the kind of horse I saw at the circus. Black as night and it had spangles on its halter.'

'That's no circus horse, miss,' the groom put in. 'Jupiter be the duke's horse. He's a thoroughbred.'

Columbine's eyes rounded. 'Is that a special kind of horse?'

'Best there is, miss,' said the groom. 'Only the master can control a horse like that.'

'You'll need to start on Bluebell,' Darius said firmly. 'Jupiter isn't for little girls to ride.'

Columbine stepped towards the horse. 'Do horses dream? How do they sleep? Standing up?'

'Mostly,' he said. 'They close their eyes and

droop their heads, and probably have lovely dreams of being out in a clover field.'

Columbine giggled.

'Sometimes, they lie flat out on the stable floor,' he added.

'Like I do in my bed. I must be a horse.'

Darius smiled. 'I'll order carrots for breakfast.'

'Talking of sleep, Columbine, you really must go for a rest,' Calista said firmly, ignoring her sister's giggle that quickly turned to a groan.

'She thinks she's better,' Calista said in an undertone to Darius. 'This is the danger period. She needs extra attention.'

'Of course. I understand.' But for him it was Calista he wanted to give his attention to. His need to hold her again was almost unbearable.

He drew her aside. 'Do you need a rest, too?'

'I'd rather take a walk,' she surprised him by saying.

He chuckled. 'I might have guessed. You're determined to make me wear out my shoe leather, Miss Fairmont.'

'It would be refreshing after the journey. I thought I saw a deer in the grounds as we came up in the carriage.'

'Indeed, you may have, in the woods. There's fine hunting on my lands.'

She shuddered. 'How dreadful to hunt such a beautiful creature.'

'It's part of country life.' Darius moved closer to her. 'I need to be alone with you.'

At Calista's smile his stomach lurched with desire.

'I'd like to see the woods,' she replied.

Chapter Nine

With woods, with fruits, with flowers, and verdant grass.

Nicholas Rowe: *The Fair Penitent* (1703)

'Why, this is beautiful.' Calista breathed in the mossy air. 'Surely these woods are enchanted.'

Darius laughed. 'That's not what the village children say. They call it haunted.'

'Surely not.' She pushed back her bonnet as the tingling caused by his nearness spread through her body. 'These trees are so green. And look at those primroses and bluebells.'

'Spring and summer paint the woods in bright colours.' The brim of his hat also shadowed his face. 'Yet in winter, when the trees are not in leaf, the woods can be a frightening place. The wind rushes through the branches, making the trees whisper as if they are people, not plants.'

'You love this place.' Calista spoke lightly, yet

her mind whirred. She realised she wanted him to tell her about his childhood, after what Mabel had hinted at. She yearned to know more about him. When he'd invited her to Albury Hall, he had said he wanted them to discover more about each other. In spite of her reservations then, now she wanted that, too.

His scent was known to her now. In the stables she'd had the strange desire to nestle against his strong neck, like the way horses did. She bit her lip. She had to control the sensations he aroused in her. But he intrigued her. Allowing time to get to know him seemed more honest than keeping him at a distance set by convention. She wasn't going to dissemble, even if he was a duke.

She smiled inwardly. His title didn't seem to matter to her any more.

Now he shrugged. 'Childish eyes make a different landscape.'

'Did you play in the woods as a child?' She asked the leading question with the light tone she used on stage.

'With many of the village children and sometimes with Herbert when he came to stay. Of course when I went away to school I lost touch with some of the children from the village. The gap between us widened, but the connection remains.'

'You were an only child. You must have been lonely sometimes.'

Again he shrugged. 'I didn't know any different.'

From beneath her bonnet she studied him. It was on the tip of her tongue to ask him more about the tragedy Mabel had mentioned. But she didn't want to spoil the moment, strolling through the woods with him at her side.

Once more, as when they'd walked together through the London streets at night, he matched his pace to hers. Or perhaps it was hers that changed to match his. She couldn't be sure. All she knew was that they fitted in time together, just as her body had fitted to his when he had first kissed her. His long stride was familiar to her now. She would almost have known him by his tread alone as they made their way deeper into the woodland, the sun lengthening their shadows.

Soon their shadows disappeared as the thicker canopy of trees overhead blocked the sun's rays. In the undergrowth she sensed hidden animal life as well as plant life. Small, scurrying creatures. And larger animals, too. Foxes, perhaps. Or maybe the deer she'd thought she had seen from the carriage as it had rolled through the gates.

The thought of a doe being hunted sent a chill down her spine.

Calista peered around the wood, suddenly

frightened. Perhaps the woodland scene wasn't as pretty and innocent as it seemed. Perhaps there was danger hidden in the undergrowth that she had never suspected.

Beneath her cloak, with a roll of her shoulders, she forced the strange foreboding away. She was often far too fanciful. It was part of being an actress, she supposed, an intuition essential to the craft, but it could lead her astray. Why, she knew little of country life. Hunting was commonplace in the country, as much for livelihood as for sport. It wasn't her place to judge.

Bringing herself back to the present, she studied the duke's attire as he strode along the path. He'd torn off his hat and his head was bare, his dark hair ruffled in the breeze. The colours of his brown leather boots and long scarf, hanging over his long tweed coat, blended into the colours of the woods.

Her stomach rippled, deep down.

Camouflage.

A hunter.

The duke was a man who would seek out his prey and never give up.

Calista chuckled.

'What brings you such mirth?' he asked drily.

'If when we met first in London I'd thought that I would be walking through the woods with the Duke of Albury, I'd never have believed it.'

'You're enjoying yourself, I hope.'

She met his glance with honesty. 'Very much.'

A slight smile curved his lips. 'That pleases me.'

'You seemed such a London gentleman,' she teased. 'I didn't expect you to suit your country landscape so well.'

He halted on the woodland path. 'I thought the same thing about you on the steps of Albury Hall.'

A leaf floated down from a branch above as she also stopped. 'You did?'

The duke's voice became husky as he pulled Calista into his arms. 'Indeed.'

Throughout the long walk in the woods Darius had waited to kiss her.

He'd waited until the branches hid them, protected them from the prying eyes at the house. Not that he minded the servants' interest. They wished him well, he knew, just as they knew that they would be treated fairly by him, always, in good times and bad. The villagers of Albury, too, knew they were more than tenants to him. He'd grown up with many of them. They might have lived in different houses, but they had shared the same landscape, season by season, year on year. That made a bond not easily broken.

Nonetheless, he had wanted to be alone with her, unseen by others, to kiss her again in the shelter of the trees. To discover if it was true, that the passion of her lips matched his own as if she were made for him alone, that in his arms she became part of his body, at one with his mind.

It was true.

The kiss in the darkened London streets had merely kindled the flame.

Beneath the boughs, now, the flame was relit, as if their lips joining could turn the leaves around them into a bonfire.

The fullness of her lips, the taste of her almost made him groan aloud as he found her again, as her slim body pressed against the force of his own.

Was it possible to taste goodness?

Surely it was in her kiss. Her character, her honour, her nobility of spirit. All that he tasted, sensed, as her arms circled his neck, and he curved her further into him, like the bough of a willow tree that bent, but did not break.

He opened her generous mouth wider to him, let his tongue taste her sweet goodness as if he could take it into his soul. It changed something inside him, kissing her. It was as if her body conveyed words in the same way she acted upon the stage.

He hadn't known she could play a character with her lips.

The unwelcome thought slammed into his mind and he jerked his body away from her.

Released from his grip, she stood gasping beneath the branches of the oak.

'Is something wrong?'

He shook his head. 'There can be nothing wrong with a kiss like that, Calista.'

Her taut body formed the shape of a question.

'I was just remembering how you showed me the secret of how you acted.' He thrust the clenched rocks of his fists into his coat pockets. 'You may recall, you demonstrated on the street. How easily you can become someone else. How you can imbue your body with the characters you play.'

She replaced her bonnet, the gesture hiding her eyes. 'It's part of the craft of acting.'

'Crafty indeed,' he drawled.

She lifted her chin. Now he could see the flash of her sapphire eyes. 'You make it sound as if I act a lie.'

'But you do act a lie, don't you?'

She became still, as still as a doe caught in the sights of his rifle. 'What do you mean by that?'

'You lie about acting.' He held up his hand to halt her before she could utter a furious reply. 'I enjoy your sister Columbine's company—she's most enlightening. I've learned a great deal about you. I know you never wanted to be an actress.'

Calista gasped. 'She told you that?'

'Not on purpose. Don't be angry with her. It slipped out.'

'It always does with Columbine,' Calista said grimly. 'I trust it's a fault she'll outgrow.'

'At the moment her fault is to my advantage. Tell me. Why are you an actress if it isn't your calling?'

'I have to provide for Columbine,' she said simply. 'I do what I must. I have no other way to earn money.'

He stepped back. He'd jumped to so many conclusions about her and all of them appeared to be wrong. 'So you don't seek the stage for fame or fortune—'

'Or a title,' she broke in with a laugh and a half-dip of a curtsy. 'No, Your Grace.'

'Yet you defend actresses.' She'd spoken up with such outrage. He would never forget her courage.

'I defend my sex,' she corrected him. 'The women of my profession.'

'But if you're not an actress by choice, how do you continue to perform on stage, night after night?' No wonder she was often so weary. 'If your heart isn't in your role…'

'You mistake my meaning.' She stared past him, into the shadowy trees. 'My heart is with my sister. I act no lie on stage. It wouldn't be possible for me to do that. I do not pretend to want to be there. I do want to, for Columbine's sake. I put all that I am into my roles and I play them in truth.'

In his pockets his fists uncurled. 'I understand now.'

'It's hard to explain.'

'You've explained well enough.' He understood her better and with that he found he admired her even more. 'Tell me about your real calling. What made you want to become a playwright? Surely it's unusual for a woman.'

'I grew up watching my father write plays. I emulated him, as many children do their parents. But it wasn't only the writing of plays I witnessed, day after day, night after night, for my father worked very hard at his art. He also took me to see plays and gave me scripts to read, too. He told me stories of the great playwrights, their lives, their works. Their triumphs and their tribulations. Shakespeare. Jonson. Dryden. Rowe. But the playwright I loved to hear most about was Aphra Behn.'

'A woman.'

'You know of her?'

'I know her name, but not her work.'

'She was a playwright in the seventeenth century. She is my role model—a woman who went her own way in life. She didn't receive the same respect for her craft as her male contemporaries, but she wrote many fine plays and other works, too, novels and poetry. Her plays are not often performed now, but they ought to be. So that's what I'm doing. I discovered my father had left a play half-finished. It's a dramatisation of one of Aphra Behn's stories. I'm completing it. '

'You're adapting a play,' he said slowly. 'Surely you would prefer to create your own original work.'

'Dramatising a novel or story is common enough. To see how a skilled playwright like my father does it is an excellent opportunity. And, yes. Perhaps I will write my own plays one day, but for now I'm still learning. It's a good story that will make a fine play. It has a strong heroine, who falls in love with a prince.'

'What's the play called?'

'The Fair Jilt.'

Darius's eyebrow reared upwards. 'And is the heroine a jilt?'

'It might be the hero who jilts her.'

'Forgive me, but the title is more often bestowed upon women than men.'

'Women are often accused of being jilts when they merely want to go their own way,' Calista replied with spirit.

He studied her silently.

'I've almost finished the adaptation,' she rushed on after a moment. 'I've been working on it for some time, but I was spurred on when I met you.'

'I trust I won't see my likeness on stage,' he said drily.

She laughed. 'I haven't made your likeness in a character. It's just that my father told me to use all of my emotions to write. Just as I do when acting on stage.'

He gave a crooked smile. 'So I've been of assistance in that regard?'

The look she gave him would have seemed coy in any other woman's eyes. Coming from her it was direct. 'I'll own you've raised many emotions in me.'

He slipped his hand out of his pocket and ran a finger over her mouth. 'Which emotions?'

'Anger. Fury.'

The duke's finger pressed lightly on her lips. 'Come now. Is that all?'

Calista breathed on Darius's skin. 'Not all.'

The tip of his finger played with her lips, almost entering her mouth.

She took a step back, out of his reach, her back making contact with the bark of a great oak tree behind her. She hadn't resisted his kiss. She wouldn't have known how. Kissing him seemed as natural as the song of the birds in the trees above them. But she wasn't about to miss her chance to find out more about him.

'You've learned a great deal about me,' she said. 'Now I have some questions for you. When we first met at that dinner with Mabel at the public house in London…'

He interrupted her with a groan. 'You're not bringing that up again, are you? Haven't I apologised enough? Or perhaps I ought to do so again. I believe I find it quite enjoyable.'

'This is serious,' she protested. 'When we first met, you said you disliked the theatre.' The memory of how he'd infuriated her at the Coach and Horses came back to her. It still rankled, yet she longed to discover what had laid behind his attitude that night.

'I said I disliked play-acting,' he corrected.

'Despised,' Calista countered. 'I believe you said you despised play-acting.'

'It's not too strong a word.' His mouth hardened. 'I learned all I ever needed to know about play-acting from the Duchess of Albury.'

'What? Do you mean your mother was an actress?'

He emitted a harsh laugh. 'Not my mother. *She* didn't have any pretence in her. I refer to my stepmother.'

Calista held herself still. Something in the way he spoke, his hands clenched by his sides, told her that she was near to discovering the tragedy in his childhood Mabel had once alluded to.

'My mother died.' His tone was clipped. He only spoke those three words, yet Calista sensed instantly how much they cost him to say.

'How old were you?' She kept her query matter of fact. He wouldn't respond to platitudes or gushing emotion. She knew that much about him now.

'Comparatively young. Eleven years old.'

'It must have been terrible for you,' Calista said, her voice low. It was hard to find any words that would suffice, but she sensed he wouldn't want an emotional outburst from her. Only by continuing to match her tone to his would she gain his further confidence.

He shrugged. 'It was bearable.'

How could it have been bearable? Desperately, she wanted to comfort him. She laid her fingertips flat against his cheek and cupped his jaw in her palm.

'That's not enough. I want to know how you felt.'

He exhaled against her hand. 'I felt how any eleven-year-old boy would feel when he hears at school that he's lost a parent.'

'Did the schoolmasters and other students show you kindness?' She prayed someone had.

He laughed. A bitter laugh that chilled her to the soul. 'I think you misunderstand what life at a boys' boarding school is like. Showing kindness is a form of weakness in such an environment.'

She trailed her fingers down his jawline. It was set like a rock. 'You showed kindness to your cousin Herbert at school.'

He shrugged. 'I protect my family name.'

'You're kind,' she insisted. 'Underneath that brusque manner of yours. Why, Columbine calls you the nicest duke in England.'

His mouth twisted. 'Does she indeed? And do you agree?'

'I think the duke is a role you play,' she said simply. 'Behind the Duke of Albury is Darius and I like him very much.'

Beneath her fingers a muscle moved in his cheek. 'You're astute. A duke does indeed have a public role. I've told you of my responsibilities, to my tenants and servants, to my family.'

She allowed her fingers to trace his neck as she took her hand away. 'There's much more to you than that. You can't fool me. I know character too well.' The thought of what he'd had to go through in his youth, all alone, made her heart ache. 'It must have been very hard for you at school.'

His smile was bleak and didn't reach his eyes. 'I don't think about it much and I certainly don't talk about it. In fact, I never talk about it at all.'

'Perhaps it's time you did.' She kept her tone

gentle. She sensed if she pried too deeply it would only push him further away.

'Was there someone at home who cared for you? Did your mother's death bring you and your father together?'

He gave another laugh, as dry as an autumn leaf. 'The contrary, I'm afraid. He had no time for me.'

'Why not?' she asked, mystified. She'd thought that surely their grief would have brought them closer together. They only had each other.

Darius faced her. 'He married my stepmother.'

'The actress! So that's why—'

'Indeed,' he drawled.

Calista's head spun. Now it all made sense. 'Tell me about her. Please.'

For a moment he was silent, his jaw clenched. 'Her name was Dorothy Bloom. An improbable name. Who knows her real name, where she came from or even her real age, for that matter? All I knew was that she appeared one morning, sitting in my mother's chair at the breakfast table.'

'Your father didn't tell you about her?'

Darius shook his head. 'No. But he was besotted with her. Within six months of losing my mother he'd married the actress.'

The actress. Calista shivered at the cold way he said it. 'No wonder you have an aversion to actresses.'

His smile was grim. 'There's more to it than that. Since my childhood I've been determined never to let another Carlyle fall prey to the Carlyle curse.'

'There's a curse?'

'My father wasn't the first man in my family to have married an actress, or to have had a relationship with one. It's an odd kink in our family tree. We seem to have a weakness for these ladies, and what generally has followed is a loss in our family fortune.'

'Is that what happened with—Miss Bloom? Did she love your father?'

His mouth twisted. 'It was a more practical arrangement for Dottie, I believe.'

'So their marriage wasn't for love?' The whole affair sounded horrible.

'Love? I'm not sure Dottie knew the meaning of the word. No, that's unfair. She was very affectionate. And not just to my father.' He paced, moving away, sending the leaves on the ground flying. 'Once she had married into my father's money, Dottie conducted multiple affairs, whilst always maintaining the façade of the perfect marriage in public. She wasn't particularly good at hiding her relationships and my father soon found out. But she always managed to convince him to forgive her.'

'That's dreadful,' Calista said.

'It was also expensive. My father didn't want to be alone, you see.' He waved a hand towards Albury Hall in the distance. 'So a perfect match was made. My father would keep his new wife happy with all kinds of expensive gifts. And my father's money kept Dottie very happy for a while. But it's a popular misconception that those in the upper classes have endless freedom and choices because they have money. It's often to the contrary, in my view. With wealth, land and privilege comes responsibility. What we have can't be squandered. It must be administered, stewarded. Husbanded.'

'Noblesse oblige,' she put in.

'That's right. Nobility obliges. Perhaps it sounds old-fashioned.'

She shook her head. 'Not at all. It sounds… honourable.'

'Perhaps I take it all too seriously, my duty to this house, this land and the people who rely on it. But I'm the head of the Carlyle family now and I feel it is my responsibility to uphold it.'

'I know you take family duty seriously,' she said slowly. 'I do myself. I don't blame you for it.'

'Now you've seen Albury Hall you'll know it's more than family duty. I'm responsible for these lands, the house, the farm, the village of Albury itself. There was a cholera epidemic in Buckinghamshire less than fifty years ago. A good lord of the manor will see to the care of his tenants in such times.'

'Did your father look after his tenants well?' she asked cautiously.

He exhaled. 'No. He did not. Not after his second marriage. Dottie's tastes became more and more expensive. I won't go into details, but there was a lot of work to be done after I inherited the title.'

'Where is Dottie now?'

'She died in Italy a few years ago, after she'd driven my father to an early grave. I didn't see her when my father died. She didn't care to keep up appearances any longer when she was merely the dowager duchess. By then she'd tucked away a tidy fortune for herself.'

'The way she behaved after your mother died…' Suddenly it clicked in her brain. 'Why, that's what you meant by play-acting.'

He exhaled sharply. 'Dottie could put any stage actors to shame. I constantly recall events like the village fête, when she would appear as the perfect duchess, or at least what she thought one would be like. She thought she had fooled everybody, but she never fooled me. I knew a real duchess. My mother.'

'What was your mother like?'

'She was tall. Slender. Full of grace. The opposite of Dottie.' He stared into the trees, appearing lost in memory. 'It was the same at Christmas and other festive occasions. When I was a boy, when she was still alive, I used to adore the big Christmas parties for everyone on the Albury estate. Then Dottie took over her role, even trying to pretend she had become a perfect mother to me. I loathed the pretence. Occasionally we had an almost pleasant family occasion, until my father inevitably had too much to drink in order to get him though the tedium of Dottie's company. Although he couldn't bear to lose her, they were extraordinarily ill suited.'

'How did Dottie treat you?'

'She wanted me to call her Mother. I refused. But she cried and pouted, all in a very over-dramatic manner, of course, until my father could take no more. He insisted I call her Mama.'

'That's terrible,' Calista murmured. She could just imagine how hurtful it would have been for a young boy to have a new mother forced upon him. 'So you were forced to act, too. That's what put you against actresses.'

'I'm against marriage and family life becoming a farce,' he said through gritted teeth. 'That's what I object to. I saw enough of it to last a lifetime.' Abruptly he shook his head. 'Come now. Let's drop such subjects. We're spoiling our walk.'

Calista opened her mouth to speak and then closed it again. The expression on his face told

her not to pursue the topic and she sensed that
he'd revealed more than he usually showed to
anyone. She'd learned more about the man behind
the duke, a man not many people ever seemed to
meet. She'd not press him for more, she decided,
especially if it would only cause him pain. Perhaps with time he would learn to confide in her
more.

'What would you prefer to talk about?' she
asked.

'I'd prefer to talk about how to spend more
time with you alone.'

'Mabel and Herbert arrive tonight,' she reminded him.

'How could I forget?' He groaned. 'Tell me instead about the emotions I raise in you.'

'I find it hard to select the right words.'

With a faintly mocking smile he shook his
head. His breath tingled against her neck, making her quiver. 'And you, a playwright.'

Calista's breathing quickened. 'I'm at a loss.'

'Let me help.'

Darius opened his coat and pulled her inside it.
Camouflaging them both, he drew her deeper into
the woods and pressed her back against a tree.

Calista gasped as he ran his finger over the frill
she'd sewn on the neckline of her blue dress and
moved lower still. Beneath her bodice the tip of
her breast stiffened beneath his touch. With a slow

finger he circled one peak, then the other, leaving a burning sensation. He toyed with the tip, bringing it to an arrow that thrust out to meet him.

Another moan escaped her lips.

Darius raised his head. 'Well?'

Hidden inside his coat the length of him pressed against her. She felt his need and her own body responded, arching towards him. Her stomach somersaulted, as if she were one of the acrobats on horseback that Columbine liked so much. She opened her mouth, but no words came out.

'It's of no matter.' Darius lifted his finger to trace the outline of her mouth. 'Your lips tell me all I need to know.'

Chapter Ten

The winds, with all their wings, would be
*   too slow*
To bear me to her feet.

Nicholas Rowe: *The Fair Penitent* (1703)

'Cold water,' the duke barked at his valet.

'Straight away, Your Grace.'

Darius ran his hand through his hair. Blast. Once again he'd been abrupt with Hammond, who didn't deserve to bear the brunt of his frustration.

But if he didn't quench the fire in his body he would no longer be able to stand it.

He must cool down.

Holding Calista in his arms had brought out a kind of primitive hunger in him. He understood now why there had been pagan rites in the woods in days of old and heaven knew what else.

In the stables he'd wanted to kiss her.

In the woods he'd wanted to take her beneath the trees and make her his own.

He tore off his waistcoat, liberating his upper body from his shirt.

He'd had women before.

He'd never known desire like this.

The kiss in the woods had barely slaked his thirst for her lips, his need to press her willowy body more firmly against him. He'd wanted to glimpse the bare flesh beneath those shabby garments, to see her legs and feet hidden all afternoon beneath her full skirt. Only the barest flash of her ankles in discreet stockings and worn-out boots had been visible to tempt him as she'd walked along the woodland path, her steps in time with his.

She had matched his stride.

She had matched his kiss.

If she matched him in the bedroom…

He groaned.

Surely those legs, those glorious legs, and the fine feet he had imagined so clearly in his mind but hadn't yet glimpsed, except in erotic night visions, deserved to be treated better. To be given better clothes. Better shoes. A better home. A better life.

He swore aloud as he pulled out his list from the drawer of his desk.

The words, written in bold black ink, in his

hand, no longer made any sense. They looked like a foreign language. Had he really written them—about Calista?

He'd changed so much since he had scrawled that list of items aimed at seducing her. The plans he'd made to woo her had been swept aside, the same way he now wanted to sweep her up the marble staircase to his bedroom, to lay her on the bed and rid her of those worn-out shoes and threadbare clothes.

He wanted to see her.

To touch her.

To hold her.

To tell her she would never wear anything but silk and lace again or he'd have her wear nothing at all.

To listen to her laugh, for she would laugh, he knew it, and that would be why he'd say it.

To hear her reply that there was nothing wrong with wool or cotton.

To see those full lips broaden into a smile, to hear that musical note gurgle from her lips, until he kissed it away.

He groaned again.

The whole farce had become just that.

A farce.

It was no play-acting for him to court Calista, not any more.

His lip curled. For a man who despised play-acting it was ridiculous. It was as if the gods were playing with him.

He wanted complete truth between them now.

In the woods he'd found himself confiding in her of matters he'd never spoken of to another living soul. Briefly he closed his eyes. She'd eased his pain. Her soft hand on his cheek had transmitted more than any words could have done.

He smiled grimly as he opened his eyes. Her calm, compassionate response only confounded the situation. That he'd found in an actress—an actress!—a woman to whom he could reveal his greatest secrets was yet another twist of fate's playful hand.

He hadn't lied when he had said he wanted her to make herself at home at Albury Hall. His relief that she'd consented to come had been overwhelming. Already her sister Columbine seemed in better health, but it was thoughts of Calista which filled his mind.

She was so different from his preconceived notions of actresses. Her passion, her innocence, had surprised him and had made him reassess his prejudices. Calista Fairmont was so much more than a title-hunting actress. He'd been so sceptical about the kind of person she would be, but he had found himself genuinely enjoying his time with Calista, and even with her sister. Being around her, witnessing her strength even with her father absent, he was beginning to see that happiness in a family might be real, rather than an act.

He'd never felt such liking, and such passion, for a woman before. It was clear she played no act with him. There was no flirtation, no ploys, just an admirable willingness to explore the connection that was growing between them, yet he sensed she would only let it go so far. He admired that, too, her honesty to herself and to him. It was curiously refreshing.

The cost, of course, was the company of Miss Coop who would appear tonight at dinner on his cousin's arm. He winced again. Still, it would give him a chance to put matters right with Herbert. No longer could he go on with any plan to deceive Calista.

Darius tore up his list and tossed the pieces into the fire.

Seizing a fresh piece of writing paper, he scribbled a note.

He couldn't hold back any longer.

When Hammond came back into the room, bearing the water jug, Darius turned to him. 'I need roses. Have someone pick a single rose in every shade of pink from the garden and bring them to me. I want to select the exact shade myself. Then I want them delivered to Miss Fairmont in her room along with this note.'

'Very good, Your Grace.' Hammond indicated

the water jug that he had placed beside the copper tub. 'Shall I assist you with this first?'

Darius shook his head. 'No. Thank you, Hammond.'

When the valet left the room he stripped off his remaining garments.

The recollection of Calista's soft body in his arms made his own harden.

Standing in the tub, he gritted his teeth, seized the jug of cold water, lifted it high above his head and poured.

Calista stood on the balcony and stared across the ground of Albury Hall. The wind whipped her hair, ruffled the silk of her pink evening gown. A slight chill hovered in the air, but she couldn't take her eyes from the view.

It was so beautiful. The setting sun had painted the sky a pink so rosy it rivalled her gown, promising another fine day on the morrow. The undulating lawns and the smooth, glossy lake beckoned. A swan flapped its wings as it glided from the sky and landed without a splash on the surface of the water beside its mate. Beyond the lawns were the woods and further still in the distance one could see the top of the church steeple.

Calista breathed in the fresh air. It felt health-giving, as opposed to London's air. Here at Albury Hall Columbine could breathe. It would do her the world of good, thanks to Darius.

Calista's breath became a shuddering sigh.

What he'd told her in the woods haunted her.

Returning to the bedroom, she sat at the golden-wood dressing table and stared into the oval looking glass. The kisses she had shared with Darius amongst the trees still burned on her lips. In the glass they appeared plumper, redder.

There, in the woods, wrapped in his coat, his embrace had taken her breath away. How could it be that the same man who had driven her to fury with his insulting assertions about actresses now filled her with such desire?

But he hadn't known her, then, and she hadn't known him. She knew Darius now, the man behind the duke. His kiss had soothed the sting of memory away, if a hard, powerful kiss like that could be considered soothing. His searching lips had seemed to learn everything about her in that passionate embrace.

She'd learned something about herself, too.

About her feelings for him.

She shivered again. Now his attitude about actresses made sense. His stepmother's behaviour had clearly hurt him at a time when he was still grieving his mother's death. She felt his pain so keenly it seemed to slice through her bodice. Now she understood why he abhorred any kind of play-acting. It brought back too many tragic memories.

She could only hope she'd helped him to view the past differently. She wanted to do that for him. He'd given her some hope about her father. Perhaps she could bring Darius some peace about his past.

Her finger still on her lips, she stared into the glass, her gaze unseeing. In her mind's eye she beheld his face, the blade of his lips, the line of his jaw, the night blue of his eyes. Just that vision made her shudder with longing. She'd wanted his kisses to go on for ever.

In the woods, he'd ignited a passion within her that couldn't be denied, the kind of passion playwrights and poets wrote about. Surely it was wrong to deny such feelings. Should she have held back? Convention would have dictated it so, but she had let her feelings speak to him through her lips. She couldn't pretend or disguise it. Such deep desire, combined with the increased liking she had for him, for the unexpected humour and kindness he'd revealed beneath the abrupt manner, plus her new-found tenderness and care for the man behind the duke—they were too powerful to be ignored.

Did it all add up to what she suspected it to be? Her head moved to and fro even as her heart thumped. All she knew was that her feelings ran so deep she had to trust them to guide her.

Calista took another peep at herself in the glass. She wore her rose-pink evening gown, of course, for it was the only one she owned. But a maid had knocked at her bedroom door and delivered a huge vase of roses, the exact shade of the bud Darius had bought her in the restaurant.

Along with a note.

She'd read it once, twice.

I must be with you. Wear my rose if you will come to me tonight. Darius.

Calista put a trembling hand to the blooms, then to her heart. There was that pang again. She could hardly breathe, recalling his mouth on hers. If they hadn't been outdoors, she'd have wanted him to keep kissing her, to explore her, body and soul, with his lips, his eyes, his hands, and for her to do the same for him, to discover everything there was to know about him. Her yearning for his touch was a revelation.

In his arms, she was a woman. A woman who wanted a man.

One man.

The Duke of Albury.

No longer could she deny it.

She loved him.

Her heart pounded. She'd known it when he had kissed her, the very first time. It had been a deep, powerful knowledge, in her body, in her soul. It had pulled her to him, again and again. No kisses would ever be the same as those she had shared with him. His kiss alone was the key that opened her heart. It had drawn her to Albury Hall, into his arms.

With the note clutched in her hand, she paced the floor. She'd never been part of the intrigues between aristocrats and actresses at the stage door. She shuddered. Men like Lord Merrick had repelled her, not attracted her. She'd resisted all entanglements.

But did she want to resist the duke?

When they'd first met, she'd made the confident assertion that she would rather be his mistress than his wife. Her words had been a distraction. Until this moment, she'd never considered being a duke's mistress.

Yet now…

She clutched the note tighter. Her mind, her body, her heart—all were in a whirl. Did Darius want her as his mistress? Was that his meaning in the note? She had no experience with men to guide her.

Still pacing, she tried to unravel her emotions. She had to admit, as her body tingled, that she was intrigued by the idea of being alone with him at night. Yet she was nervous, too. The flutters in her stomach told her she was also excited and wary. She'd never felt that way about a man before.

Her feelings. So powerful and passionate. A tumult, a tide, sweeping her onward, towards one destination: the Duke of Albury's arms.

Were they leading her to his bed?

Calista took a deep breath as she sat once again at the dressing table and stared at her reflection, at the lips that Darius had searched. He'd awoken a desire inside her that refused to be ignored. Surely she had to trust her feelings and let them guide her.

The adjoining door to her room was flung open. Columbine burst through from the bedroom next door. With a skip and a jump she came and stood at the dressing table.

'Why, Cally! You look beautiful!' Columbine leaned against her. 'Will you read me a fairy story tonight?'

Calista kissed her sister's cheek before tucking away the note. 'I'd like to, Columbine, but it might have to be Martha. I'm going downstairs for the evening.'

'That's all right,' Columbine said cheerfully. She looked so much better and her breathing had no trace of a wheeze. 'The duke might read me some tomorrow.'

'You found the book of fairy tales in the nursery, then.'

'Oh, yes. There's a nursery at the top of the house and there are so many other books and toys to play with I couldn't choose. Then this afternoon after my nap Martha and I walked down to the lake. We're going to take some bread tomorrow for the swans and in the afternoon I've got a riding lesson on Bluebell. Oh, Albury Hall is the nicest place in the world! And I told you the Duke of Albury is the nicest duke.'

Calista glanced at the vase of roses on the dressing table as she stood and turned to her sister.

Columbine bounced on the bed. 'Why, your room is even prettier than mine. Look at those blue curtains. They're like the sky. And I've never seen wallpaper before with all those pictures of pretty ladies and lambs and people dancing on it, and this eiderdown on your bed is so soft!'

'Don't jump on the bed, Columbine.'

She giggled. 'I'm not jumping, I'm testing it. Like the real princess in the fairy tale. Do you think there is a pea under your mattress? Oh, Cally, don't you feel like a princess here at Albury Hall? You look like a princess from a fairy tale tonight.'

'I'm not a fairy-tale princess,' Calista said firmly.

Taking Columbine by the hand she led her sister towards the door of her own bedroom. 'Come along now, it's time to get ready for bed.'

She was no princess.

Yet just for tonight, she admitted, as she caught sight again of the roses in the vase, she felt like a duchess.

Calista seized a single rosebud from the vase. With shaking fingers, she tucked it into her bodice.

Chapter Eleven

Calista, now be wary.
Nicholas Rowe: *The Fair Penitent* (1703)

'Calista!' Mabel's squeal pierced Calista's ear as she descended the marble staircase.

In the vast entrance hall below she saw the butler wince as Mabel rushed over to her and squealed once more. 'Oh, look at us. From the stage of the Prince's Theatre all the way to Albury Hall! Whoever would have thought?'

A wave of Mabel's floral perfume engulfed her as they embraced.

Calista smiled. She'd not revealed to her friend her own hand in Mabel's invitation. 'It's lovely to see you, Mabel. You look beautiful this evening.'

Her friend preened. 'Yellow's my colour, that's what Herbert said when he gave me my lovely fur. So when I saw this yellow silk in a shop window on Bond Street, I said, "Oh, Herbie, wouldn't you love to see me in that gown?" And so he made me a present of it.'

'You look very fine.' Gold and diamonds sparkled in the crevice of Mabel's deep-cut, ruffled gown, Calista noted. 'And that's a beautiful necklace.'

Mabel's fingers played with it as she released a huge sigh. 'It's only a necklace. Not a ring. I don't know what's happened to my Herbie. He was all ready to propose, then...' She snapped her fingers. 'Something changed his mind. I don't know what it was, though I have some idea. Still, we're here now. That's a good sign.' She tucked her arm into Calista's and glanced about the hall. 'Where do we go? There are so many doors.'

The butler opened the door to the drawing room. 'This way. The gentlemen are still in the drawing room, I believe. The bell for dinner will be rung at eight.'

He opened the door to the drawing room. Chandeliers of fat white candles lit the room to a blaze. Thick green-velvet curtains framed the mullioned windows. The long room was half-panelled in wood and paintings, mostly of men and women Calista presumed were Carlyle ancestors, overlooked her and Mabel as they made their way across the patterned carpet.

Darius stood by the fireplace, dressed in his

long-tailed dinner jacket and a pristine white shirt. He spun around as they entered.

Calista's heart thumped so hard she put her hand to the rose at her *décolletage*. Her reaction to this man almost frightened her as he crossed the room to greet her. His gaze went instantly to the rose, then to her eyes.

As they looked at each other Calista felt as if his lips were once again on her own.

A moment passed between them.

A question. Her answer.

His smile.

His glance glided to where her fingers touched the rose petals. 'So you received the gift from my garden?'

She nodded. 'Thank you. They're beautiful.'

He shrugged and gave a taut smile. 'It's not a ruby bracelet.'

'I'm very glad of it. You know I like flowers best.'

'I believe I've come to prefer them, too.' The tautness of his smile relaxed. 'Was all to your satisfaction in your bedroom?'

She nodded. How he could think the lovely wallpapered room might not meet her approval she couldn't imagine. It was a far cry from their tiny rooms in London. 'I left Columbine being read a fairy story by Martha. She's so much better. I think she believes she's in a fairy tale here at Albury Hall.'

'I trust she's enjoying her stay.'

'She's become your devoted fan.'

'That's fair,' he whispered in her ear, 'for I've become yours.'

Mabel broke the spell between them. 'Good evening, Your Grace!'

Darius turned to her with a bow. 'Miss Coop.'

Mabel dipped one of her eye-popping curtsies. 'I knew we'd meet again. I said that, didn't I, Herbie?'

'You did, Mabel.' The duke's cousin managed to drag his gaze away from her friend's cleavage and address Calista. 'Delighted to see you again, Miss Fairmont. Hope we'll manage to finish our dinner this time, eh, what?'

Calista smiled at Herbert in his dinner jacket that appeared to be straining somewhat around the waist. His sandy hair and red cheeks were oddly endearing. So, too, was the adoration with which he surveyed Mabel. He was clearly besotted. It did seem a shame that he hadn't proposed and she was suddenly glad she'd intervened with Darius on their behalf. 'It's a pleasure to see you again, too, Sir Herbert.'

'Do call me Herbert,' he urged her. 'We're all on first-name terms here, aren't we, Darius?'

'If we must be,' he drawled.

'Darius.' Mabel giggled. 'That's a funny name.'

The duke raised an eyebrow. 'Darius was a great King of Persia in the third century. The name has been used many times over the years in my family. It was brought back from the Crusades, I believe.'

'Along with many other treasures,' Herbert told Mabel.

'Treasures?' Her face brightened.

'Antiquities,' said Darius. 'Made of stone.'

Mabel's mouth drooped. 'Oh.'

'It might have been worse,' Calista said to Darius lightly. 'You might have been named from a play.'

'Such as *The Fair Penitent*?' His darting smile sent her hand again to the roses at her bodice. 'That would make me Lothario.'

Herbert chortled. 'There have been a few Lotharios in the Carlyle family, eh, what, Darius?' With a quick glance at the duke's face his chuckle became a cough. 'Not in this generation, of course.'

'Lothario,' Mabel mused. 'We did that one once at the Royal, I remember now. He's the villain in that play, isn't he?'

Calista nodded. 'It's a tragedy. He seduces Calista and breaks her heart. She dies in the end.'

'That's so sad,' said Mabel.

Herbert's cough turned to a choke.

'It's just a play,' the duke said drily.

The door opened and the butler and two foot-men entered. Herbert lifted Mabel's hand.

'Shall I show you your seat, Mabel?'

Mabel giggled her assent.

As they turned away, Darius silently took Calista's hand, lifted the palm to his lips and kissed it.

Darius glanced at Calista seated to his right at the long, linen-covered table. Once before he'd sat in such a position at the table, with Miss Fair-mont at his right and Miss Coop at his left. From the left he could smell again that overwhelming a floral fragrance, so sickly-sweet it could spoil the bouquet of a good wine. From the right, as usual, Calista seemed not to have doused herself in cheap scent. Instead, there was her own fresh scent that he'd come to know so well, that deli-cate fragrance from her hair and clean skin, com-bined with the scent of the rose—his rose—that she wore tucked into her bodice.

It soothed him as he listened to Miss Coop's chatter.

The sound no longer bothered him.

Meeting Calista, confiding to her about his childhood, had healed an old wound inside him. There was more he'd never tell her, of course, such as the way his stepmother had attempted to seduce him in his teenage years, in this very dining room. The way she'd taunted and teased his father and demanded jewels with a stamp of her feet. He could still recall when his father had given Dottie the ruby bracelet and she'd sat on his father's lap and dangled it with a triumphant look in her eye.

He had thought those memories would tarnish Albury Hall for ever. But now, having told Calista his story, seeing the understanding in her eyes, tasting it on his tongue...

She'd taken the sting of the memory away. She'd changed his view on actresses, done away with his prejudices. No longer could he see them all in the same damning light. He saw her dignity, her courage, her beauty. She lit up the world around her, not just the stage. No shadow could survive that light.

Previously he'd gritted his teeth, listening to Mabel's screeching voice. It had reminded him too much of Dottie, he realised. Now, it was merely background noise as his ear sought out the sweet solo violin of Calista's tones.

Darius hid his rueful smile behind a mouthful of claret. He'd ordered the finest vintage from the cellar and Herbert, his face puce, was drinking freely as he tucked into a fine meal of roasted duck. But Calista drank and ate lightly, as he'd noted before.

His heart clenched as he watched the pink rose moving up and down on the ruffles of her evening gown as she breathed. The sight of it sent a surge of desire through him.

Had she understood the full meaning of his invitation? He frowned inwardly. He wasn't entirely sure. The innocence in her kiss—it had thrown him off guard. But he was sure of one thing.

He wanted her. He needed her.

Tonight.

For a moment he allowed himself to envision touching the tip of her slipper with his toe, sliding it off, and caressing her feet beneath the cover of the long linen tablecloth, with no one else aware. He forced himself to take another sip of claret to blot out the thought of it. Of those legs, so tantalisingly close to his beneath the table.

She'd brought new life to this place. For so long he'd loathed the dining room at Albury Hall. It had always held too many painful memories of farcical family occasions, after Dottie had taken his mother's beloved place. But tonight, he could see how happiness might change the past, put his home back where it belonged.

Calista suited the dining room particularly well. With her actress's skill, she appeared perfectly at home. An image of her at the other end of the table flashed before his eyes. A morning scene, her with coffee pot in hand, him with a newspaper. A domestic idyll, the kind of scene he would have thought nonsense, until now. He was genuinely enlivened by her presence, in a way he'd never expected to be.

Over time he'd have to convince her to prefer jewels to flowers, among other things.

Yet her worn rose-pink evening gown and hair done up in a simple twist had grown on him, just like her company. Her dark hair was burnished by the candlelight to a rich shade like the wood panelling behind her.

He watched her mouth as she took a sip from her crystal water glass. To keep his mind and body from going astray again at the sight of her full lip caressing the edge of the glass, he focused on his duties as her host and forced himself to wonder if she might care for some other wine than claret.

He smiled, almost chuckling aloud. How the gods must be laughing at his interest in the tastes of an actress.

Beside him she laid down her glass. 'You seem to enjoy some private jest.'

'I'm reflecting upon our first meeting. So much has changed since then.'

'Indeed.' She borrowed his word.

He smiled. 'It's strange that these four players find themselves together again.'

She raised one elegant eyebrow. 'Are we in a play, then?'

'The great Bard put it that way, did he not? All the world's a stage.'

A delicate sip of claret reddened her lips. 'Shakespeare's writing always fills me with admiration.'

'You'll have admirers for your own play-writing before long, I'm sure.' He leaned in. 'Do you mind me knowing your secret? That you're more than an actress?'

Her sapphire eyes glowed as she shook her head. 'You don't mind me knowing yours.'

'I want you to know everything,' he said quietly.

'What are you talking about?' asked Miss Coop, from the other side of the table.

'About the theatre, Miss Coop. Your place of employ,' Darius said quickly.

'Ooh, I'd give up the stage quick as a wink if the right man asked me.' She fluttered her lashes at Herbert, who turned an even more unfortunate shade of puce.

Herbert had almost ruined everything talking about Lotharios in the family, but Darius had managed to quell his cousin with a glance. He'd talk to him later, set him straight on matters.

He sighed. Herbert appeared more besotted than ever with Miss Coop. Never would he have imagined himself in the same position with an actress. But it indeed seemed to be the fate of the Carlyle family. Inwardly he continued to battle with himself. To have found a woman he liked and respected in an actress still staggered him. To feel that unexpected comfort and understanding that she brought him, along with the refreshing promise of passion that blazed between them. Indeed, his feelings for Calista, growing stronger by the hour, couldn't be denied.

Tonight.

He shook his head and reached for the claret jug. No, he could no longer condemn his cousin.

The Carlyle curse had surely struck again.

Calista laid down her spoon and refrained with difficulty from licking her lips. The gooseberry tart for pudding had been delicious, especially served generously with both custard and cream.

She peeped sideways at Darius. All of her senses seemed to be heightened with him beside her. She was constantly aware of him, of his eyes, his mouth, his body near hers, beneath the table. He, too, appeared at ease, as if they were a married couple entertaining friends.

What a notion, she chided herself.

Yet there was an ease between them which she couldn't deny.

It was difficult to get a word in, though, with

Mabel at the table. She glanced across at her friend with affection. Oh, she knew Mabel might be considered the worst kind of title-hunter, but she wasn't unkind. And Herbert, he had a good heart, too.

She studied the duke's cousin with puzzlement.

A few times during the evening she'd caught him looking at her with a strange expression, the meaning of which she simply could not make out.

What was it? Some kind of embarrassment? A warning? He had hastily looked the other way whenever she'd caught him.

It didn't make sense, but with her habitual focus upon the expressions of others, she knew she wasn't mistaken. He was even staring at her now, but when she smiled at him he took a hasty bite of gooseberry tart.

'I say, that was delicious,' Herbert said when he'd finished, keeping his attention averted from Calista.

'What's next?' Mabel giggled. She'd drunk far too much claret and was now drinking a second glass of golden-coloured dessert wine that matched her dress.

'Perhaps a quick game of billiards,' Herbert suggested.

'Ooh, I love to play billiards. Herbert's been teaching me,' Mabel added.

'Indeed?' the duke drawled, before he addressed Calista. 'Do you play?'

Calista nodded. 'My father taught me.'

'Then perhaps we shall all have a game tomorrow night.' Darius took a sip of wine.

'I say, marvellous idea,' agreed Herbert.

Mabel yawned loudly, and then giggled again. 'Ooh, excuse me. It must be time to turn in.'

Herbert finished his wine with a splutter.

Darius raised an eyebrow in question as he turned to Calista. Her heart drummed as she lifted her eyes to his.

'I believe it's time,' she said.

Chapter Twelve

I see she has got possession of thy heart;
She has charmed thee, like a syren, to her
*   bed,*
With looks of love, and with enchanting
*   sounds:*
Too late the rocks and quicksands will
*   appear.*

Nicholas Rowe: *The Fair Penitent* (1703)

Darius paced the bedroom carpet. From the drawer of his desk he took out the black-velvet box he'd retrieved from the family vault. He clicked open the lid and stared at the sapphire blue.

He'd always been so cynical about happy families. The dream of a happy marriage had been just that—a dream, with no chance of it coming true. But now, instead of the memories of his stepmother at Albury, the memories of his own mother and his father were coming back. Happy memories, of a happy childhood, before it had all gone wrong.

In the woods, talking to Calista had released him from the pain of the past.

For the first time, since his childhood, he wanted a future.

At dinner she'd worn his rose. Yet he wasn't entirely sure if she'd understood his message. Would she appear?

He slid the ring box back into the drawer and slammed it shut. Striding to the fire, he stripped off his evening jacket and shirt and flung a robe over his half-naked body.

That afternoon it had been as if one of the woodland gods had sent a clarion call to his soul. He was even more certain now. How could he pretend to himself any longer?

He was in love.

It was no pretence. No farce.

Pacing the patterned carpet again, he tried to think back to when the thunderbolt had first struck him. No mere arrow from Cupid's bow had made him fall for her. There was substance to his feelings, drawn from the strength of her character, as desirable to him as her lovely face.

So when had the bolt struck? In Hyde Park? When he had seen her fresh-faced beauty and her concern for her sister? On stage at the Prince's

Theatre, when he'd first caught sight of those long, shapely legs clad in tights? When he held her in his arms in the foggy street?

Be honest, man, he told himself. The thunderbolt had first struck him, he realised now, at their meeting in the Coach and Horses, when she had first raised her pointed chin and declared she would never marry a duke. The challenge in her eyes had been irresistible.

Oh, yes, there was fate's playful hand in this.

He, the Duke of Albury, had fallen in love with an actress.

He threw another log on to the fire, seized the poker and prodded the flames to new heights. The force that drew him to her was so powerful, yet he'd suppressed it at first. He'd fought love's shaft and convinced himself that he had sought her company only to protect Herbert. Now he could no longer protect himself from the power of his feelings.

His courtship in London had started as a sham. Here at Albury Hall his courtship was in earnest.

He clenched his fist around the poker. Tonight. In his arms. He'd set it all right with her.

A knock came at the door. Darius strode over and threw it open.

'Calista.' He tightened the cord of his robe.

She was still clothed in her pink evening dress. He opened the door wider to let her in and followed her glance around the room, watched her eyes roam over its dark-oak furniture and long red curtains. It was one of the older rooms in the house, and the ceiling was lower than in the later-built parts, but he preferred it.

Calista moved towards the fire, the light gilding her profile. The angle of her face was like one from an ancient coin: high forehead, fine nose, pointed chin. It was as if nobility were bred into her bones. No wonder she played such roles on stage so well.

'How is Columbine?' he asked, knowing she would have checked on her sister.

'She's sleeping so peacefully. I can't quite believe how easily she's breathing.' She took a deep breath. 'Thank you.'

Darius crooked an eyebrow. 'For what am I receiving your thanks?'

'For allowing Columbine to come here. She told me earlier she loves it here.'

'The air is better than in London.'

'It's more than that. You've been so kind. Not only having us here for Columbine's health and making us so welcome.' She took another lungful of air. 'You've made a difference in regard to my father's disappearance, too. I plan to start my enquiries anew, make a renewed search to find him. There's an old theatre acquaintance of my father's I can write to. I won't give up.'

'So you're holding on to hope now,' he said gravely.

Calista raised her eyes to his. 'Because of you.'

He moved closer to where she stood by the fire and took her in his arms. He stroked her hair. 'This is unfathomable.'

She laid her head against his chest. 'It is for me, too. It wasn't so long ago I swore never to have dinner with you.'

'And now you're in my home.' He pulled her tighter against him. 'And in my arms. And that pleases you too?'

'You know it does, Darius.'

His name on her lips went straight to the centre of him, re-igniting the flame that had flared almost out of control in the dining room.

'I like the way you say my name.' His voice came out hoarse. 'Say it again.'

She raised her head. 'Darius.'

'Let your lips say it.'

He leant down. With his mouth he opened her parted lips, the lips which had told him of the longing they shared without any words.

Now they told him more.

Passion.

Heat.

Fire.

He parted them wider to quench his thirst for her and found more heat, more fire within.

When they parted for air he ran his finger down her neck, along the ruffled neckline of her evening dress. 'Your gown becomes you.'

In reply her laugh was shaky. 'It's my one and only evening gown. You've seen it before.'

'Indeed,' he said. 'And every time I see it I like it more. The shade brings out the roses in your cheeks and is the same colour as your lips.'

Now his finger brushed her the neckline, dipped deeper to find the tender point of her breast. 'I'll wager this is rose pink, too.'

He lowered the ruffle, set her breast free. Once more he toyed with the tip. 'Does this taste as pink as your lips?'

'Pink is a colour,' she said faintly. 'Of what could it taste?'

'I'll have to try it and see.'

Her breathing quickened as he took her in his mouth, sucking then biting gently until the tip was hard on his tongue.

'Yes,' Darius murmured when he finally raised his head. 'As pink as your lips. But it's not your lips I want to taste now.' He felt her tremor of pleasure as he leaned to whisper in her ear, 'Will you let me?'

Her reply came out in a rush of air. 'You said you wanted to explore what's between us. So do I.'

'Have you…explored before?'

'You know I haven't,' she said with the honesty that so disarmed him. 'Does it matter?'

'Not to me,' he said, 'although it may to you.'

For a moment she was silent. Then she reached for his hand and took it to the first tiny button of her bodice.

Darius bit back his groan. Slowly the ruffles fell open as one by one he undid the silvery buttons that ran down the front of her gown.

Calista moved towards him. Her bare skin tingled, the silk bodice of her gown open to his surmise. Desire for more, for his lips, his hands, surged through her, from the deepest place inside.

She would trust her feelings.

She would trust Darius.

Desire flared in his eyes, too, brighter than any footlights on a stage.

When she'd stood in the hall outside his bedroom, she'd hesitated, unsure if she possessed the courage to go to him. Before he had answered the door she almost returned to her own bedroom. Then she'd stepped over the threshold, into his private domain. His bedroom reflected wealth and power, the private room of a man who believed he could have anything he wanted. The ceiling, painted in white and gold. The mahogany furniture. The dark hangings. The gold-framed paintings. The red-curtained four-poster bed. The rich luxurious carpet that cushioned her tread.

Now Darius stood in front of her, in a red-brocade robe piped with gold, the sheer force of his masculinity overwhelming her. His hair was dishevelled, as if he'd been running his fingers through it, a habit she'd noted in him. She wondered how his fingers might feel running over other parts of her body. She bit her lip, striving to calm the sensations surging through her at the thought of such a powerful caress.

Her evening slippers brushed the carpet as she stepped closer, so close her full corset brushed against him. His eyes shut, then opened, his gaze returning to hold her as he drew her even nearer to him. Reaching out, she slipped both hands beneath the lapels of his robe. With a shock she encountered warm, bare skin.

He raised his eyebrow.

She gulped and lifted her chin. Beneath the robe she let her fingers trail across his warmth, to trace the bulging muscles and the whorls of hair at the centre of his chest. His muscles tensed beneath her exploring hand.

The feel of him. All else vanished from her mind as she explored the breadth of his chest with her fingers, her touch tentative at first, then growing bolder as she found herself lost in the dizziness of the contact whilst at the same time still staring into his eyes.

Those eyes darkened to night.

She trailed her hand lower.

He reached out, held her wrist. 'Are you sure you want to go further?'

Calista's heart pounded.

'Yes. I'm sure.'

He searched her with his gaze before it darkened once more to desire as he released her hand.

'Please,' she whispered.

He leaned down, pulled her close, as if to kiss her, then put his mouth to her neck.

Tremors ran through her as his lips found the tender place below her ear. All her nerves focused on that one place. The sensation rippled through her limbs, like rays from the sun. That he could do this to her, by finding such a sensitive place on her body, one she never knew existed, was incredible. Her breathing came faster as he moved his mouth up her neck and over her chin.

His lips were almost on hers. 'Still want to explore?'

Her breath mingled with his. She could only incline her neck, that tender place still tingling from his mouth.

He laughed, low, as he pulled away. Then with a swoop he lifted her into his arms and placed her on the bed.

Calista fell back amidst the softness of feathers and pillows as he pushed the bed curtains wide. At the foot of the bed he stood staring down at her. He pulled off his robe. The firelight silhouetted his bare torso, his broad shoulders, his powerful neck.

'My God,' he groaned. 'I've longed to do this.'

She caught her breath as with strong hands he tugged her ankles and pulled her closer to him. Lifting the ruffled hem of her skirt, he reached for her evening shoe and slipped it off. Her breath caught in her throat as he knelt and slid one hand up the inside of her thigh. Then he lifted her leg and put his lips to her foot.

'I imagined doing this.'

'You imagined my feet?'

His smile gleamed in the candlelight. 'The sight of you on stage in those breeches. Your boots. I've wanted to know what was inside them. They're just as I pictured them to be.'

She quivered as his fingers caressed her instep, as he trailed his fingers across her sensitive sole, sending darts of ticklish sensation through her somewhere between pleasure and pain.

It was nothing compared to the feeling when he put his lips to her bare foot. As his tongue made contact with her tender skin a flame shot up through her lower body.

Calista closed her eyes. Never had she experienced such unexpected pleasure.

Slow, tantalising, the pressure played on her skin. His kisses were light, soft. Then hard, unyielding. Just as she became used to one kind of touch it altered, sending her further into spirals of pleasure.

Just when she thought she couldn't take any more his lips trailed upwards, found the arch of her foot.

The ticklish sensation made her moan aloud.

He lifted his head and smiled. 'What will I find if I go higher?'

'Find out,' she gasped in a voice she barely recognised. All she wanted was him. All she needed was him to keep caressing her with his lips as he covered the inside of her ankle in hot fast kisses.

Higher. She needed him to go higher. As if he possessed a secret map of her, as if he knew the way.

Her calf.

His tongue.

Higher.

Please. Was it a word? A thought?

Above her knee.

She tensed, then yielded to his hand. With both legs apart, in the cuffs made by his hands, she shuddered with anticipation.

Gently he pushed her skirt and petticoats up

to her thighs. Still he tantalised her, his lips playing on the tender inside of her thigh towards the wide lace edge of her pantaloons, while his fingers reached inside.

Higher.

Instinctively Calista lifted her lower body to meet his hand. She wanted him. Needed him. All thoughts were gone, replaced by the feel of his fingers reaching…

He stopped.

With a curse Darius released her. He ran his hand through his hair. 'Blast it, Calista. I refuse to make love to you.'

Darius stared at Calista as she struggled to sit up against the pillows. Her hair had come loose, tumbling over her shoulder. Her *décolletage* was pink, her cheeks coloured with a tantalising blush. The lights of the candles flickered from her chin to the slender column of her swan-like neck, dipping into the shadow between her breasts. How he wanted to follow that light with his lips.

'My God.' It took every fibre of his mind to force his body to move away from her. The smoothness of her skin, the taste of it… 'I'm finding it hard to resist you.'

'Don't resist.' Her voice was as hoarse as his. 'Please, Darius. I don't want you to stop.'

Her long legs were revealed beneath her petticoat. He longed to tear her clothing from her, put his lips to the rest of her. Yet he forced himself to look away.

'No.' With every ounce of will power he had left he dragged himself another step away from her tantalising form and re-tied his robe. 'I'm not going to let this happen. Not tonight. Not yet.'

She sat up straighter. 'If not now, then when?'

'When we're married.' The words shot out.

There was silence from the bed.

He, too, fell silent. Inwardly, he cursed. He'd jumped the gun. Those were words he'd once never thought he'd say in earnest. Yet it felt so natural, so obvious, so right. Just as she fitted naturally in his home, his arms, his bed.

In the candlelight he saw her mouth open, then close. 'What?'

Her voice was a whisper. It wasn't surprising. He'd shocked her. He'd shocked himself.

'Forgive me. I didn't mean it to come out like that.' Darius shook his head in disbelief. 'Surely you've realised it wasn't only for Columbine's health that I invited you to my home? It's you I want at Albury Hall. Always.'

'What of the Carlyle curse?' she gasped.

'To hell with the Carlyle curse.'

He vaulted beside her on the bed and pulled her warm body against his bare chest.

'Don't you understand? I love you. I loved you

from the moment we had that ridiculous argument at the Coach and Horses. No one ever dared to stand up to me before as you did. Your courage. Your beauty. Your talent. You care so much for others, yet you bear so much alone. I want to care for you, protect you, love you as you deserve to be loved.'

Calista's quivering mouth parted in reply.

Darius brushed against it with his. 'Tell me you feel the same, Calista. No words. Tell me with your lips.'

She told him.

Chapter Thirteen

*Is this well done, my lord? Have you put
   off
All sense of human nature? Keep a little,
A little pity, to distinguish manhood,
Let other men, though cruel, should dis-
   claim you,
And judge you to be numbered with the
   brutes.*

Nicholas Rowe: *The Fair Penitent* (1703)

'Oh, Cally. I've been waiting all day. There's something I must tell you!'

Calista turned to look at Mabel.

At the drawing-room door Mabel took her by the hand and pulled her inside. Her eyes were wide, almost scared.

'What is it, Mabel?' Calista asked dreamily.

The whole day had passed in a blur. All she'd been able to think of was Darius.

He loved her.

He *loved* her!

They'd had no time to be alone together since their whispered farewell in his bedroom the night before. She was too tempting to have in his bed another moment, he'd told her, before he had done up each button of her evening gown with a touch that had tantalised her almost as much as when he'd undone them. Back in her own bed, her sleep had been almost feverish with desire.

The morning had been taken up with Columbine's riding lesson on Bluebell and, in the afternoon, Darius had taken them all on a tour of Albury Hall and its grounds.

Albury Hall. Where he wanted her to stay.

As his wife.

Always.

They'd told no one yet of their intentions. Yet she wondered if anyone could miss what was between them. Darius's slightest glance brought heat up from her core, racing up her neck to her cheeks.

Could it be true? Calista put her hands against her warm cheeks. Had the duke's proposal the night before been part of a dream? Even now she was barely sure if she was awake or asleep. All she knew was that she was the happiest she'd ever been in her life, in love with him.

Perhaps they'd find a moment alone together before dinner, if she hurried. Her heart quickened.

'Must we talk now?' she asked Mabel. 'I was about to go and dress for dinner.'

Back into her pink silk evening dress. Her body seemed to melt, recalling the way he had opened it so slowly, button by button.

'Herbie said I wasn't to tell you, but I can't hold it back any longer!' Mabel exclaimed.

'What is it?' Calista asked. 'Is it about Herbert?'

Mabel shook her ringlets. 'It's about the Duke of Albury. Oh, Calista, you have to know!'

In the drawing room, Mabel seized her hands and pulled her over to the leather club chairs by the fireplace. Even with the fire in the grate, the vast room was chilly after the warmth of the sun outdoors.

Calista shivered as she perched on the edge of the red-leather chair. It felt slippery beneath her dress. She breathed deeply, trying to fight off the dreadful sense of unease building inside her. Her heart pounded.

'What do you need to tell me about the duke?'

Mabel's blue eyes were wide. 'Oh, Calista, I don't know how to tell you...'

Calista gripped her fingers together. 'What is it?'

Mabel shook her head. 'I don't know where to start.'

'Mabel! Just tell me! Out with it.'

Her friend paused dramatically. 'It's all a play!'

'What on earth do you mean?'

'It's a play. The duke made an agreement with Herbert. He's acting a part, pretending to care about you.'

'What?' Calista gasped. 'I don't believe it.'

Mabel's round eyes were sympathetic. 'I'm sorry, Cally, but it's true. It's a sham courtship.'

Her lips turned numb. *A sham courtship.*

She stared from her clenched fingers resting in her lap to the leaping flames in the grate and back again, trying to focus on the facts. Her shivering body told her it all made terrible sense, yet her mind refused to grasp it.

'I don't understand,' she managed to stutter. 'Start at the beginning, Mabel, please.'

'Well, you know what the duke said about actresses when we met?'

Calista remembered all too well. 'He said every actress in Covent Garden wanted to marry a lord or a duke.'

Mabel nodded. 'You told him you didn't want a coronet.'

'I went further than that,' Calista recalled. 'I told him I'd rather be a mistress than a wife to an aristocrat like him.'

'He didn't believe you,' Mabel wailed. 'That's just it, you see. That's why he told Herbie and Herbie told me, even though he wasn't supposed to, and I told you. I mean, I didn't mean to but what else could I do? I had to tell you…'

'Mabel, please! Tell me exactly what Darius said to Herbert!'

'He said even though you declared you'd never wed a duke, the duke swore to persuade you to accept a marriage proposal from him.'

'What?'

Mabel's ringlets bobbed as she nodded. 'The duke's courting of you was all to prove his claim. And he has been courting you, hasn't he?'

Inside her chest Calista's heart became a cold stone. In spite of the fire, chilly vapours spread inside her body.

Images flashed through her mind in quick succession.

The duke walking her home. The duke collecting her in his carriage. The duke taking her to dinner. The duke inviting her to his home. The duke giving her roses.

The duke kissing her.

The duke's proposal.

Her fingers trembled as she put them to her frozen lips. 'I suppose he has been courting me. But I don't understand. Why would he do such a thing?'

Mabel leaned forward. 'The duke told Herbert that if he could persuade you to marry him, then he would have proved all actresses want a title. Poor Herbie. That's why he hasn't proposed to me yet, you see. He's waiting to see if the duke is right.'

'So your fate rests upon mine?' Calista exclaimed, shocked. 'That's so callous, so conniving.'

Mabel nodded. 'Herbie was all ready to propose. I was sure of it. Did you not suspect anything?'

Calista shook her head.

'No,' she whispered. 'I thought Darius was being…kind.'

The kindest duke in England.

'They call it the—'

'Carlyle curse.' Calista finished Mabel's sentence. 'I know about it. I just didn't know it applied to me.'

She clambered to her feet. Beneath her skirt her legs trembled as much as her hands. Her petticoats suddenly seemed terribly heavy.

'Cally.' Mabel jumped up in alarm. 'You look quite faint. Are you all right?'

'Yes. No. I don't know.' Calista grasped the edge of the carved wooden chimney piece. Her fingers seemed as frozen as her lips as she struggled for words. 'I have to go upstairs. I need to lie down.'

Mabel reached out to put an arm around her. 'I'll come with you.'

Calista shook her head. 'No. I want to be by myself.'

Her head spun. There was so much to take in.

A sham courtship.

A sham proposal.

The Carlyle curse.

'I shouldn't have told you,' Mabel fretted, her pink lips in a pout. 'I never could keep a secret. Herbie will be fearfully cross.'

'I'm glad you told me,' Calista said. 'You're a good friend, Mabel. It's not your fault.'

She let go of the mantelpiece and stumbled. Her leg slammed against the edge of a side table.

'Cally! Let me help you.'

'No!' The words came out louder than she expected. 'I need to be alone. I'm fine.'

She rushed from the room.

'I say. This is an excellent drop,' said Herbert. 'You always did have a taste for the finest of everything, Darius.'

Darius sipped his whisky and watched his cousin gulp his as if it were a blackberry cordial. It was on the tip of his tongue to remind his cousin that if he drank so fast his palate would never improve, but some new compunction stopped him.

Calista's goodness.

It had got into his system and banished the bitterness.

If he kept kissing her he'd surely become some kind of saint.

His lip curled. That was unlikely. But she'd made a change inside him. He couldn't deny it.

He glanced at his cousin.

'So you've been teaching Miss Coop to play billiards?' he enquired of Herbert.

'What? Yes, that's right. We'll have a good game tonight after dinner. Between you and me, Mabel's not very skilled, but she's pretty to watch. Very pretty.'

Darius wondered how Calista would play the game. She would become skilled quickly, he imagined, for she appeared to have the right kind of dexterity for the sport. She would handle a billiard cue with ease. At the vision of Calista with a billiard cue in hand he seized his glass and drank some more, gulping almost as fast as Herbert.

'It will be pleasant to play with the ladies.'

'So you're on the way with your bet?' asked Herbert. 'It certainly seems so. I say. That was quick work.'

Darius's frown deepened. 'I need to talk to you about that.'

'I never thought Miss Fairmont would fall for it. What's your trick?'

Glass in hand, Darius studied his cousin. 'It's not a trick.'

'Eh, what?'

Darius swirled his whisky in the glass. 'It's not a trick. I've not had a chance to tell you. I'm calling it off.'

Herbert goggled. 'You mean you're not duping Miss Fairmont? Well, that's quite a relief, I must say. It never seemed to be your kind of lark. I know you wanted to make your point about actresses, but—'

'It's off,' Darius broke in. 'It was an ill-founded plan and a plan I'm not particularly proud of, I'll admit. My only intention was to stop you proposing to Miss Coop, and halt another Carlyle male from making a terrible mistake. You know our history.'

He wished he'd had a chance to clarify that the wager was off with Herbert before matters had gone so far with Calista, but it couldn't be helped. He couldn't wait any longer. He now knew for certain she was the woman he wanted to spend his life with and she had deserved to be the first to know.

Herbert whistled. 'That's a turn-up for the books. Never expected to hear the Duke of Albury admit he was wrong about anything. I can't imagine anyone believing me from school or up at Oxford. What changed your mind?'

Darius gritted his teeth. Calista Fairmont had changed his mind. He hated to be wrong, but he had to admit he'd been completely mistaken about her, right from the start. He'd misjudged her. He couldn't use her to make a point about actresses being all alike when she was the most original woman he'd ever met. She was refreshingly candid and direct, with no falseness in her nature.

And so, he'd own his error to her, too. No more pretence. There would only be honesty between them from now on.

Darius rubbed his jaw. His conscience had been bothering him more than he cared to admit. It was a relief to have called it off with Herbert for certain. It had never sat well with him, he realised, even if his intentions had been in the best interests of his cousin and the family name. 'Let's just say fate played a part.'

Herbert reached for the whisky decanter. 'Fate, eh? So the Carlyle curse has struck again?'

Darius rescued the decanter from his cousin's grip.

For some reason, the mention of fate made him uneasy.

He ought to have told Calista everything the night before. But he hadn't trusted himself to keep her in his bed a moment longer. The temptation had been too great. Her response when he'd proposed to her…

Words were unnecessary between them, he'd said to her.

But some words must be said. He owed her the same honesty she had given him. He wanted to give her an explanation. He had imagined he would have had a chance to talk to her during the day. But it would have to wait.

Could he ask her to come to his bedroom again tonight?

He shook his head as the mere thought of it aroused him. No, she was too tempting. He meant what he'd said. He wanted to wait. He wouldn't take her innocence out of wedlock. He wanted to make her his wife.

But curse the stars, it had better be soon.

Calista Fairmont must be his bride.

It had all been so sudden the night before, he hadn't given her a ring. He'd make a proper proposal of marriage, he promised himself, after he'd cleared up the other matter.

'Where can the ladies be?' Herbert exclaimed.

Now Darius frowned as he stared around the empty drawing room. The gold-fringed curtains were pulled and the lamps were lit. The large room appeared warm and inviting. The red-velvet sofa, where for some reason he had imagined Calista would be seated waiting for him, was empty. So, too, were the leather chairs by the fireplace.

It shocked him how much he wanted her to be there.

He went to the bell by the fireplace and seized the cord.

'Where is Miss Fairmont?' he demanded when the butler appeared.

'Miss Fairmont went upstairs a little earlier, I believe, Your Grace.'

'And Miss Coop?' Herbert asked.

'She followed Miss Fairmont not too long after.'

'How peculiar!' Herbert exclaimed when the butler left. 'Did they not understand they were to meet us before dinner?

Darius stoked the fire. There was an odd chill in the air and a faint but distinct scent of roses.

There were no flowers in the room, only some potted ferns in blue-and-white china pots. He must be imagining it.

Darius stabbed at the wood with the red-tipped poker. It clanged as he dropped it into the silver pot by the hearth and he tried to shake off the strange sense of unease.

Where was Calista?

Chapter Fourteen

*Witness, ye holy powers, who know my
    truth,
There cannot be a chance in life so miser-
    able,
Nothing so very hard, but I could bear it,
Much rather than my love should treat me
    coldly,
And use me like a stranger to his heart.*

Nicholas Rowe: *The Fair Penitent* (1703)

Somehow Calista had managed to stumble out of the drawing room. In the vast hallway she had stared up at the swirl of the marble staircase. Her skirt clutched in her hand, she'd raced up the stairs, faster than Cinderella fleeing from the royal ball.

How could she have been so stupid?

She pulled open her bedroom door. Once inside, she stood trembling with her back against the wood.

The duke had lied to her all along.

Fragments of scenes danced in her head, as though she was watching a play performed at speed.

How clearly now she saw the plot!

Why, he'd laid it out as if he himself were a playwright to rival the Bard.

Again the images flashed before her eyes, like rehearsals, practised over and over.

The duke waiting outside the stage door.

The duke offering her his carriage.

The duke taking her to dinner.

The duke inviting her to Albury.

The duke walking with her in the woods.

The duke holding her in his arms.

And when he had kissed her…

A moan escaped her lips.

Calista put her trembling fingers to her mouth to silence the noise.

An act. All an act.

How cleverly he'd duped her. He had played his part to perfection. She'd never suspected him of such perfidy, such lies. The attentiveness, the courtesy, the kindness. All had been designed to reel her in. He'd got her measure and realised she wouldn't respond well to the usual gifts and seductions as another actress might. Brilliantly,

he'd allayed her doubts as to the purpose of his
attentions and gained her trust. He had played the
role of kind benefactor superbly, played on her
weakness, her need, the vulnerability she kept so
hidden from the world. Somehow, he'd sensed she
had needed him. Why, he'd even involved Columbine in his scheme.

The kindest duke in England.

And she was an actress!

Yet she, Miss Fairmont of Prince's Theatre,
Covent Garden, hadn't seen through his play-acting. Why, it was the Duke of Albury who ought
to be on stage. She prided herself on being able
to judge character, of being a great observer of
it, as an actress and a playwright. But Darius had
deceived her from the very first.

How harshly he'd spoken to her that night at
the Coach and Horses, hurling insults, yet even
then she'd felt some extraordinary attraction lur-
ing her to him. Why else would she have forgiven
him, allowed him to walk her home, to befriend
her sister, to pay his attentions, to court her? To
encourage her to cling to faith in her father's return, to believe that the future might still hold
some hope?

Her feelings for him had led her into a cruel
trap.

In the woods she'd recognised the hunter in
him. She'd been wary, but not wary enough. She'd

once sensed him to be arrogant and dangerous, but she'd soon discerned something else in him, a deeper, more powerful connection.

A meeting of souls.

She had understood him. At least that's what she'd believed. She'd perceived his snarling and barking to be no more than the instinctive defence of a dog who'd been kicked as a young pup. He used his sharp teeth to keep people at bay. To protect those he cared for, as well as himself, from further hurt. She'd known that, somehow, from the start. And when he'd confided in her about his childhood, it had all fit together.

Calista's eyes snapped shut. The back of her head hit against the door as the realisation almost winded her.

She clutched the linen towel as if it were a lifeline thrown to a drowning sailor in a storm. But the storm raged within her. It was impossible to say when her love for him had begun, only that it was the truth. In his arms all her good sense had vanished. She hadn't allowed herself to consider where those kisses might lead, but had just given herself up to him, in what she'd thought had been the honesty of the moment. She, who prided herself on her caution, had been deceived by a truly masterful performance.

No dinners with dukes.

Her hand now on her mouth, Calista rushed to

the pitcher and basin. For a moment she thought she might retch. The tea she had drunk with such pleasure earlier now churned in her stomach. Sweat covered her brow. She seized the towel from beside the basin and put it to her forehead, wiped the beads of perspiration away.

She'd told him she wasn't naïve, but that's exactly what she was. He thought her a hardened actress, a woman of the world who played at love. Yet she had never played such acts. She'd let no other man get close to her, only Darius.

Now she knew. It was he who had played with her, for purposes of his own.

He'd even gone so far as to propose marriage.

The night before, he'd held back, saying he wanted to wait until marriage. And she'd believed him! Why, that, too, must have all been part of his method of snaring her.

No doubt the duke was planning to take the seduction further tonight, with his promises of marriage. His proposal was a sham. He'd given her no ring, not that she cared for such jewels. But he surely knew that now, after the incident with the ruby bracelet. He hadn't risked the same mistake.

Still clutching the towel, she sank on to the stool in front of the dressing table.

She stared at her reflection. Her skin was waxy, all colour gone.

'Fool,' she said aloud. 'Fool.'

Her voice broke the word in two as the tears came.

Great gushing tears that she always held at bay and never allowed to release.

Tears of loneliness. Tears of sorrow. Tears of fear. Tears of worry.

Now they all flowed out, forced out of her body, racked by the mighty flood of the realisation of her love for Darius.

Her companion.

Her protector.

He'd sent arrows of pleasure darting up her body to her core. Sent her into a wildness she never knew existed.

She moaned aloud. It had all been part of his act, but she hadn't been acting. Not once, not when he'd held her against him, lifted her into his bed.

A bitter laugh escaped with her tears.

How completely she'd let her guard down, allowed herself to fall into the trap he had laid. Like a silly chorus girl she'd indulged in the most ridiculous romantic dreams, even as she denied those dreams to herself. Why, in the past few weeks she'd begun to appreciate what it might be like to have someone travel alongside her in the journey of life, someone to turn to, someone who cared.

'Lady Calista. Countess Calista. Duchess Calista. Is that your secret hope, like all actresses?'

Like a chill, the memory of his mocking voice when they'd first met came to her mind. So that was the true Duke of Albury.

Shivering, she put the towel to her lips to muffle her shattered cry.

As she did she caught sight of the new vase of roses Darius had sent to her room. She'd intended to wear one for him again. As the secret symbol of their love. But Darius didn't love her.

He never had.

He never would.

Calista seized the roses from the vase and hurled them into the fireplace.

'Cally?' Mabel popped her head around the bedroom door. 'Please let me come in. Are you all right?'

Quickly Calista wiped her eyes on the towel. 'Come inside, Mabel.'

With a glitter of diamonds Mabel crossed the bedroom floor. 'I know you said you wanted to be alone, but I'm worried about you. Why, Cally, you're crying!'

Calista gulped. 'I'm fine.'

'I knew you'd fallen for the duke,' Mabel said. 'I just knew it.'

Calista took a deep breath. 'What you told me

was a shock, that's all. I've been overwrought of late. I should have known better. I broke my rule.'

'Some rules are made to be broken,' said Mabel.

'Mine wasn't.'

Calista stood and went to the window and drew in some air. Trying to regain her composure, she pushed aside the curtains. It was dark outside now. She'd missed the beautiful Albury sunset.

Of course. She was just an actress to him. Nothing more. Someone to be played with and cast aside.

After another deep breath she spun about. 'I have to leave Albury Hall.'

'Now?' gasped Mabel. 'You can't go back to London at this time of evening. It's far too late.'

Calista twisted the towel in her hands. 'What else can I do? It's impossible for me to stay now that I know the truth.' Her voice shook. She steadied it and went on. 'I must take Columbine and return to London. I ought never to have brought her here in the first place.' It had been a terrible error of judgement. The power of the duke's charm had driven away her usual caution and good sense. Columbine would be disappointed, but there was no help for it.

'Must you go tonight?' Mabel asked.

'I have no choice.' She seized the carpet bag

and started tossing clothing into it. They must leave Albury Hall without delay.

How could she face Darius? She couldn't go down to dinner. She'd never lacked courage before, but to stand before him knowing how he'd played with her heart—surely that was impossible.

'I thought you were planning to stay here at Albury Hall for a week,' said Mabel. 'To have a proper break.'

How far away making plans for a happy holiday now seemed! Only two days ago they'd arrived in the carriage with such excitement.

'I can't stay here,' Calista said. Albury was the last place she wanted to be. 'Not under such false pretences. Believe me, I wouldn't return to London if I didn't have to.'

'Oh, Cally,' Mabel mourned. 'I feel just dreadful. Perhaps I oughtn't to have told you.'

Calista bit her lip. 'Of course you ought to have told me, Mabel. I needed to know the truth. But—'

'But what?'

Calista wrung her hands together. 'I just can't believe it. I'm from the theatre. Surely I'd know if the duke was acting.'

'Maybe he's got a talent for it.'

Calista put her face in her hands. His words. His hands. His lips. All lies. Was it possible?

It couldn't be. Surely she knew him, the real man behind the duke. Surely the man she knew, the man she loved, wouldn't treat her in such a manner. She must be a better judge of character than that. If only there was a way to find out for certain. She must know for sure.

Thoughts buzzed in Calista's head, like lines from a play.

Wiping the tears from her cheeks, she stood up and studied herself in the mirror.

Could she do it? Could she play the role?

Calista lifted her chin. She was an actress, after all.

Tonight, she would give the Duke of Albury a performance he'd never forget.

Chapter Fifteen

~~~~~~~~~~~~~~

And cry'd aloud for vengeance, and
   Lothario.

Nicholas Rowe: *The Fair Penitent* (1703)

The drawing-room door opened, bringing in a draught of cold air.

At the fireplace Darius released his grip from the chimney piece and spun around.

To his relief Calista entered, followed by Miss Coop.

'I say!' Herbert sat up in the club chair. 'We thought you'd forgotten dinner.'

'How could you think so, Herbie?' cooed Miss Coop, with a flash of her bosom as she bent over him.

Darius studied Calista and frowned.

Her blue eyes were brilliant and on her cheeks her colour was higher than her pink evening gown, the same gown he'd removed from her body the night before.

He looked again at her face. Was she wearing rouge?

He'd only ever seen her face painted in such a way on stage, except for that first occasion at the Coach and Horses. Yet the skin on her fine cheekbones was suspiciously crimson. And she was no longer wearing one of his pink roses.

That punched into his stomach, like a blow.

Had she changed her mind about them? Perhaps she was unwell. At that possibility he experienced yet another of those now familiar grips of concern.

Darius moved towards her. 'Are you quite well?'

'Very well,' she cooed.

'Jolly good,' said Herbert. 'After dinner we've got our game of billiards. Don't want to miss that.'

Darius turned to Calista. 'Do you still want to play?'

Her voice was low and husky. 'The games have only just begun.'

He rubbed his jaw. 'Are you sure?'

She gave a throaty chuckle and flashed him a sapphire glance. 'I'm sure.'

Darius stared.

She'd never given him such a glance before.

Her expression was generally so frank, so—
wholesome.

Yet the look in Calista's eyes tonight spelled
out a very different message.

He ran his hand through his hair. Perhaps she'd
had too much sun on the tour of the grounds. He
hadn't been an observant host. He'd been thinking of Calista too much.

Now, with unprecedented alacrity, his cousin
jumped to his feet.

'Let's go into dinner.' With a gallant air Herbert tucked Mabel's arm in his. 'Then you'll see
the most marvellous billiards room we have here.
It opens on to a delightful terrace, should we need
to take the air.'

'I'm sure I'll need to take the air if you do,
Herbie.'

Darius took another step towards Calista. She
looked different, but he wasn't sure why. 'It's been
a long day. If you're too weary…'

Calista lifted her chin even higher. 'I'm ready
to play.'

Calista took in a deep gulp of air, the same
kind of breath she took when she stood in the
wings, about to go on stage in the Prince's Theatre. All the skill she possessed, all the talent,
she summoned up now as they entered the billiards room.

The room was painted a dark green to reflect the colour of the baize table top. Paintings of sporting scenes—hunting, fishing, shooting— were framed in gold on the walls. Dark-red paisley curtains lined one wall. They were open in one section, and she glimpsed through the glass doors the paved terrace beyond.

It took more self-possession than she feared she owned to face the duke. What an actor he was! Inwardly she scorned him as he enquired as to her health with all the appearance of civility, of concern. Over dinner he'd been most attentive, but she knew it to be a sham.

He was almost convincing, so much so that she was tempted to believe the tenderness in his eyes was a message just for her, tenderness that she alone brought out in him.

No. It was a play.

The duke was just performing his part.

Now she must play the role he'd set her.

'You said you were familiar with the game,' Darius said to her, as with a slight bow he allowed her to pass before him.

'I've grasped the rules.'

He took a billiard cue from a rack by the door. His fingers brushed against hers as he gave it to her. She forced herself not to jump. Instead, she let her own fingers slide over the tips of his long fingers in reply.

He frowned as he took his hand away. 'Have you played often?'

'Not as often as you, I believe.'

'Here you are.' Herbert handed Mabel a cue. 'Do you remember what I taught you?'

Mabel fluttered her eyelashes. 'I think so, Herbie.'

'Shall we form teams?' Darius asked brusquely.

'The gentlemen against the ladies?' Herbert suggested.

'Surely it's the aristocrats against the actresses,' Calista put in.

She felt rather than saw Darius's sharp glance at her.

Mabel pouted. 'I want to play with you, Herbie.'

'Oh, I say, of course, Mabel.'

'Would that suit you, Calista?' Darius asked.

With a coquettish shrug she peeped at him over her shoulder. The coquette wasn't a role she'd ever played on stage, but she'd observed it often enough to know how to perform it. The affectation had always seemed to her a betrayal, a sham of real love. 'I'm sure we'll play admirably together.'

Darius ran his hand through his hair. 'Let's get started.'

Herbert bustled over to the table. 'Now, Mabel. Try to remember. There are three balls. The red ball…' he touched it with his cue '…and these two whites. This white is Darius's ball, he's playing with Miss Fairmont, and this is ours. It has a black dot so you know it. We try to hit the red ball and their white ball. If we strike both of them in a shot, it's called a cannon. If they go into a pocket, that's called a hazard. There are winning and losing hazards, of course, depending on which ball goes in first.'

'Oooh,' Mabel breathed. 'It's all so confusing.'

'Are you clear on the rules, Calista?' Darius asked. 'A winning hazard is when the red ball is potted, or striking our opponent's ball and potting it. A losing hazard is if our ball strikes another and is then potted.'

She surveyed him from under her lashes. 'I'm familiar with the difference between winning and losing.'

He narrowed his eyes.

Mabel was still fluttering her hands by the table. 'I'll count on you to tell me what to do, Herbie.'

Herbert puffed out his chest. 'Don't worry, dearest. It's all in hand.'

'Shall we string to begin?' Darius asked impatiently.

Mabel giggled.

'That means shall we see who gets the best

shot to go first,' Herbert clarified. 'I've told you that before, Mabel. You tried it.'

'We've tried so many things, Herbie.'

'Two players take a shot at the same time. Whoever gets closest to the lower part of their table gets to start the game. It's called the baulk. I'll play for us.'

'And I'll play a shot for our team, if that suits my partner,' Darius said.

Calista threw him another coquettish look. 'Whatever pleases you, Darius.'

She made her voice an invitation.

His eyebrows met in a frown. Turning away, he reached for a cue of his own and inclined his head toward his cousin. 'Ready?'

Herbert nodded.

Darius and Herbert both aimed their cues.

The balls ricocheted across the table.

'Oh, dear, never mind, Herbie,' said Mabel.

Herbert shook his head. 'I say. That was an excellent shot, Darius. I never could beat you at billiards.'

The duke leaned on his cue. 'A lucky shot, I'm sure.'

'Perhaps it's your lucky night,' Calista said, daringly.

Darius inspected her through narrowed eyes before placing the red ball on the spot at the top of the table. 'Our team can now play. Would you care to take a shot?'

Calista raised her cue. 'I'd like nothing better.'

Darius watched Calista move towards the billiards table. The grace with which she normally walked, the grace he admired so much, had tonight become something more.

Liquid.

Her back to him, she leaned over the table.

His mouth dried up. The curve of her waist and her straight back were accentuated as she leant towards the baize.

She straightened suddenly. 'It's been a while since I've played this game. I fear I need some advice, too.'

'Is that so?' he managed to reply.

Her hips swayed slightly. 'Perhaps you will be kind enough to help me.'

His cue gripped in his fist, he approached her. 'What is it you need?'

She glanced over her shoulder, moved her hips again. 'I'm unsure of the right angle.'

He moved to stand beside her. Even as he kept a safe distance between them, he could still sense the vitality between them.

With his cue he demonstrated the gliding movement required. 'You move like this. Do you see?'

She bit her lip. 'Might you guide my hand?'

After a moment he laid down his cue. 'Of course.'

He stepped closer and put his arm around her as she leaned deeper over the table. Even through her petticoat he discerned the soft shape of her. He gritted his teeth as he laid his hand over hers and slid the cue in her hand. 'Can you feel this?'

'Yes,' she murmured. Her fingers were tense as she shifted beneath him.

The back of her swan-like neck. The scent of it, sweet yet with a deeper muskier scent that made him want to put his lips to her soft skin.

His body flared to life.

Instantly he stepped back so that he wasn't pressed against her. 'You seem to have it.'

'Why, yes, I believe I've got it.' With a slide of her fingers, Calista flicked the white ball within inches of the red. 'Almost.'

'Well played, Miss Fairmont,' Herbert said heartily. 'Now it's your turn, Mabel.'

Miss Coop approached the table and took aim.

'Not that one,' Herbert said hastily. 'You must aim for our ball, not theirs.'

'Oops.' Mabel giggled.

As she jerked up her cue Darius winced for the baize top. Two balls cracked and the red jumped off the table.

'That's a foul,' said Darius.

'Oh, are we playing by the rules?' asked Calista.

He turned to her sharply. 'How else would we play?'

She lifted her chin. 'I'm not sure that dukes don't make their own rules.'

He released a short laugh. 'Don't actresses?'

'Not every actress. Not in my experience,' she replied. 'Although perhaps all actresses must learn to do so, in time.'

Darius frowned. That arch tone was there again in her voice. It held something else, too, something brittle and fragile.

'It's your turn, Darius,' said Herbert.

He strode to the table and raised his cue. Almost without thinking he potted the red.

'Excellent, excellent,' his cousin said, trying to hide his dejection, before making his own shot that fell short of a cannon.

Herbert sighed. 'Your turn again, Miss Fairmont.'

Darius tried not to watch as Calista ran the cue up and down in her hand before making a passable shot.

'Now it's your turn again, Mabel,' Herbert said. Miss Coop appeared to have lost interest and had moved to stare out of the French doors that led to the terrace.

'Oh.' She turned to the table and languidly

picked up her cue. Once again she took aim. This time she failed to make any connection with the ball.

'Another foul,' said Darius.

Mabel pouted. 'Billiards are boring.'

'Have you had enough, my sweet?' Herbert asked.

Darius moved towards Calista and spoke in an undertone. 'Do you still want to play tonight?'

She aimed her cue. 'The game isn't over yet.'

Chapter Sixteen

*Enthusiastic passion swelled her breast,
Enlarged her voice, and ruffled all her
  form.
She call'd me Villain! monster! base betrayer!*

Nicholas Rowe: *The Fair Penitent* (1703)

Darius groaned and slammed the leather-bound folio shut.

After the extraordinary billiards game, and too many glasses of champagne to cope with Calista's disturbing presence, he'd gone to the library to find a printed script of Rowe's *The Fair Penitent*. He had been sure that the vast library, with its wood panelling and floor-to-ceiling shelves, would house a copy and it did. The library was a room he usually avoided. It was strange how certain rooms brought back memories, and painful ones at that.

It had been the room where he'd hidden after his mother had died.

Now back in his bedroom, holding the leather-bound book, Darius shook off the recollection. If he dwelt on such episodes the whole house might become a graveyard of memories. He refused to brood on the past, especially now.

Darius frowned. What in the blazes could be the explanation for Calista's strange behaviour in the billiards room? The look she had given him…

Instantly his body remembered.

That unmistakable invitation.

Her disappearance before dinner and her re-emergence that had held such an air of brittle playfulness troubled him greatly. Again he wondered if she was unwell. In the morning he'd send a maid to enquire if she needed anything, but not at this late hour, when she'd retired.

Darius ran his hand through his hair, thinking about what he had to tell her. His plan wouldn't put him in the best light. She had to forgive him.

If only he'd told her *before* he'd proposed about the ridiculous sham courtship, his own notion, heaven forgive him, which had brought them together. Now he knew his feelings were so powerful, he loathed even more the idea of her labouring under false pretences. Even worse was the knowledge that the ill-founded plan had been at his instigation.

'Blast,' he said aloud.

He'd make her understand. He'd kiss those lips until they told him she forgave him yet again.

He cursed aloud. If only he didn't have to put her forgiving nature to the test.

A knock came at the door.

God knew why Hammond was knocking at this hour. 'Come in,' Darius called.

The knock came again.

He strode to the door, flung it open and took a step back.

'Calista.' He tightened the cord of his robe. 'What are you doing here?'

In answer she stepped inside the room and closed the door behind her. She was encased in a dark blue dressing gown, her feet in slippers. The dressing gown had the well-darned look that so many of her clothes possessed. Her hair was in a loose bun, curls clustering about her face. He hadn't known her hair curled that way. It was usually up in a more formal style. The curls suited her.

'I couldn't sleep.' Her voice was low and husky. 'Could you?'

He shook his head. He hadn't even tried. Her company all day had been far too stimulating for sleep. 'I'm reading this instead,' he said, holding up the copy of *The Fair Penitent*.

She raised an eyebrow. 'Rowe's play. So you're

re-acquainting yourself with Lothario? The villain of the piece?'

'Something like that.' He frowned. Her voice still contained that strange brittleness. It didn't sound like her usual musical notes that rang out as clear as a bell. 'Are you quite well, my darling? Have you caught cold in your bedroom? I promised you every comfort. I can have a servant build up the fire in your room or attend to the curtains if you require.'

She laughed in the arch manner that sounded so different from the irrepressible gurgle that had previously escaped her lips. Her laugh was usually the same as her sister's. He wondered what she'd been like as a child. Very like Columbine, he expected. Her own children would be similar. A flashing vision of Calista's own daughter laughing made him choke back his own breath, the image was so vivid.

'There's nothing wrong with my bedroom.' She pouted. 'Except that I want to be in yours again tonight.'

Darius stared. Was she fluttering her eyelashes? Blast. It seemed she had taken up with the powder and paint again. Some kind of black lined her lashes. 'Are you sure you're all right?'

Yes. She was definitely fluttering her lashes. He'd never seen her do that before.

She moved close to him, stood on her tiptoes.

Her breath fanned his neck. 'I'm more than all right when you're near me, Darius. That's why you brought me here to Albury, isn't it? So that we could be together. So that I'd be at your command.'

'Not entirely,' he managed to reply as his body hardened.

'But you'll take advantage of the opportunity, won't you?' She raised herself on tiptoe, her mouth inches from his. Then she stepped back and threw off her dressing gown.

Darius exhaled. Beneath the serviceable wrapper she wore the most extraordinary nightgown, so diaphanous it revealed more than it covered. It was made of some gauzy material, frilled at the front, the loose ribbons an open invitation. It was the most extraordinary article of clothing Darius had ever seen and the most stimulating.

He frowned. He couldn't deny the nightgown's effect, yet it was odd night attire for her, unlike the worn dressing gown that had clearly seen better days and her sensible slippers. He almost groaned aloud as she stood still, as if she were on stage, as he studied her from head to foot.

She'd slid her feet out of her slippers at the same time as throwing back the dressing gown as if it were a pair of stage curtains. There they were, as delicate as he remembered, joined to those stupendous legs, marble white beneath the gown. Slender yet strong. Her hips formed a curve as beautiful as a stringed instrument made to play a song. Then there was her waist that he'd only ever seen encased in a corset. It didn't have that too-tiny shape he loathed, crushed out of proportion. It was slender, yet not ridiculously so.

And her breasts. Fuller than he remembered. Ripe. Fruitful. The sheer fabric, frilled at the neck, played tricks with his eyes as she breathed and the movement shifted her breast up and down.

'That's an exceptional garment.' His mouth was so dry he wished for another glass of wine. Hell, he needed it.

Her lips curved. 'I wore it for you. I had hoped you'd like it.'

His body did. Yet his mind's instruction was clear. There was too much unspoken between them. Fighting back his visceral response, Darius retreated a step. 'Aren't you chilled in that nightgown?'

Calista shook her head, sending her curls to kiss her cheeks as stepped closer to him. 'Not if you hold me.'

'Calista—' Darius's voice held warning.
She ignored it.

Earlier, in the billiards room, she had examined him from beneath her lashes. He had held a billiards cue in his hand as easily as he might hold a hunting rifle, every inch the athlete. When he'd leaned over her to show her how to aim, she'd sense the muscled strength of his body, the power and heat of it burning. His hold had heightened the flare of attraction between them.

The flare she must now ignore.

It was pretence, on his part, no matter how desperately she longed to believe otherwise.

Her performance as a coquette had taken its toll. Yet she had to entice him to make his false proposal again.

Surely it couldn't be true! When he'd put his arms around her to demonstrate how to make a better shot, holding her so close to his chest, she'd feared herself about to swoon, so powerful had been her yearning to lean back against him and allow herself to sink into the safety of his arms.

But the Duke of Albury wasn't safe. He was dangerous.

'Please,' she whispered now, holding back the choke of her tears. 'Hold me again.'

The lines came from her mouth as easily if she were in a play, yet to her consternation she realised they came from somewhere deeper inside her, too. Her body couldn't lie, as his could.

'You're tempting me, my darling.' He brushed a finger over her lips, something between a caress and a stop. 'I told you I want to wait.'

She bit her lip to stop the pain. How could he be so cruel?

The nicest duke in England, she thought bitterly. If he was the nicest, she'd hate to meet the worst. She'd been so mistaken in him. It shook her to the core.

'We don't have to wait,' she cooed. 'Let's play.'

She trailed her hand down to brush against his lower body. To her own consternation, the feel of his arousal sent desire surging through her.

'You're not playing fair,' he growled.

'You don't play fair,' she choked out.

A muscle flared in his cheek as he stepped away, evading her touch. 'You don't seem yourself tonight, Calista. Is there anything you need?'

There was that tender note in his voice that had so misled her. How easily he had duped her with such pretended concern, when for so long she'd felt so desperately alone.

Companion.

Protector.

Feigned kindness was his perfect weapon.

Her anger re-ignited, she raised her eyebrow. 'You always seem to have my welfare in mind. Are you always so assiduous to your guests?'

'You're not a guest here any more,' he murmured. 'I told you. I seek to please only you.'

He sounded so sincere, but she mustn't be

fooled. He was capable of anything. She knew that now.

He was a man who believed he had the right to play with other people's lives.

And with their hearts.

'Then kiss me,' she whispered, pressing herself against him. She made her voice an invitation, even as it threatened to break.

For a moment he hesitated, his eyebrows drawn together. Then with a groan he leaned in and touched his lips to hers.

The moment their lips met he drew back.

Darius frowned. 'Something's wrong. What is it?'

Calista swept a mocking curtsy.

'You've been outplayed, Your Grace,' she hissed.

Shock played over Darius's face. His head jerked back as though she'd bitten him. 'What are you saying?' he demanded.

As if he didn't know.

Shaking from head to foot, Calista faced him, her chin raised high. 'I know all about your wicked scheme. The sham courtship to prove that I'm a "title-hunter like every other actress". Mabel told me.'

'Miss Coop. I might have known,' he muttered under his breath.

'You can't blame her! She told me everything.'

He gripped the cord of his robe so tightly his

knuckles whitened. 'Of course I don't blame her. I take responsibility for my own actions. But let me make it perfectly clear. Miss Coop doesn't know "everything". Listen to me, not to the tittle-tattle of your friend. I regret you heard about it that way, but I'd already called it off.'

'So you don't deny it?' Calista felt sick. She'd hoped so desperately he would tell her Mabel had made a terrible mistake, that it had all been a mis-understanding.

'I can't deny it. But I assure you, I have a sat-isfactory explanation,' he said tightly.

'There can be no satisfactory explanation!' She threw his words back at him. 'You've used me as a plaything.'

His mouth thinned. 'You must give me a chance to explain.'

'Explain the low esteem in which you hold the women of my craft? I believe I know enough of that. I thought you a villain when I first met you. But you're even worse than I suspected.' Calista's voice shook. 'You...you...Lothario!'

'You're calling me a seducer?' He ran his hand through his hair. 'After your performance just now? Hellfire, Calista! Don't you realise? I wasn't acting last night. I asked you to marry me!'

'That was all part of your plot to seduce me,' she said scornfully. 'I know the whole terrible scheme. I wanted you to have a taste of your own medicine. To know how it feels to have someone play-acting love to you. That's why I came here tonight.'

He seized her arm. 'And what were you planning to do?'

Calista gulped. She didn't know how to reply. All reason slipped away when he held her, but it seemed impossible to explain that now. She pulled herself free of his grip. 'I told you I'd be your mistress before I'd be your wife.'

He seemed to grow in size as he loomed over her. 'What of your virtue?'

His question stirred her to fresh fury. 'My virtue? What do you care for my virtue? You cared little for it when you determined to seduce me. What were you going to do? Seduce me and then jilt me?'

He swore beneath his breath. 'No! Blast it, Calista. I'll admit it to be an ill-conceived plan, but my family's reputation was at stake.'

'So *my* reputation could be sacrificed,' she said bitterly. 'I'm only an actress, after all.'

He leapt in front of her, spun her to face him. 'Don't you understand? I'd called it off.'

She flung herself away. 'So you say now.'

'I was planning to tell you tonight, before you appeared in that…that…' He seized her wrist. 'Where did you get that damned nightgown?'

Beneath his grip her pulse raced. 'It's not my nightgown. It's Mabel's.'

He cursed. 'I might have known.'

Tearing herself from his grip, she pulled the sheer material over her breasts. 'It was my idea to wear it tonight. I thought it suited the part you expected me to play.'

He reached out and fingered the fabric of the nightgown. 'You think I want you to wear garments like these?'

She curtsied as if she were on stage. 'I've taken my lead from you, Your Grace. Your game of courting me—that was masterful. It was sadistic and cruel,' she said, her voice low.

In the pockets of his robe she saw he clenched his fists. 'I'll own it hasn't worked out well.'

'I made a mistake coming to Albury,' she said, low. 'But my biggest mistake was to trust you. It's one I'll never make again. I expected more of you. You're a nobleman, yet you play with hearts, with dreams. You're no better than Lord Merrick!'

'I'll admit this doesn't represent my finest hour,' he said through gritted teeth. 'But I'm no Merrick. You have to understand. I didn't know you as I know you now. My rank and title called on me to protect my family name from further scandal.'

'From me? Am I such a threat?' Her voice threatened to break, like her aching heart.

She twisted away. She couldn't bear to look at him any more, as tears started to pour down her cheeks. 'How could you have proposed marriage to me?'

His hand gripped her arm and spun her back to face him. His eyes blazed into hers.

Now her tears gushed from her eyes. She wiped her cheeks with her hand.

'Calista, listen. My proposal wasn't for the reason you think.'

'What other reason can there be? I thought, I hoped, that Mabel had it wrong, that she had misunderstood what Herbert had said. That was why I carried on with the act tonight. It was the only way I could comprehend such villainy.' She choked. 'I trusted you. I believed in you. I believed you to be better than all other men. But you're not. You're much worse.'

Darius held her arm, his grip firm. 'It wasn't an act. Listen to me, Calista.'

'No!' She wrenched herself free. 'I beg you, stop. I can't take any more. There's no point in play-acting any more.'

'Damnation, listen to me! I can explain.'

'No more! I beg you. Let me go!'

Calista rushed for the door and flung it open. The ribbons of the nightdress flew behind her as she raced out of the duke's bedroom as fast as her bare feet could take her.

* * *

In the guest bedroom Calista stripped off the frilled nightgown. If it hadn't belonged to Mabel she would have thrown it into the fire, never to see it again. Instead she tossed it aside. Putting on her petticoat she wrapped a thick shawl around her shivering body.

Her hair loose and dishevelled, she went out on to the balcony. The tiles were cold under the soles of her feet.

The cold wind slapped at her face. It was still wet with tears.

'Cally? What are you doing out there on the balcony?'

Wiping her eyes, Calista hurried back into the bedroom. 'What's wrong, Columbine? Can't you breathe?'

'I'm quite all right. I'm just so excited about my next riding lesson. I love it here. Everything is nicer here at Albury. It's the nicest place in England. Do you think Albury is the nicest place in England, too?'

Calista clenched her hands into fists. 'No!'

'What?' her sister asked in amazement.

'No.' Calista bit her lip. She lowered her voice, but kept her tone firm. 'I'm sorry. There'll be no riding lesson tomorrow, Columbine. First thing in the morning, we're returning to London.'

Columbine's eyes widened. 'Why, Cally? What will we tell the duke?'

Calista's stomach lurched. After what had happened in his bedroom… Her cheeks burned. 'I've already told the duke.'

'But I don't understand. Why won't you let us stay, Cally? I love it here. We were meant to holiday at Albury for a week.'

'I'm not going to go into the reasons now, Columbine. Believe me, I wouldn't have us return to London if we didn't have to.'

'I don't want to go home. Please, Cally…'

Calista put her hands to her temples. 'Stop it, Columbine.'

'But…'

'That's enough!'

Calista saw her sister's mouth drop open. She'd never spoken that way before. 'There'll be no argument. We're going back to London in the morning and that's that.'

Stony-faced, Darius watched the carriage pull out of the courtyard.

It was only after the wheels had rolled away across the gravel, bearing Calista out of his life, that he realised he'd stood and watched her leave with the same kind of numb, internal horror he'd experienced when the funeral cortège had taken his mother's body away.

The pain almost brought him to his knees, but he stayed courteous, upright. He'd been unable, no, unwilling to halt Calista leaving his home. Her distress had been so evident, so real. She already had too much to bear. He loathed that he'd brought her more suffering.

She didn't deserve it.

Darius shook his head.

He'd been forced to let her go. He'd had no choice.

His teeth gritted. It was useless to rehearse his regrets, though it was all he'd done for the past hours. The whole plot had been confounded. Yet if he'd not started the whole affair, he would never have got to know the jewel she was. He would never have walked her home from the theatre that night, when he'd first discovered that Calista Fairmont was someone unique, a woman to be prized.

The woman he wanted for his own.

He clenched his gloved fists.

He ought to have spoken to Herbert and called off the plot the first night he'd walked her home.

In his heart he knew he had.

He hadn't realised at the time how effectively she'd pierced the armour he'd held in place since his childhood. The iron cladding around his heart had come away when he had begun to care more for her than he did for himself.

He hadn't known it to be possible, to have thoughts of another person fill his days and nights.

Her comfort. Her ease. Her happiness.

She'd changed him, made him more of the man he had always wanted to be. The man behind the duke.

He'd have convinced her of it, if he'd had more time.

With his words.

With his hands.

With his lips.

Darius stifled a groan.

He remembered Calista's sapphire eyes filled with tears. She'd been so vulnerable. She'd suddenly looked no older than her young sister.

If he had managed to explain, to get her to see the humour, or at least the irony in the situation instead, they might have laughed together. They might have fallen on to his bed with her in his arms where she belonged, their anger turning to passion. He still would have refused to make love to her then, he wouldn't have broken his word on that, but he'd have kissed her again.

Blast.

He'd have kissed her feet.

And then…

Herbert appeared at his elbow. 'I say. This is all a frightful mess, Darius.'

Darius gritted his teeth. That was an understatement.

His cousin coughed. 'I don't suppose it's a good time to ask, Darius, but with everything considered…'

'What is it?'

'It's about Mabel. I'd like to propose to her, with your permission.'

Darius sighed. Family occasions marred by the screech of Miss Coop's voice at table at Albury Hall appeared to be part of his destiny. But she was Calista's friend. He'd been proved wrong about actresses.

'I'll not stand in your way,' he said finally.

He wasn't a hypocrite, after all.

Herbert beamed. 'I say! That's marvellous. Mabel's been the model of patience, waiting for me to pop the question. I've made it up to her, of course.'

With furs and silks and diamonds, Darius presumed. It was the kind of thing he'd tried on Calista, but she was a very different woman.

He clenched his fists. He'd let Calista go. But not out of his sights.

Chapter Seventeen

Oh, my heart!
Well may'st thou fail; for see, the spring
  that fed
The vital stream is wasted, and runs low.
Nicholas Rowe: *The Fair Penitent* (1703)

Calista stared out the window at the falling rain.
The raindrops glistened in the faint sunlight, but
there was no rainbow. The early morning had
held promise, but the day proved to be less bright
than she expected.

As was her habit she laid her forehead against
the cold glass. Her forehead was hot, her eye-
lids heavy. She put her palm to her bodice and
breathed deeply. In. Out. In. Out.

Two weeks had passed since they had left Albury Hall. The pangs in her chest were lessening
now, surely. The sharp pain that came whenever
Darius crossed her mind no longer sliced into her

quite as often. Just in the mornings when she first awoke and late at night before falling asleep, and once or twice during the day when she had a moment alone, as she did now. It wasn't so much, any more. And the nausea, the sickness in her stomach, had almost disappeared, although she still didn't have much appetite and her costume at the theatre was still loose at the waist. And the taste of ashes in her mouth that replaced the usual flavours or food—that was fading. She'd eaten some fish for luncheon and had noted it tasted more of the sea than usual, or perhaps that was because she'd managed to get it fresh by rising and going to the market early that morning.

'Our lovely holiday at Albury Hall,' Columbine mourned as the carriage had carried them back into London.

Calista had offered no explanations as they'd left Buckinghamshire and the Duke of Albury far behind them. For a moment she wondered if she had been too hasty in refusing to listen to what the duke had to say. She shivered, recalling the look in his eyes as she replayed the scene so many times in her mind, as if she were performing it over and over again.

So many different emotions had run through her body that night in the duke's bedroom.

Fury and passion. Anger and desire.

Now her rage at the duke had vanished.

All that was left was heartache.

In. Out. In. Out. She breathed.

No dinners with dukes. How she wished she'd never accepted the invitation! How sensible she'd been to vow never to rely on anyone. She'd been foolish in the extreme to indulge in romantic dreams. Her determination never to marry had been renewed. She had her sister to care for and she would shoulder the responsibility of her up-bringing alone.

Bitterly she exhaled. Never again would she allow herself to become so vulnerable to a man. She would never accept any invitation—whether for a carriage ride, a dinner, a walk, a stay in the country. She would certainly never accept a marriage proposal.

Because no other gentleman is Darius, a voice in her head whispered.

There was no hope of forgetting the Duke of Albury.

She clutched her hands to her hair.

'Cally?' Columbine called from the sitting room. 'I thought you were getting the playing cards.'

'Just a moment, Columbine.' Calista replied in a bright voice.

She pressed her palm harder against her bodice.

In. Out. In. Out.

Calista seized the wooden box of cards and went back to where Columbine sat by the window.

Her sister gazed on to the street. 'Look, the rain has almost stopped. It's made an enormous puddle.' She sighed. 'I did hope the duke would come and visit us. If he did so he might take me out to tea at Gunter's. I'd be able to go out in the carriage.'

Calista bit her lip as she took her seat. Darius's kindness to her sister had been sincere. She was sure that, with the uncanny discernment of a clever child, Columbine would have seen through anything else, but it didn't change anything. She had to forget him and so did Columbine.

She shuffled the cards. 'What shall we play? Whist?'

The girl shook her pigtails. 'We played that yesterday afternoon. Can we play Old Maid?'

Calista swallowed hard. 'Yes, of course.'

Before she dealt she took a joker from the card box and slipped it into the pack.

Columbine took her cards. Her brow furrowed as she arranged them into a fan that was almost too large for her hand to hold. 'Why, the King looks like the duke!'

Calista shifted one of the cards in her own hand. 'We call it a Jack, Columbine.'

Her sister shook her head with a giggle. 'That's

not what I mean. Look! The King of Spades looks just like the Duke of Albury.'

Martha came and leaned over Columbine's shoulder. 'Ooh, I see just what you say, Miss Columbine. It's him to the life.'

'Look, Cally.' Columbine slid the card across the table.

Calista took the card in her trembling fingers and stared.

It was true. There was a strange resemblance in the dark sardonic face, the piercing eyes.

'I shall have to show him if the duke comes to call on us,' Columbine said.

It was on the tip of Calista's tongue to tell her sister that the duke would never call on them again. Instead she said, 'We can ask Mabel to come and play cards with us. She can make up a four.'

Columbine would forget about the Duke of Albury, in time. They all would. They must.

'Here.' She dealt another card. 'You can't use that one. I know who it is.'

Calista slid the King of Spades back into the pack of cards.

Darius stared out of the carriage window at the streets of Covent Garden. London was always at its best in the early summer. Late afternoon sunlight gilded the pavement, made the streets appear paved with gold, though the shadows were lengthening. The lamps hadn't yet been lit. It was still a few hours before the theatre crowds would come and the doors would open.

Hammond appeared from the alley beside the Prince's Theatre.

'Well?' Darius asked impatiently.

Hammond nodded as he climbed into the carriage. 'It's all been done as you wished, Your Grace. I've got the information we need.'

'And you understand my instructions?'

'Yes, Your Grace. I'll deliver it personally.'

'It may take some time,' Darius warned.

'You can count on me, Your Grace. I'll make a start right away.'

Darius rapped on the carriage for the driver to start the horses. 'Let's go.'

Calista turned the corner towards the Prince's Theatre.

For a moment, outside the theatre, she thought she caught a glimpse of a familiar black and gold horse-drawn carriage driving away.

Wearily she rubbed her eyes.

Perhaps she'd imagined it, the same way she'd taken to imagining someone beside her on her pilgrimages to and from the theatre, when the loneliness seemed almost too much to bear. It had never felt lonely before, but now she found herself yearning for that tall shadow, that long stride, that unexpected gleam of a smile beside her. More than once, Herbert had offered her a lift with Mabel in his carriage after a performance, but she always declined. It was better to rely on herself alone.

Better not to be reminded of Darius.

Calista put her hand to her bodice, tried to blunt the pang in her chest.

She would never see Darius again. Their paths would not cross. An actress and a duke were hardly in the same social circles. More than once she scolded herself for peering through the fog outside the stage door, hoping to see his unmistakable figure waiting for her to walk her home, like he had once before. How easily she'd grown accustomed to his presence. Now she knew she must grow accustomed to forgetting him.

She shuddered. Fear had returned to her nightly walks, without Darius at her side.

She had to run the gauntlet again. And Lord Merrick, as if sensing her vulnerability, had taken again to lying in wait and leering at her.

She lifted her chin as, instead of turning down the alleyway to the stage door, she went around to the front of the tall building. How grand it was. She rarely entered the stage from the front, with its two flaming torches on either side on the main door, which weren't yet lit for the evening.

Under the portico, the wide main doors were locked. She took the side door into the foyer, lush with red-velvet carpet. The carpet was worn in places, especially up the central staircase that led to the stalls, where so many pairs of shoes stepped night after night, but the brass gleamed and the wood shone. Even on the soft carpet her boots seemed to echo in the vast space. The cloakrooms and desk were closed, the foyer empty. There was something strange about the room that would be packed with people in just a few hours. The air seemed full of past excitement and anticipation.

Her gloved hand glided up on the curved railing as she climbed the stair to the door at the top and slipped into the empty theatre.

Calista stared. She would never forget the first time she had seen it. To her, the Prince's Theatre was the most beautiful in Covent Garden, though it was not as grand, people said, as some others. It wasn't the largest either, but there was room for more than two thousand people to watch a play within. She loved to spend time in the empty space, where only echoes remained of the plays performed there, night after night. It was her favourite place to come and think.

The theatre had been her world.

But not any more.

Everything had changed. She no longer belonged on the stage as an actress. She felt it in every part of her body as she spoke and bowed and walked across it. Each night it became harder to perform. She stood in the draughty wings, experiencing something akin to stage fright. Her hands became clammy, her throat dry. Her heart wasn't in it any more, even though she tried hard not to let it show. The audience paid good money. She refused to let them down.

The performance must go on. She was still playing Rosalind, though there was only a week left for the play to run and she hadn't secured her next part. She barely had the energy to get up in the mornings, let alone to pursue a new role. Work was no cure. Acting a role on stage only reminded her of play-acting, of deception and pretence, and all she wanted to forget.

Fred, the doorkeeper, came into the theatre and gave her a curious look. 'Thought I heard someone in here. All right, Miss Fairmont?'

'Oh, yes, Fred. Thank you. I'm quite all right.'

Calista put her hand to her bodice as she made her way backstage.

In. Out. In. Out.

Darius glared at the stage.

In the bright lights a dark-haired, slender figure bowed, sweeping her hand, her wide mouth curved in a beaming smile as she accepted the call of the crowd.

'Bravo!'

'Miss Fairmont!'

'Bravo!'

With the grace he now knew so well she dropped a straight-backed curtsy as flowers landed at her feet.

'Miss Fairmont!'

'Bravo!'

Night after night he watched her perform and give all she possessed to the audience.

Night after night he watched her fade. His glare became a scowl. No one else seemed to notice her deep exhaustion, the disappearance of that inner flame that had once made her burn so bright on the stage.

Darius noticed.

It wasn't visible on her face or in her body. It was internal. Her spirit. Her soul.

The first night he'd returned to London he'd been unable to resist coming to watch the play, slipping into the back row of the high gallery in the darkened theatre just before the first act had begun and leaving before the first of the crowd spilled out on to the street. And even from that first night he'd witnessed the change in her.

A light had gone out in her.

He'd done that to her. At Albury Hall he'd watched her flame burst into vivid life, only to turn to ash before his eyes.

Now, he watched Calista give one last wave to the crowd and disappear into the wings. She'd seemed better tonight, had performed with more vivacity. He knew every nuance of her performance by now. Some of her old energy had returned this evening and he wasn't sure why. Perhaps she'd managed to find some time to rest.

The curtain came down.

Darius gripped his gloves as he tugged them out of his coat pocket and made his way out of the theatre on to the street to his post near the alleyway to wait for her to emerge from the theatre and start her journey home.

A good hunter, he'd become adept at keeping a good distance from Calista in the inky darkness, camouflaged in a black cloak and shoes padded with leather to reduce their echo. The London fog hid him from her view, though once or twice she'd peered over her shoulder as if she sensed him.

At first he had resisted the idea. He'd sought to restrain himself from shadowing her home each night, escorting her from a secret distance. He didn't want to frighten her. But the thought of her walking alone by night, unprotected, punched him like a fist in the centre of his stomach.

So he'd had made a black broadcloth cloak at his tailor's in Bond Street. It was a strange garment for a duke, but it did the job well. Last night, however, he'd had the strangest notion that

Calista had known he was near, her silent, hidden guard. There was a connection between them he couldn't explain. She'd stopped unexpectedly once or twice in the street and he'd quickly stilled his footsteps.

He refused to let her walk alone, even if she didn't know it.

For now, it was all he could do.

Chapter Eighteen

I have not since we parted, been at peace,
Nor known one joy sincere;

Nicholas Rowe: *The Fair Penitent* (1703)

'Oh, I say!' Herbert backed out of the doorway. 'Frightfully sorry, Miss Fairmont. I thought Mabel was the only one in here.'

Calista spun on the dressing-table stool. 'It's all right. I'm finished here.'

Herbert bowed. 'So sorry to intrude. You were quite marvellous tonight, if I may say so.'

Mabel appeared from behind the wooden screen in a flounced, low-cut gown. She pouted. 'What about my performance, Herbie?'

'I barely took my eyes off you for a moment,' Herbert replied hastily.

Mabel sighed and fluttered her lashes. 'Only one more week and this play is finished. I'll take my final bow on stage. You'll have me all to yourself soon enough, Herbie.'

Calista hid her smile at Herbert's goggle-eyed expression. Yet beneath her joy at their happiness, worry gnawed. The end of the play's run meant the end of her income. She would only be able to make her savings stretch for so long. She must try for another part as soon as possible, perhaps even at another theatre.

Even the thought of it wearied her. No one in the company had noticed or commented, but she knew her performances had changed and not for the better. She was no longer able to slip into character completely on stage. There was always some part of her that longed for Darius. Not for the duke, not for the part he played to the world, but for the man she'd thought she had discovered behind the performance. He was an intensely reserved man and he'd let her into his private world.

Or so she'd believed.

'May I offer you a lift home in my carriage tonight, Miss Fairmont?'

Calista came out of her reverie and winced. Travelling in a carriage that didn't contain the Duke of Albury was too much to bear. She would rather walk, even though the terror of her nightly walks had started again. Fear had once more become her companion on her way home, instead of Darius. And the streets were once again unnerving, even though for the past few weeks the sense of a protective presence hadn't quite disappeared on those long lonesome journeys. It was a strange comfort.

She couldn't risk the price of a hansom cab, not this time, not with the run of *As You Like It* coming to an end. Knowing how precarious earning a living was in the theatre, she'd tried to put aside savings, but who knew how long they would have to last. The thought of finding her next part filled her with dread. Conjuring up more performances on stage seemed beyond her capability any more. But she must.

'It's very kind of you.' She smiled. 'But I wouldn't like to take you out of your way.'

'Not at all,' Herbert protested. 'It's not far from our destination.'

'We're going to that lovely new restaurant in Mayfair,' Mabel added. 'You know the one, Calista. You told me about it.'

Calista swallowed hard. The memory of that dinner with Darius swept through her mind. Would the recollection of being in his arms ever fade?

She shook her head. 'Thank you, but, no.'

She needed time alone, even if the walk tired her, even if she still felt haunted by thoughts of the duke on the journey. Why, tonight she'd even imagined him in the theatre while she'd performed. She fancied his presence everywhere.

Companion.

Protector.

She must let such imaginings go.

'I could use the solitude. I have a few scenes to consider.'

'Your performance as Rosalind is perfect!' Herbert protested. 'I beg you, do not reconsider it in any way.'

Mabel wrapped her fur over her bare shoulders. 'She means the play she's writing.'

'I say.' Herbert's eyes threatened to pop out. 'You're writing a play? How extraordinary. I fear to offend, but I've never heard of a woman doing such a thing before.'

Calista smiled. Yet beneath it came another needle of pain. Darius had known of women playwrights. He'd told her so, as they had walked through the woods at Albury. 'I can only try.'

'You've nearly finished it, haven't you, Cally?'

'That's right.'

She'd kept writing *The Fair Jilt*, as though through it she maintained some kind of connection with her father, but she had to admit her hope was fading. She'd sent another letter north, but had received no reply. She might as well face it. Their father wasn't coming back.

Don't give up hope for your father, until you know for certain. That would be a mistake.

That's what Darius had said when they'd sat at dinner together. She'd clung to those words, like a lifeline. At the time his message had rung so true, but it had all been part of the duke's act.

Her chest tightened so much she could hardly breathe.

Perhaps it was time to abandon hope.

About her father.

About Darius.

She stared into the mirror at her red-painted cheeks.

You need no artifice.

A deep voice echoed in her head.

Calista's fingers trembled as she picked up the pot of *crème celeste* and rubbed the bright colour away.

Darius pulled the black cloak more tightly around him. He'd been guarding her for weeks now on her walk home, unbeknown to her.

He'd remembered her routine. How she came out later than the rest of the cast. How she walked briskly, confidently, showing no fear, no matter that she felt frightened sometimes. She never let it show. She kept a brisk step, her chin up. And then there was her extraordinary ability to change her shape, to become almost invisible on the street if anyone appeared to show too great an interest.

Almost invisible. *Almost.*

Usually, her performance worked.

But tonight was different.

Darius spotted it straight away, the dark-painted carriage that had pulled out behind her at the theatre. He expected it to turn right or left, to the more salubrious districts of London. Instead, it continued into the darker, poorer streets.

Darius narrowed his eyes. There could be no doubt. The carriage and its two black horses were not on the same street as Calista by chance.

Miss Fairmont was being followed and not only by him.

Onwards Calista walked.

Onwards the carriage wheels rolled stealthily behind her.

Onwards Darius continued, keeping pace behind.

He didn't know if he wanted her to notice the carriage and hasten on, or whether seeing it there it would terrify her.

The lamplight became even sparser as they reached the area close to her home. How he wished he could take her away from that responsibility, offer protection. But he didn't have time to dwell on that now. Still the carriage followed.

Darius picked up his pace.

At last they reached her street.

Calista stopped at the corner where she normally crossed the street to her lodgings. Her long neck turned to and fro as she stepped out.

Beside her, at the roadside, the carriage came to an abrupt halt. The door flung open.

A man in a top hat leapt out.

Darius broke into a run.

Calista screamed.

A hand clamped on her mouth and stifled the noise. 'You'll be quiet, if you know what's good for you.'

As the man dragged her backwards she began to kick beneath her petticoats. She bit down on his hand, hard, but her teeth didn't go through his gloves.

The man swore. 'You little vixen.'

Suddenly Calista recognised the man's voice. Lord Merrick! The realisation sent her kicking, fighting hard to free herself from his grip.

With his other hand he clutched her hair, dragging her with it. 'Be quiet, I said. I'll listen to you scream later.'

At his words she bit down even harder on his hand.

He cursed again and let go.

As she spun around she realised it wasn't her bite that had stopped him.

Calista's boots slipped on the pavement and she almost slid to the ground. 'Darius!'

Darius sent his black cloak flying as he hauled Lord Merrick off Calista, sending him to his knees.

'Get out of here, Calista,' he ordered her. 'Go home. Now!'

Calista couldn't move.

'Go!' he shouted again as Merrick clambered to his feet.

Her eyes wide with fear, to his relief she didn't argue. Picking up her skirts, she raced away, across the street.

Darius spun back to Merrick, who'd raised both of his fists. 'You ought to stop interfering in my affairs, Albury.'

'You don't know what's good for you, Merrick. I told you not to come near Miss Fairmont again.'

'She's a harlot,' the other man spat. 'I thought you'd finished with her.'

'It's you I'm about to be finished with,' Darius said through gritted teeth. 'You deserve a hiding. And, by God, I'm ready to give you exactly what you deserve.'

Merrick rushed at him, his fists flailing.

Darius raised his own fists as he stepped aside to evade Merrick's blows.

'This reminds me of our schooldays,' he said

almost conversationally as he took aim. 'Do you remember my favourite pastime?'

With a right hook Darius knocked Merrick to the ground. 'Boxing.'

With one hand Darius opened the carriage door. With the other he seized Merrick by the scruff of the neck and hurled him sprawling on to the floor of the carriage. 'Take my advice. Get out of London.'

Darius slammed the door shut and rapped on the side of the carriage. 'Drive on.'

Chapter Nineteen

What if, while all are here, intent on
 revelling,
I privately went forth, and sought
 Lothario?

Nicholas Rowe: *The Fair Penitent* (1703)

Darius nodded to the doorman as he entered his club. 'Good evening.'

'Good evening, Your Grace. Your cousin is in the drawing room.'

Darius flung a cursory glance around the club-room. Merrick hadn't had the nerve to show his face, he was pleased to note. Darius had heard earlier that day that he was planning to go to the Continent, on some kind of hastily arranged Grand Tour. Frankly, Darius didn't care where Merrick was or where he went, as long as he went nowhere near Calista.

He'd stayed outside her house until he had been

sure there'd be no further trouble, but he hadn't knocked on her door. He didn't have the right to see her, to speak to her.

He frowned as he made his way to the club drawing room. The play's run was soon to end. She would no longer be walking home and he'd no longer be needed to shadow her to safety.

Pain shafted in his chest so hard he faltered in his normal quick stride across the room. At their usual table Herbert sat staring out of the window, wearing the same beaming, sappy smile he'd worn since Miss Coop had accepted his proposal of marriage.

Darius sighed. Perhaps he'd become accustomed to Miss Coop's screech echoing in the corridors of Albury Hall, over time. But time couldn't heal all wounds. He knew that, better than anyone.

'Herbert.'

His cousin jumped. 'I say. Didn't see you come in, Darius.'

Darius raised a brow at the waiter, who rushed off to bring his whisky. 'Lost in thoughts of your impending connubial bliss?'

Herbert sighed happily. 'I've been making all kinds of arrangements. One wants to give the woman one loves the world, you know.'

Darius fell silent for a moment. He knew.

Oh, he knew.

The play's ending bothered him on another level, too. The thought of Calista continuing to struggle financially bothered him greatly. He'd toyed with the idea of leaving money on the doorstep, providing some kind of windfall, but he knew she'd reject something so obvious. Her pride would never allow her to accept charity.

The waiter returned with his drink. The whisky scalded his throat as it went down.

'How is Miss Coop?' he forced himself to enquire, for Calista's sake more than anything else. Some of her goodness still swam in his system, it seemed. 'I hope you gave her my very best wishes.'

Herbert beamed. 'We've been keeping an eye on Miss Fairmont, as you requested.'

'How does she seem to you?' Darius asked brusquely. 'Backstage, I mean.'

Herbert hesitated. 'It's hard to say. I don't know her well enough, but Mabel's worried about her, I know that. She's very caring, Mabel.'

Darius's estimation of Miss Coop raised a notch. It seemed she was indeed a good friend to Calista. Herbert had been most apologetic about the matter of Mabel revealing everything to Calista, but Darius couldn't blame Miss Coop.

He took responsibility for his own actions.

'Now Miss Fairmont's working on her play.'

Herbert shook his head. 'Mighty unusual woman, if you ask me, I mean—'

'What?' Darius interrupted. 'She's writing?'

Herbert nodded. 'So she said. She's almost got a play all done, she told Mabel.'

Darius took another swig of whisky, let it burn down his throat. It must be the adaptation of her father's which she'd hoped to complete, based on the story by Aphra Behn.

His mouth twisted as he recalled the title.

The Fair Jilt.

He glanced out the window. The stars were beginning to appear in the twilight.

Darius threw back the last of his drink and leaned towards his cousin.

'There's something else I need you to do.'

'I'm sorry, Mabel.' Calista removed the paint she wore as Rosalind for the last time in the dressing room of the Prince's Theatre. It felt strange knowing she wouldn't play the role again. When she'd curtsied to the audience, for curtain call after curtain call, there had been that familiar moment when she came back and became her own self again. Yet the final bow to the applauding crowd had been different this time. It had come as a relief more than anything else. She needed to be alone. 'I'd prefer not to come to the cast party.'

She had to have some time to think.

Darius had saved her from Lord Merrick.

She'd been so distraught the night before that she'd obeyed his curt instruction to go home. By the time she'd raced outdoors again, unable to stay away, the street had been empty.

'Oh, Calista.' In her mirrored reflection over Calista's shoulder Mabel's full mouth pouted. 'That was my last-ever performance on the stage. I won't perform once I'm married. You simply must come to my final cast party.'

Calista gave a small smile. 'It's no use pouting at me, Mabel. I'm not Herbert.'

Her friend giggled. Her reflected expression changed to seriousness. 'Please come tonight. You've been my closest friend at the theatre. We've always shared this dressing room. My last theatre party won't be the same without you.'

Calista picked up her hair brush. 'Where's the party to be held?'

'At the Coach and Horses Inn...' Mabel faltered.

Calista swallowed hard. The Coach and Horses. In the upstairs dining room of that very inn where she had first met the duke.

She brushed her hair with long, hard strokes.

'Please, Calista.' Mabel entreated. Her blue eyes welled with tears. 'It's not a big party, but Herbie has ordered champagne and lobster for everyone. It's all going to be perfect, but it won't be if you aren't there, too.'

Mabel burst into tears.

'Oh, Mabel.' Calista stared perplexed at her friend. 'Please don't cry.'

She continued to sob. Her shoulders shook in her pink silk dressing gown.

Calista crossed the room and put an arm around her. She knew from Mabel's performances on stage that she could cry on command, but it didn't alter the effect, and she realised she would miss her friend's company backstage. It was churlish to spoil the happiness of others simply because her heart still ached.

And then it came to her.

Herbert was Darius's cousin. She'd convince him to tell her how to find the duke to thank him. Of course!

'Perhaps I could come to the Coach and Horses for a while,' she said slowly.

Mabel raised her head and wiped her cheeks with a lacy cuff of her dressing gown. The remnants of her tears sparkled prettily in her eyes. 'You will?'

'Not for long,' Calista warned her. She would need time afterwards to follow through with her plan.

A knock came at the door.

'Come in,' trilled Mabel.

One of the stagehands put his head around the door. 'Message for Miss Fairmont,' he said.

He handed Calista a folded paper.

Calista frowned, perplexed.

'It's a message from the manager of the Prince's Theatre.'

'What does it say?' Mabel asked.

Calista scanned the letter. 'Why, I don't believe it. He wants to talk to me about putting on one of my father's plays. This note says they have a new investor interested in promoting his work. The investor has already invested a considerable sum as a sign of good will.'

Mabel squealed. 'Oh, Cally, that's marvellous news!'

She read on in amazement. 'Apparently the investor is going to attend the final night party tonight. He's keen to meet the cast.'

'That's perfect.' Mabel smiled radiantly. 'You must come now, Cally. You can talk to this investor and have some champagne, too.'

She refolded the letter and clutched it in her hand. This news contained a spark of hope. An investor who wanted one of her father's plays to be performed, at last. If only he could be there to hear the news!

'You can come in the carriage with Herbie and me to the Coach and Horses,' her friend offered.

'Thank you, Mabel. That's very kind.'

'Wonderful!' A cloud of rose scent enveloped her as Mabel gave her a hug. 'You won't regret it.'

Calista sighed. In spite of the promising news, her heart tore at the thought of visiting the place where she'd first met Darius. 'That's what you said last time.'

But this time she wouldn't be sorry.

The Duke of Albury had shadowed her home to safety, had rescued her from Lord Merrick.

Tonight, Calista vowed, she would find him.

Darius stared into the fire. In the grate the fire leaped in bright colours: red, yellow, orange, with blue at the centre. A paler blue than the sapphire of Calista's eyes.

He was almost out of time. The final performance of *As You Like It* would be just finishing at the Prince's Theatre.

He winced. Tonight he had missed her performance. He paced the room.

The thought of not being able to see her on stage, to protect her from this point onwards, was unbearable. He'd dealt with Lord Merrick, but how many others would there be?

Nothing had been right in his life since he had met Calista Fairmont. She'd turned his world upside down.

A scratch came at the door.

The butler entered. 'Apologies for the interruption, Your Grace, but you told us to let you know immediately if word came from your valet.'

Darius sprang across the room. 'He's sent word?'

'Hammond is downstairs, Your Grace. And he's not alone.'

Calista sipped her glass of champagne in the private dining room of the Coach and Horses Inn. The golden liquid bubbled in the glass, yet it tasted flat on her tongue.

She took another sip. Perhaps it might revive her. The other members of the cast were laughing and telling stories about the run of the play. Forgotten lines, incidents in the wings, squabbles backstage. Everyone seemed to be having a marvellous time, especially Mabel, who was decked out in a red dress, flashing the diamond ring Herbert had given her.

Calista glanced down at her own blue dress. It was an old favourite with a high ruffled neck, made over more than once. It had seen better days, but the colour matched her eyes perfectly, or at least that was what her father had told her.

Herbert Carlyle turned to her, his face red-cheeked. 'I say, drink up, Miss Fairmont.'

Calista smiled at him and took another sip of champagne. 'This is delicious.'

'Only the best for Mabel.' Herbert beamed

with pride across the table to where Mabel sat squeezed between two admiring members of the cast. 'She'll never have less again.'

'I'm very happy for you both.' Calista took a large gulp, almost finishing her champagne. 'And I hope you'll both be happy, too.'

'Oh, we will be, you can be assured of that.' Herbert picked up the champagne bottle. 'May I pour you some more?'

'No, thank you.' The new investor hadn't put in an appearance at the cast party after all. Perhaps he'd changed his mind. Investors in the theatre were notorious for doing so. It was an insecure business. 'I really must be going home.'

Herbert appeared alarmed. 'What, already?' He called across the table, 'I say, Mabel, Miss Fairmont says she's going home.'

Mabel's eyes widened. 'Not yet! Please, Calista, stay longer. We haven't eaten the lobster.'

Calista shook her head. 'I don't have much taste for lobster these days.'

'Then let me order you something else,' Herbert pressed. 'Mutton? Beef? Something sweet, perhaps. I'll ring for the serving boy.'

He leapt up, knocking over the champagne bottle. Just in time Calista seized it, set it upright.

'Really, there's no need.' She turned to Herbert and spoke low. 'There's something I need to ask you before I go.'

The dining-room door opened.

Calista's legs buckled beneath her skirts.

'Darius!' Herbert leapt up. 'You're just in time.'

'Am I?' the duke asked, staring straight at Calista.

Her pulse raced faster than the times she'd stood in the wings before a performance. She'd forgotten how his presence dominated a room, how everyone else in it melted away when his eyes met hers. But the shade of his dark eyes, the sardonic tilt to his mouth, the hard line of his jaw, she hadn't forgotten those. She saw them every night in her dreams.

'What are you doing here?' she managed to ask. Her voice was hoarse, the words like stones scraping her throat.

He bowed. 'You received a letter about a new investor for your father's work to be performed at the Prince's Theatre, did you not?'

Calista's mouth fell open. Something in her mind clicked. 'The new theatre investor is you.'

'I understand it can be an excellent investment with the right play. The work I'd particularly like to see on stage is *The Fair Jilt*.'

'The play I've been working on for my father?'

'Indeed.' An almost teasing expression came over his face. 'I look forward to discussing terms with him.'

She wiped a trembling hand across her eyes

and stepped forward. 'My father is gone. You know that. Do you mean to taunt me?'

The duke's face changed. The teasing expression vanished.

'Calista—'

Her breath heaved from her chest. It wasn't Darius who spoke her name this time. Another man stood in the doorway.

Calista blinked. For a moment she wondered if she was hallucinating. She blinked again through her tears.

'Papa.' The name fell from her lips.

His familiar voice that had once filled so many theatres came to her across the room.

'Cally, my dearest girl.'

'Papa!' With a choking cry Calista rushed into her father's arms. 'Oh, Papa!'

All the tears she'd held inside for so long burst out, gushing down her cheeks, on to the ruffled neck of her gown. 'Oh, Papa, I thought I'd never see you again! I'd almost given up hope!'

Almost, but not quite. The duke's determination for her not to had seen to that, in spite of what had happened between them.

'There, there, Cally. I'm home now.' Her father held her tightly.

Wiping her eyes, she pulled back to study him. His blue eyes, the same shade as hers, were dulled and set deep into his face, yet they still managed to sparkle at the sight of her, just as they always had. But his hair was greyer than she remembered, his face lined and sallow.

'Papa! You're not well. You're so thin.'

'This is William Fairmont, Calista's father,' said the duke to the assembled company.

Mabel gave a shriek. 'He's back at last!'

Herbert rushed to give him a chair. 'Sit down, sit down.'

William Fairmont bowed his head. 'Thank you.'

He clutched the back of the chair before subsiding into it and breaking into a fit of coughing.

Calista knelt beside him, clutching his hand. 'Papa. What happened to you? Why didn't you come home? Where have you been?'

Her father tried to speak through his coughing.

'Have some champagne.' Herbert proffered a glass.

'He needs water, Herbie, not champagne,' Mabel said. 'Give this to Mr Fairmont.'

Calista took the cup of water Mabel poured and held it to her father's lips. 'Better?'

He stroked her hair. 'Much better for seeing you, my daughter.' Now she realised his voice sounded reedy, not strong and rich as it used to be.

'What happened, Papa? You've been gone so long.'

His face was gaunt, too, and his clothes hung

off him. She tried to disguise her shock at his emaciated state.

'Your father's been ill,' Darius said smoothly. 'I've been making enquiries for some time. I finally received word that he was in Leeds, in a very poor state. Fortunately, we hit upon a lead and we were able to find him.'

Calista twisted her neck to look up at the duke's impassive face. 'You made enquiries about my father?'

He shrugged. 'It seemed prudent to protect my investment.'

'I've wanted to come to you and Columbine for so long, Cally.' William Fairmont coughed, a deep, racking hack that shook his frame. 'But I wasn't able to, there were problems...'

'Let's not discuss that now,' Darius said.

Releasing her father's hand, Calista climbed to her feet and moved closer to Darius.

'What aren't you telling me?' she asked him in an undertone.

He raised a brow. 'You know all you need to know. Your father is home.'

She shook her head. 'There's more to it than that.'

His eyes held a warning. 'Perhaps now isn't the time to discuss it. He's been seriously ill. He needs your care.'

Calista bit her lip. 'Yes, of course.'

She crouched once more by her father and took his hand. 'We must get you home. It's the middle of the night, but I know someone who will be just as pleased as I am to see you.'

'Columbine.' Her father's eyes lit up with something of their old twinkle. 'How is she?'

'She's well, Papa, very well.'

'I knew you'd look after her, Cally. I always counted on you.'

Calista's eyes brimmed. 'I did my best.'

She stood, turned back to Darius.

He was no longer at her side.

Once again, the Duke of Albury had vanished.

Chapter Twenty

Is your fair mistress calmer? Does she
   soften?

Nicholas Rowe: *The Fair Penitent* (1703)

Darius strode through Albury woods.

Haunted. That's what he'd told Calista the village children called the woodland grove that lay
between his estate and the village.

Never had it been more true.

The trees were in even more vivid leaf than
when he'd walked the flower-strewn path with
her. Above in the branches, a woodpecker made
a determined attack on a tree trunk. He admired
its persistence.

It was cooler in the woods than close to the
house, where the summer sunshine blazed on the
lawns. It was darker, too, with a wind that seemed
to whisper a name.

He'd told the bearer of that name that the wind

played tricks in the woods in the wintertime. But today, even in the height of summer, he could hear the call.

Calista.

He clenched his jaw.

It wasn't the voice of the wind.

Soon after he arrived home he'd realised he couldn't escape the yearning for her presence in the country any more than he could in town. Albury Hall echoed with emptiness. Her visit had been so brief, yet every room he entered only reminded him of Calista being there. The drawing room. The dining room. The billiard room.

His bedroom.

His body hardened at the memory.

At the final night party, when he'd delivered Calista's father to her arms, he'd witnessed her face light up like fireworks blazing across the sky.

Yet when she'd first seen him, Darius, she'd paled like one of the waxworks created by Madame Tussaud at the Baker Street Bazaar. He'd viewed them once, those strangely lifeless figures. Calista's waxy face had resembled one of them for a moment, as if he were a ghostly apparition, as if he'd been haunting her, the way she haunted him.

Darius fisted his hands in his coat pockets.

He touched the ring box inside his waistcoat pocket. He still hadn't been able to bring himself to return the engagement ring to the vault. There was a kind of bitter irony in it all. In his horror of repeating his father's mistake, he'd made the opposite mistake of his own.

The actress he loved would never play false. She was true to herself and her feelings. He knew that about his Calista.

His Calista. He ran his hand through his hair. If only there was the opportunity to play it again, to see her cross the threshold of Albury once again.

He'd forced himself to leave the party, to leave London, once Calista was safely in her father's care. At least he'd been able to do that much, to take from her slender shoulders the burden of keeping the family and her sister.

Now Calista would be provided for.

She was no longer his concern.

He wouldn't need to think of her any more. He wouldn't need to shadow her home, silently guarding her in the dark London streets. He wouldn't need to watch her play Rosalind from the gallery of the Prince's Theatre. He wouldn't need to worry if she was tiring or if rain was going to fall.

He wouldn't need to care.

The pain hit Darius in the centre of his body, like a blow. He almost doubled over.

The night before he'd been unable to sleep. He'd lit a lamp and taken up his copy of *The Fair*

Penitent, but soon reading Calista's name over and over had grown too much to bear. He picked up instead his copy of the new novel, *The Whale*. It was making a sensation across the Atlantic, he understood, published in New York under a new title, *Moby Dick*. It was an extraordinary work and the book was absorbing, but when he'd come to a page about the fates being like stage managers he'd snapped the volume shut and blown out the lamp.

Perhaps, after all, the loss of Calista had been his fate. His plan of a sham courtship had been a cruel trick, but in the end, the trick had been played on him.

Above in the trees the woodpecker stopped his hammering.

Leaves scattered underfoot. His long coat flew behind him as Darius made his way back to Albury Hall. Dusk would soon fall and he must face a night alone in the drawing room and the dining room. He'd avoid the billiards room.

But he couldn't avoid his bedroom.

His fist tightened around the ring box. He didn't have to be alone. If he chose, a man of his means could fill Albury Hall with mistresses, with actresses. Yet he felt no desire to witness any other woman's performance. He wondered if he ever would again.

As he emerged from the woods he crossed the

lawn. The gardens were at their best in the ripe late afternoon sun, with dusky shadows dappling. A single white swan glided on the lake, the picture of elegance with its long neck.

Swans.

Ghosts.

His boots sent the gravel flying in front of the house. He stopped for a moment to admire Albury Hall's perfection, its symmetry. Yet even the sight of his home failed to soothe him.

With a frown he entered and stepped on to the marble that paved the vast hall. Jenkins wasn't at his post. He would bark out a reprimand later.

Darius ran his hand through his hair and chuckled wryly. He might as well admit it to himself. There would be no reprimand to the butler later. He'd hardly barked at his servants since Calista's kiss had taken the bitterness from his veins.

She'd changed him, made him the man he always knew he could be. But it was too late. His swan had taken wing and flown.

His shoulders squared against the emptiness to come, Darius pushed open the door into drawing room.

He bit back his sharp intake of breath.

A woman stood at the fireplace.

An actress.

The only actress he longed to see.

* * *

'Calista.'

Her petticoat swirled as she spun around. Her pulse raced. She hadn't been waiting long, yet each minute ticked out by the gold clock on the chimney piece had seemed an eternity. It had taken all of her courage to come to him.

Hungrily she took him in. At the Coach and Horses she'd been too overcome to study him. Now she saw lines around his mouth, tightly held like a horse's bit, his emotions under control.

He wore the same attire as when they'd walked in Albury's woods together. She knew the scent of that tweed coat. She knew the scent of him.

She struggled to control her yearning to throw herself into his arms. The ache inside her became a sharp pain at the sight of him standing before her. What he'd done for her and her family, the kindness of it. She hadn't been mistaken about the man behind the duke.

He was very much the duke now as he inclined his head in a courteous bow. 'I didn't expect you.'

Her voice shook. 'You disappeared before we finished our business.'

He raised a familiar sarcastic eyebrow. 'Is that so?'

'Yes.' Using all the skill she possessed she steadied her voice. 'Are you still interested in backing the production of my father's play at the Prince's Theatre?'

He narrowed his eyes. 'Whatever else you may believe of me, I don't change my mind about my investments.'

She wove her fingers together tightly as a darn. 'So you're still invested?'

A muscle worked in his cheek. 'Indeed.'

She gulped. 'Then I'd like to discuss the business of putting on one of my father's plays as soon as possible. He's still recovering from his ordeal. I'm here on his behalf.'

'You're here on your father's behalf.' He paused. 'I see.'

She craved to tell him that she was there on her own behalf, that since she'd seen him at the inn she'd yearned to set matters right between them. Yet his austere expression halted such revelations.

He studied her with a hard gaze. 'I see no difficulty in discussing business with you.'

Now her words came. They rushed out like a waterfall. 'I know what you did for my father. That's why I'm here. I came to thank you.'

He brushed her words aside. 'I require no thanks.'

Calista raised her chin. She'd come to thank him and she would. 'Did you truly think I wouldn't want to express my gratitude?'

The duke's eyes shone with intelligence. 'Your father told you more than I wanted you to know.'

The tale had horrified her. 'Yes. He told me the whole story. I know what happened now. You found my father…in a debtors' prison.'

Darius moved swiftly towards her, made to reach out his hand, and then dropped it by his side.

'It wasn't your father's fault. He wasn't to blame.'

Calista steadied herself with a deep breath.

'I understand he made an investment in a theatre company on the promise that his play would be performed. But—'

'But the theatre manager he took up with was the most unscrupulous character,' Darius broke in. 'He left your father with the company's debts.'

'I can't believe my father did such a thing.' Calista shook her head. 'It's unlike him to show such poor judgement. And he was so thrilled at the start. Poor Papa.'

'Desperate times make for desperate acts and can lead to desperate errors. He wanted the play performed in order to provide for you and your sister. Surely you of all people understand.'

'I suppose I do.' Darius's explanation made sense, but it still appalled her that her father had been driven to such actions.

'Don't blame your father. His intentions were

honourable.' His mouth twisted. 'He's a good man. How is he now?'

'He's better, now he's at home. He's suffered so much, but Martha is fussing over him and Columbine is—well, Columbine's reaction is as you'd expect it to be. She's the happiest girl alive.'

'I'm sure your father will make a good recovery in time. Yet I should warn you, the conditions he was found in were almost intolerable.'

Calista gripped her hands even more tightly together. 'He'd still be there, in the debtors' prison, if it wasn't for you. He might have...'

His coat billowed as he moved even closer, then stopped, his fists clenched.

'Your father was found and released in time. Don't think of it.'

Tears choked her throat. 'He told me you paid his debts. How can we ever repay you?'

'There's no need for recompense. I owed you a debt,' he said, his voice low. 'My behaviour towards you did me no credit. The least I could do was to restore your father to you.'

She bit her lip. He'd done it out of a sense of honour, not for any other feelings. 'You didn't owe me that.'

He shrugged. 'I knew you would never stop taking the responsibility for Columbine on your shoulders until your father returned. I could no longer witness your strain on stage—'

Calista jerked her head up. 'Have you been watching the play as well as following me home?'

After a moment he gave a brief nod.

'Every night? But I didn't see you.'

'I watched from the gallery, not from my usual seat.'

'That must have been a sacrifice.' There was a glimmer of amusement in her voice.

'Some sacrifices are worth making,' he said drily. 'And your performances made it worthwhile.'

'I sensed you there,' she said in wonder. 'And on my walks home, even before you rescued me from Lord Merrick—'

'I couldn't let you walk alone,' he broke in.

Her companion.

Her protector.

So she hadn't been mistaken. The sense of him being so near…

'I felt you beside me. I knew you were at my side,' she whispered.

He gave another of his shrugs and his eyes remained down. With soft tread he moved even closer. 'So you sensed my presence.'

Her heart thumped. 'Yes.'

He surveyed her silently.

She broke the hush between them before he could discern the throbbing of her telltale heart. 'I'll take the news back to Covent Garden. May

I tell my father *The Fair Jilt* is to be performed at the Prince's Theatre, then?'

'If you wish.'

She nodded. 'Thank you. It will lift Papa's spirits more than I can say.'

'Will he be happy with the work you completed on his behalf?'

'I think so.'

'Then your name will be in the playbill as playwright and lead actress. I assume you have the main role?'

She shook her head. 'Oh, I won't play the lead.'

'Why not?'

'Now my father's home...'

'You don't need the income.'

'Not any more. I don't have to tread the boards to provide for Columbine.' She took a deep breath. 'Thanks to you.'

His gaze narrowed. 'I sensed your weariness in your performances. No one else would have noticed, I believe, but I did. I knew you needed a rest before you took another role. If your father hadn't returned in time, I would have organised for one of his plays to be put on at the Prince's Theatre in any event. I'd already put Herbert on to it.'

'So you'd have been my benefactor, not just my father's.'

His voice became husky. 'It's not your benefactor I want to be, Calista.'

She bit her lip, hard.

'Tell me,' he insisted. 'Is it solely because of financial reasons that you've given up the stage?'

'It's not for that reason alone.' She took a deep breath. 'You see, I don't want to be an actress any more. Do you remember how you put it, in the woods when we walked there together? My heart isn't in it. Not any more.'

'Where is your heart?' Darius asked.

Calista's heart stilled. She couldn't reply.

He closed the gap between them until they were so close his lips were but a breath from hers.

'Where is your heart?' Darius questioned again, even more intently. 'Where does it belong?'

'Here.' Calista's single word was a sigh. 'I left my heart at Albury Hall. With you.'

Darius pulled Calista to his chest, crushing her against his lips, hot against her forehead, her eyes and her cheeks.

Then her lips.

He tasted the truth on them.

He took her lip gently between his teeth, yearning, needing to know for sure. With equal fierceness she met his question, telling him all he needed to know.

She longed for him.

She yearned for him.

Her heart was his.

At last they sought for air.

Calista took a deep shuddering breath that filled her corset. He felt it against his own chest.

'Tell me something, Calista. If I'd asked you to marry me in the woods, before everything went so wrong, what would you have replied?'

Her sapphire eyes blazed with honesty. 'You'd have won your bet.'

He tangled his fingers in her hair. 'That's what I hoped you'd say.'

'Surely you realised I'd fallen in love with you.'

'When?' he demanded.

She bit her lip. 'I think it must have been your apology when you gave me that awful bracelet.'

He laughed aloud. 'I shall have to continue my habit of apologising to you.'

'Please do,' she whispered with a grin, but not before he saw the flash of quickly hidden pain in her eyes.

A shaft seemed to pierce his heart. 'Calista. That terrible night. To have you in my bed and then to argue—I couldn't explain...' He took a breath. He'd hurt her and he would always regret it. 'I've had time to think about it, too much time. You didn't deserve any of it. Surely it was unforgivable.'

Now her sapphire eyes were grave. 'Not unforgivable.'

He shook his head in a kind of wonder. 'You're a saint. Or some kind of angel.'

'Darius,' she reproved him with a laugh. 'I

played along. Coming to you that night, wearing Mabel's nightgown, it was hardly angelic behaviour. I'm an actress, after all.'

He pulled her closer and whispered in her ear, 'I wouldn't have you any other way.'

He felt her quiver. 'I expect there will always be fireworks between us.'

'I hope so,' he drawled, revelling in the softness of her in his arms. Yet there was strength of character beneath that softness.

'My temper was as hot as yours that night. I left before giving you a chance to explain.'

He tightened his hold. 'You were distressed, in shock.'

She nestled into his arms. 'I misjudged you.'

'We misjudged each other. I judged you by Dottie's behaviour, tarred you with her brush. I'll always regret it. It was beneath me, beneath you.'

'You rescued me from Lord Merrick.'

'I'm as bad as he.'

'No.' She shook her head fiercely. 'You protect the ones you love.'

He smoothed back her hair. 'I wanted to protect you from the moment I saw you in the park with Columbine. I saw you cared so for your sister, yet there was no one to care for you. I yearned to protect you, to keep you safe. Yet I fought it.'

'You've made up for it,' she said gently.

Finding William Fairmont and returning him

to his daughters had been the only way Darius could conceive to show her his feelings, to make an apology with actions, rather than with words. It spoke louder, he hoped.

She didn't know the whole story of the rescue and she never would, he vowed. He would never reveal to Calista the near-starving state her father had been in when he'd been found in the prison, or how much money it had cost to free him. Calista's father had agreed not to tell his daughters. He was a brave man and a good one. It wasn't his fault that he had ended up in such appalling circumstances. It was best to put the episode behind them.

He stood back and let his gaze trawl over her, witnessed her shiver.

'Made it up to you? Not yet, I haven't. But we're going to break the Carlyle curse and be the happiest duke and duchess ever to live at Albury Hall.'

She flushed, her cheeks as pink as when he first met her, and she'd been wearing rouge. There was no need for it, now. The urge blasted through him to see other parts of her turn that rosy. 'Perhaps we can let the curtain fall on the past. Or lift a new curtain.'

'Is that possible?' Her voice was soft, but her eyes held a playful spark of flame.

'You're the playwright. You can make the script as you like it.'

She smiled. 'I can't believe you still came to the play each night in London.'

'Where else would I have wanted to be?' Didn't she understand by now? 'I've listened to you speak lines on stage night after night. I only wanted to hear you say one word.'

She put her fingers to his cheek. 'Is it this word? Darius?'

On her lips his name was a breath of air.

He pulled her close against the hardness of his body again. His desire flared into life. 'Not my name. I asked you a question once before. Do you remember?'

Her mouth a circle, she nodded. 'Of course.'

'Give me your answer,' he demanded. 'Now.'

She raised her eyebrow. 'Is this the proper proposal you promised me, Your Grace?'

'Don't play with me now, for pity's sake,' he ground out. 'I vowed to marry you and I will.'

'And I vowed never to marry you,' she reminded him with a half-smile.

Loosening his hold on her, he took a step back. 'Do you still seek to test me?'

Calista lifted her chin. 'I seek fair play. We both made vows at our first meeting. Yours was to make me your wife. Mine was to be your mistress. Must only you win? Surely we can reach a compromise.'

Darius shook his head obstinately. 'There'll be no compromise. You'll be my wife, Calista, or nothing else.'

The fire flashed in her eyes blue. 'Is that so, Your Grace? This hardly augurs well for conjugal happiness. I wouldn't begin the married state under such a command.'

He ran his hand through his hair. 'Blast it. Is this an act? I tell you, I won't back down.'

Her lips set firm as her chin made the dangerous tilt he'd come to know so well. 'We're in a quandary, then. Nor will I back down. My vow is to be your mistress.'

'Mine is to make you my wife.' He put his finger on her pink lips to soften them. 'Don't you trust me to marry you?'

She took his hand from her lips, laid it against her smooth cheek. 'I trust you with all my heart. I want to show it.'

A muscle worked in his jaw. 'And am I to trust you?'

'Do you doubt me?' She took his hand to her mouth, his fingertip just inside.

'Calista…' He reached for her again with a groan.

She pulled away from him and snapped her fingers. 'Why, I have it. I can be both mistress and wife.'

He clenched his teeth. 'That's impossible.'

'Not at all. If the Carlyle curse can be broken,

why, nothing is impossible.' She laughed aloud. 'I've a way to satisfy both our vows.'

Darius shook his head and groaned. 'What now?'

Mischief lit up her face as Calista curtsied. 'We have one last game to play, Your Grace. May the best player win.'

Calista slid the cue through her fingers.

'Is that your best shot?' Darius drawled from the other side of the billiards table.

Calista righted the cue and surveyed the duke. His eyes glowed black as coal. He'd removed his long coat and wore only his white shirt and dark-brown waistcoat, striped with forest green that matched the baize of the table.

Calista ran her finger along the lacy collar of her dress. Darius had built up the fire in the room before they'd begun to play and the room was warm. She wished women could remove items of clothing as easily as men.

The thought only made her even warmer.

'Can you do better?' she demanded.

He shrugged. 'I play to win.'

Casually he made a shot that struck Calista's cue ball and the red ball.

'That's a cannon,' said Calista reluctantly. 'Two points.'

He bowed his head, yet not before she caught the glimmer of amusement on his face.

'You're beating me,' she said.

'Your honour is at stake,' he reminded her.

'I can take care of my own honour.' Calista gripped her cue and made her next shot. As the balls connected they made a satisfying crack before the red ball entered the pocket.

Darius raised an eyebrow. 'A winning hazard. Three points to you, Miss Fairmont. You continue to surprise me. The last time we played, I didn't realise you were so skilled.'

'I grew up in the theatre,' she reminded him. 'There's a lot of waiting around between performances. I learnt how to play many years ago.'

'Ah. Now I understand why you were so eager to play.'

'It's a fair challenge.'

He raised an eyebrow. 'You're hardly playing fair tonight.'

'But you've agreed to my terms.'

'Just for tonight.' His words made her shiver.

She couldn't tear her gaze away from him as he made his next move. He strolled about the room with his now-familiar easy stride.

She groaned as he made an almost identical shot to hers, making three points. 'Another winning hazard.'

'It seems we're well matched,' he whispered

in her ear as he passed her by. 'It's going to be a long night.'

His breath on the skin beneath her earlobe made her shudder with desire. She forced herself to focus on the game and re-spot, but her next shot sent her cue ball jumping over his.

'Blast,' she muttered under her breath.

His dry chuckle reached her as she crossed the room to where sandwiches and wine were laid out on the sideboard. She picked up another cheese-and-pickle sandwich and bit into it. The relish was particularly delicious and made with local apples, she imagined.

Everything is nicer at Albury, Columbine had declared.

Her sister was right. Calista couldn't believe she was back at the hall, back at the billiards table, playing against Darius as if they did this every night.

'It's your turn,' he said.

Quickly, she swallowed some wine and returned to the game.

She had to focus.

She had to win.

On they played.

The fire burnt low as the clock chimed in the hall outside. Darius built the fire up again.

'We're getting close,' he commented with another half-smile.

Calista bit her lip. At the start of the game

they'd determined that the winner had to reach the usual three hundred points. Already, the duke was in the lead, while she trailed behind.

With every nerve stretched she leaned in and played her next shot.

From behind she heard his low whistle. 'A perfect ten.'

'Is it?'

'Indeed.' Darius pointed. 'You struck the red first before you potted them both. Then you got a losing hazard.'

Calista counted the combination. 'So I have. I must say, I never liked it being called a losing hazard. Surely a winning shot is a winning shot and must be called such.'

'I had no idea you were so competitive.'

His eyes glinted with amusement before he placed the ball in the appropriate place on the table. 'We must continue to play in hand, following your hazard, the type of which I shall not mention.'

He played another shot that made her bite her lip. Her own, played next, kept him still in the lead.

He studied her face and laughed. 'Don't fret.'

She lifted her chin. 'I want to win this game.'

'The stakes are high,' he conceded, as he casually made another cannon.

The tension in the room tautened her every nerve as they continued to play. Her stomach som-

ersaulted as she took the lead. Then on her next
turn she missed a shot.

He frowned. 'Are you too tired to continue?
Would you prefer to concede?'

'What, and have you say you beat me? Never.
This game is mine.'

He waved his hand. 'Then we must play on.'

With every nerve stretched she aimed again.
As soon as the cue connected with the ball she
knew.

'Another winning hazard. My, my. You really
are very good. You ought to have warned me.'

'Do you expect me to give away all my secrets?
Why, you hardly revealed your own skills at the
game. You must be a champion player,' she accused him.

He smiled. 'I too, like to win.'

'You're not going to win tonight.'

He studied her for a long moment before he
made his shot.

It brought their scores equal.

Calista's shoulders slumped. 'Oh.'

He leaned on his billiards cue. 'There's only a
few balls left in it. How far will you go?'

Determinedly she lifted her cue and made yet
another cannon. 'I'm not going to lose, if that's
what you mean.'

'Nor am I.' He took another shot.

Her stomach lurched. It looked like a perfect
ten. Then she peered closer.

'Stop!' She hurried to the table and retrieved the white ball from the pocket. Sure enough, the white globe had no marking. Triumphant, she held it up. 'Your ball was marked with black. You played my cue ball!'

'My, my,' he said. 'So I did. I lost concentration myself for a moment.'

She stared at him suspiciously. His expression was impenetrable. Was it possible he'd done it on purpose?

He prowled around the table. 'It gives you another chance.'

'I'd have to get a perfect ten to win now,' she objected, as her heart began to pound.

'I think you can do it. Here.' He cast aside his own cue and wrapped his arms around her. His hand covered hers. 'Can you feel this?'

'Yes,' she whispered.

He moved the cue back and forth within her fingers. 'And this? Try now.'

The cue shot across the table. The balls cracked as one by one they tumbled into the pockets.

Calista spun inside his arms. 'I've won the game.'

The colour of the duke's eyes darkened to charcoal. 'Indeed.'

Chapter Twenty-One

Let the God of Love
Laugh in thy eyes, and revel in thy heart,
Kindle again his torch, and hold it high,
To light us to new joys.

Nicholas Rowe: *The Fair Penitent* (1703)

Calista laid down her billiards cue. Her stomach somersaulted as she moved around the baize-topped table towards Darius. Her shoes pressed into the thick carpet, making no sound.

'So you concede I've won?' she asked softly.

His expression was impenetrable, the cue still fisted in his grip. 'So it seems.'

'Does this mean I'm the better player?' She couldn't resist teasing him, even as her heartbeat raced so hard it hurt.

He raised an eyebrow. 'That remains to be seen.'

When she reached him she raised her hand to his cheek. 'You know our wager.'

A muscle flared beneath her fingers. 'I do.'

'Let me play the mistress tonight,' she whispered. 'Before I become your wife.'

Their connection stretched between them, vibrating into life.

'For tonight only,' he said at last. 'Those are my terms, as I told you. Just for tonight.'

'Just for tonight,' she echoed softly.

He clenched the cue again in his fist before he laid it across the table. He moved his head so that his breath was hot on her palm.

She gave a sharp intake of her own breath as his lips found her skin.

He reached for her wrist, cuffed it in his fingers. His lips trailed down the inside of her wrist to find her beating pulse.

His dark-blue eyes gleamed black as he raised his head. 'My mistress. Does that mean you're at my bidding?'

Her heart pounded.

'I won the game,' she said boldly, even as his hold on her wrist tightened.

'But this is a new game, isn't it? For you?'

Her body quickened in response to his touch.

'You know it is,' she whispered. 'I want to play it with you.'

Startling her, Darius pulled Calista into his arms. 'We'll play by our own rules.'

* * *

Calista opened the bedroom door.

Darius stood by the fire, waiting for her. He wore his dark-red robe, over his loosened shirt and trousers. His feet were shod in leather carpet slippers.

Her own feet were bare. Her soles pressed softly into the patterned carpet that lay in front of the hearth.

His gaze went first to her feet, then her ankles, then upwards.

She shivered in spite of the heat that came from the fire.

In the bedroom that she'd occupied before, she'd opened the glass doors and paused, momentarily, on the balcony and stared out across the grounds of Albury in the black-velvet sky, lit with stars.

It was there, on the balcony, she'd found it. In wonder she'd lifted it up and run it through her fingers, sleek and soft.

And smiled.

As if in a dream she'd returned to her bedroom. She'd taken off her blue dress. Her corset. Her petticoats. Even her stockings.

Now Darius trailed his gaze over her, as she stood clad only in her chemise. The white-cotton shift was so worn it was almost as sheer as Mabel's nightgown. She hadn't brought anything with her to Albury Hall. Her chemise was all she had to wear for him.

Almost all.

She grew warmer still, as his gaze roamed over her neck, her lips, her hair.

He crooked a smile. 'What's that in your hair?'

She touched it lightly. 'A swan feather. It must be from one of the Albury birds. I found it on the balcony outside my bedroom.'

Sweeping her hair up into a simple chignon, she'd tucked the long feather in the back of it. In the mirror she'd gazed at her reflection. It made her lift her head proudly, made her neck appear longer, more elegant.

He reached out to touch it, too. 'Your feather makes a fine costume.'

'Do you like it?'

'Very much.' His expression became grave. 'This is no play, Calista. You said you want to be my mistress, but you can still change your mind. Are you sure you want to be here with me tonight?'

She nodded, felt the feather move up and down. 'Yes.'

For a moment, as she'd stood on the balcony, she'd hesitated, it was true. But when she'd found the feather, she'd taken it as a sign. And now, with his dark-blue eyes deep with love, she knew she hadn't needed to hesitate.

'It belongs to you,' she said. 'This swan feather.'

'Indeed?' He raised a brow. 'Then do I have your permission to remove it?'

'Don't you want me to wear it?'

He moved closer. 'I'll make use of it to show you how much I like it. Later.'

Her stomach rippled at the idea.

'Loosen your hair,' he said, his voice low.

In silent assent she bowed her head. He took the feather, cast it aside. It floated for a moment, before landing on the floor. Then he freed her hair from its simple knot, sent it cascading over her chemise.

Amidst the loose tendrils he put his hand on her neck, and then trailed his finger down to where the tiny buttons held the cotton together. 'This garment is yours, isn't it? Not Miss Coop's this time. I can tell.'

'How so?'

He brushed a finger over the bodice. 'Its softness.'

'It's my chemise,' she managed to reply as his finger began to circle.

'I prefer it to your previous attire,' he murmured. 'But there's something I believe I'd like to see more.'

'There is?'

'Indeed.' Leaving his finger still resting on the bodice of her chemise, he leaned in. His lips brushed hers. 'There's a part of your body I need to explore, Miss Fairmont.'

'You already checked my feet the first time I was here in your bedroom,' she said softly, still close to his mouth.

His mouth curved. 'That was merely a rehearsal.'

Slowly he undid the buttons of her chemise and slipped his hand inside.

She shivered. Not from the cold, for his fingers were warm, but from the touch of them on the tender point of her breast.

Soft.

Teasing.

Playful.

Then hard.

Just as she felt her body sway with pleasure he moved his hand away from her breast, up to her shoulder.

'This is where your wings would be. If you were an angel, as I suspect you are.' Still with his hand beneath her chemise he swept across to the other shoulder. 'Or here.'

'Perhaps if you need to be sure, you need to use your eyes,' she whispered.

His hand stilled on her skin. 'My eyes. Or my lips.'

He stepped back, surveying her.

Her fingers trembled. She lifted her chin and stood still the way she did on stage. She refused to hide her body from him. From the man she loved. Lifting the cotton hem, she raised her chemise over her head and let it fall away. 'Use both.'

He devoured her with a glance. Without words he told her how much he liked what he saw.

The trembling in her limbs passed. She wanted him to look, she realised in amazement. She pushed her hair back, over her shoulders.

As if from his box at the theatre he watched her.

At last he smiled. 'I was right. You don't have wings, but you're an angel.'

She slipped her hand inside his robe. 'And what are you?'

He released a mocking laugh. 'No angel, I assure you.'

'I didn't expect you to be. But I still want to see you, as you are.'

In reply he shrugged off his robe, tossed it on to a chair. As he'd done with her chemise, she undid the buttons on his shirt until his chest was bare.

His shirt joined the robe, cast aside.

A strange sense of ownership came over her as she put her hand on the place where his heart beat beneath his muscled skin. The feel of him had registered memory in her fingers, as she traced a line down the centre of his stomach.

He stopped her at the buckle of his belt. 'We've been here before.'

'I don't believe I was naked, last time, Your Grace.'

'I wanted you to be.' His voice was hoarse.

'Tell me how much,' she murmured.

'I wanted you more than any other woman I've ever known. I wanted you so much it almost killed me to stop.'

She kept her hand on the buckle. 'Tell me what you planned to do to me.'

He put his mouth close to her ear. 'I planned to eat you up like the wolf in the story.'

She shivered with desire. 'And then?'

'I would make you mine.'

'Tell me how,' she begged, in a voice she hardly recognised, that she'd never used for any role on stage.

'I'll do better than that.' Darius pulled Calista into his arms. 'I'll show you.'

Calista gasped.

She never dreamed it would feel like flying.

That when Darius took her, when everything between them was stripped away, all barriers gone, he would take her so high. That all around them would fall away, as if their surroundings were no more than a stage, as if nothing else was real, except his body, seeking hers. That once the stab of pain when he entered her and found the place deep inside her that she longed for him to find, had passed, the curtain torn, that she would go beyond that pain to find him. To soar higher, to meet him.

Skin. Hand. Lips. Teeth. Inside. Outside.

Her mind dizzied.

Higher. Higher.

He shafted harder, deeper, inside her.

For a moment she tensed. Drew back.

She was too high. Too deep.

His lips, breathed words on hers. 'Come with me, Calista.'

She opened her eyes to his strong and steady gaze.

The swirling in her mind became a current of air.

She lifted to him.

And flew.

Darius watched over Calista as she slept in his arms amidst the white, tumbled sheets, her head resting on his chest.

In the moonlight slanting through the window her skin held the sheen of a pearl.

Beside her lay the swan feather.

His body hardened again. He wouldn't have thought it was possible, to desire her again, so soon, yet he suspected his need for her would never leave him.

Wanting her.

Caring for her.

He'd met his match.

He groaned inwardly. He'd known it, all along, that it would be this way. They hadn't even made it to the bed. He'd made love to her in front of the fire. The first time, gently, light as a feather. He hadn't wanted to hurt her. She'd opened her eyes to him, at the moment he knew she'd joined with him as one. She'd bit her lip.

He'd kissed it.

Afterwards, she'd surprised him.

Darius groaned aloud.

She'd seized the swan feather, played with it. With her lips, her hands, her teeth.

He ran his hand through his hair.

Afterwards he had grabbed the feather and carried her to his bed, where she belonged. Where he wanted her to stay.

Always.

He frowned.

'Darius?' Calista stirred and tilted her head to look at him. 'What is it?'

Calista raised her head from Darius's chest. She'd revelled in the sound of his powerful heartbeat with her ear pressed to his warm skin. 'What kind of problem?'

'I still haven't proposed to you properly. It seems you successfully sidetracked me, Miss

Fairmont.' His tone was light, but she saw the intensity in his eyes. 'I haven't yet given you a ring. And I know exactly the ring I have in mind.'

'You do?' she asked, amazed.

Naked, he strode across the room and retrieved the ring box from his waistcoat pocket before returning to her. 'This one.'

Calista's mouth fell open at the same time as the lid lifted. 'It's so beautiful.'

'It's my mother's ring. The sapphire is as blue as your eyes.'

'It's lovely,' she choked.

He raised her hand to his lips. 'On this hand it will be lovely. I retrieved it from the family vault when I got the ruby bracelet you disliked so much.'

She winced. 'You're not pulling that out next, are you?'

He breathed into her ear. 'It's not what I had in mind.'

She leaned in, let the sheet fall. 'Is that so?'

'Indeed.' His teeth played briefly with her earlobe. 'Now stop distracting me. Let me propose.'

Her heart pounded. 'Hmmm. What will that make me?'

'What do you mean?' He drew back and frowned, half in jest. 'Your title? Is that what you're asking?'

She laughed. 'Don't you trust me yet, Darius?

No, I'm not enquiring about the specifics of my title if I wed you.'

His frown deepened. 'I thought I'd persuaded you to let the curtain fall on my errors of the past.'

'I'm sure you could persuade me of anything,' she said with a grin.

'Then what in the devil are you asking?'

Retrieving the sheet, she sat up straight. 'Well, right now I'm your mistress. If I marry you, I will become your wife. That meets both our wishes. But the moment I agree to your proposal, what will I be?'

'Isn't it obvious? You'll be my fiancée.'

She fell silent, thinking deeply. 'How long do we have to wait to marry?'

'It can take some time. A few weeks, at least. I'll have the banns read at Albury church this very Sunday. I won't delay.'

'A few weeks.' She sighed. 'Oh, dear. I'm not entirely sure that's what I want.'

'You don't want to marry me?' He sounded incredulous. 'We settled this with your game. If you won, you would be my mistress for one night. Then you agreed to become my wife. That way we were both to be satisfied.'

'I'm satisfied,' she replied with a flutter of her eyelashes, 'but I don't think I want to become your fiancée. Not tonight anyway.'

'Blast it, Calista, what are you playing at?' he

said. 'You can't become my wife unless you agree to be my fiancée first!'

'I want to remain your mistress for a while longer, tonight.'

His broad shoulders relaxed. 'Ah. So what you're saying is you will give me an answer, but not yet.'

Suddenly shy, she nodded. Her heart fluttered as if she were taking off into the sky, on wings.

'Then you'll give me the answer I want,' he clarified.

'Don't you usually get what you want, Your Grace?'

He seized her. 'Don't act any more. Tell me. Will your answer be what I seek?'

'Yes,' she whispered. She had accepted his proposal in words, this time.

He covered her hands with his. 'We'll both make vows that will not be broken.'

Calista's heart soared. 'This is my vow. Whatever my title, for as long as I live, I will love you, Darius.'

He smiled as he picked up the swan feather and ran it through his fingers. 'In that case, Miss Fairmont, I believe we have time for an encore.'

Chapter Twenty-Two

Let this auspicious day be ever sacred,
No mourning, no misfortunes happen on it:
Let it be mark'd for triumphs and rejoicings;
Let happy lovers ever make it holy,
Choose it to bless their hopes, and crown
  their wishes,
This happy day, that gives me my Calista.

Nicholas Rowe: *The Fair Penitent* (1703)

The rice flew in the air like wings of tiny white birds.

'Hooray!' shouted Columbine, as she threw handfuls high into the clear blue sky. Her cheeks were as pink as her silk dress and the roses in her hair. 'Hooray!'

Calista laughed and ducked as the rice fell about them as she exited the front door of Albury church with Darius at her side, her hand tucked securely in his arm. Clustered by the church porch, the guests and villagers cheered and called.

'Congratulations, Your Grace!'

'Best wishes to our new duchess!'

With a start Calista realised they were calling to her.

'Duchess…' she murmured.

Darius sent her a sideways smile. His breath fanned her ear as he leaned close. 'I've won the game, I believe. You now have a title.'

'This round goes to you,' she admitted. 'But we have many more games yet to play.'

Darius raised an eyebrow. 'I hope so.'

Calista bit her lip.

He tucked her hand more firmly inside his elbow. 'A title suits you.'

She couldn't resist teasing him. 'I'm sure I can play the part of duchess well enough.'

He tightened his hold. 'The role fits you to perfection. You won't need to act.'

Columbine rushed up to them. 'Oh, Cally! You look beautiful!'

Calista reached down and hugged her. There had been no further attacks for her sister, since their father had returned home. His presence had eased her worry. 'Thank you for being my bridesmaid, Columbine. You did a wonderful job with my lace train.'

The long veil was looped up now to keep the

ancient lace out of harm's way. It was the only part of her wedding attire that had come from the Albury estate. She'd hesitated to wear it, then she'd noted the look in Darius's eye when he mentioned that his mother had worn it. She had recognised that look. Had seen the trace of the lonely boy inside the man.

'I'll be proud to wear your mother's veil,' she'd told him softly. 'It can be my something borrowed. It means your parents are part of our wedding.'

She'd refused, however, the Carlyle jewelled tiara for her hair.

William Fairmont came up behind Columbine. He'd put on weight at last and looked almost his old self, though Calista suspected he'd never entirely put his ordeal behind him.

Her father nodded towards Darius, who responded with an easy smile. The two men had become friends, the playwright and the duke. Something else Calista never expected.

'Columbine is right,' William said. 'You do look beautiful, Calista my dear.'

She pointed to the coronet of feathers that crowned her veil. Her dress, too, had feathers at the neckline and the *décolletage* was embroidered with crystals before it swirled into a full satin skirt, held out by layers of snowy petticoats. 'Fine feathers.'

'It's more than that, Calista,' her father said. 'You're as lovely as your mother was on our wedding day. She'd have been proud of you.'

Calista cleared her throat. Two mothers were missing that day, but somehow she sensed they were near, watching over both of their children's happiness. 'Thank you, Papa.'

Columbine jumped up and down. 'Are you going to throw your bouquet, Cally?'

'Of course.' Her arm released from Darius's grip and she took the posy of orange blossom and white roses in both hands, turned away from the crowd and threw it high in the air. Her diamond-and-sapphire engagement ring with the new gold wedding band beside it flashed in the sun, sent rainbows scattering.

A roar of laughter came from the crowd.

'Oh, my goodness!'

Calista spun to see Martha beaming beneath her best bonnet, the bouquet of roses in her hands.

'Ooh.' Martha blushed. 'I hope it's my turn next, Miss Cally. I mean, my lady. I mean, Your Grace.'

'Do you mean that footman you like to talk to, Martha?' Columbine asked with interest.

Darius chuckled as Martha hushed her.

'Albury Hall is going to be a different place with Columbine there,' he said to Calista.

'A happier place, I hope,' she replied.

In answer he simply took her hand, folded it beneath the wing of his elbow. He, too, wore a wedding band on his left hand, as well as the now-familiar signet ring on his right. 'More than happy. Alive.'

She stared up at the tall, broad-shouldered man beside her. His immaculate grey morning coat and dark-blue waistcoat, a similar deep blue-grey to his eyes, emphasised the broad chest and muscled torso she knew lay beneath.

Her own stomach rippled. It was two months since she'd spent a night in his arms. Their wedding night was worth waiting for, Darius had insisted. And he had refused to give in, no matter how she'd tried to persuade him. To her consternation she'd never again managed to beat him at billiards. She wondered if she ever would. Somehow, she suspected not.

Mabel bustled up the path to the church porch, wearing an enormous bonnet trimmed with yellow-and-red flowers.

Herbert followed behind her. He beamed as he shook Darius's hand. 'Congratulations, Darius, and best wishes to the bride. Who'd have thought it, eh, what? Another Duke of Albury to marry an actress.'

Darius shrugged his shoulders. 'Fate played and won, it seems.'

Mabel squealed. 'Where are you going for your honeymoon?'

Calista shook her head. 'We're staying here at Albury Hall.'

'What?' Mabel's forehead furrowed beneath her bonnet. 'You're not going on a proper honeymoon?'

'I assure you,' Darius drawled, 'it will be a proper honeymoon.'

Calista's stomach rippled with tension again. She smoothed her satin skirt.

'Your dress is so pretty, Cally,' Mabel said. 'Did you go to a London dressmaker?'

'Not exactly.' She glanced briefly at Darius. She hadn't told him yet. 'My dress was made by the costume designer at the Prince's Theatre.'

'It's a stage costume?' Mabel gasped. 'Not a real wedding dress?'

Darius threw back his head and roared with laughter.

Calista grinned. 'It seemed appropriate. I am an actress, after all. Some ghosts needed to be put to rest.'

He met her eyes. 'It's time for us to go.'

On the road outside the church, an open carriage festooned with flowers waited for them. It was an Albury tradition, Darius had explained, for the bride and groom to ride up to the house for the wedding breakfast. The wedding party and guests followed behind, on foot.

More rice flew above their heads.

Calista gave Columbine one last hug before Darius helped her into the carriage.

Martha stepped forward and helped her to remove the lacy veil and wrap her in a white-hooded cloak, trimmed with blue silk ribbons for the short journey. Beneath her petticoats her white stockings were also held up with blue ribbon garters, trimmed with feathers.

'Hooray! Hooray!'

The guests and villagers shouted good wishes as the carriage pulled away. She could hear Mabel protesting about her new shoes getting dirty on the woodland walk as they drove off.

Tears of joy hazed her vision of the countryside as they passed. The flowers in the fields and lanes were in full bloom. In the sunshine, buttercups glistened and cornflowers glowed a vivid blue, and the fields of wheat and barley had turned to bright gold.

A skylark flew overhead as they drove through the gates of Albury Hall and on to the long oak-lined drive. Beyond were the woods, dark and green.

'It's a lovely tradition for wedding guests to walk up from the church to the house through the woods,' she said. 'Why, the church was so full! I didn't expect to see so many villagers and all the servants from the house, too. They're fond of you, Darius.'

He shrugged. 'I didn't see why any should be stopped from attending, if they wished to do so. The preparations are all in hand, I understand. They'll follow behind us, soon enough.'

A wedding breakfast had been prepared in the dining room. Columbine had taken part in many of the festive plans, to her great delight.

Calista smiled.

He gave her a sideways glance. 'Happy?'

'Alive,' she replied, borrowing the words he'd said earlier.

Darius pointed to where three white swans glided on the lake shimmering ahead. 'They've come to greet you,' he said.

Her throat tightened with emotion. She squeezed his hand, ran a finger over his signet ring.

He leaned close and whispered in her ear, 'Swans mate for life, remember? Welcome home, Duchess.'

Daisies dotted the lawns that led up to the house. It looked more like a castle from a fairy tale than ever, with its balconies and turrets, tall columns and central portico. The white front gleamed in the sun.

'Do you remember Columbine said Albury

Hall looked like it was covered in royal icing?' Calista asked.

Darius chuckled. 'All I remember is that you reproached me for the size of my house.'

'Well, it is like something from a fairy tale.'

'It's better than that. It's real life. You belong here,' Darius said. Then he frowned. 'Are you sure you don't want to go to Europe for a honeymoon?'

She shook her head. 'I don't want to go anywhere, except be here with you.'

His shoulders relaxed. 'I wondered.'

'I'll always tell you the truth, Darius. There's no pretence between us now.'

'You won't miss Covent Garden? I could have a theatre built in Albury village, if you desire it.'

She laughed. 'You must stop showering me with gifts.'

'Never,' he vowed.

The carriage wheels crunched on the gravel drive as they drew to a stop in front of the house.

Darius put his hands on her waist to lift her down from the carriage. To her surprise he kept his hold and swirled her into his arms.

'Darius! What are you doing?'

His smile glinted in the sunlight. 'What do you think I'm doing? Carrying my bride over the threshold.'

'You can't carry me!'

'You're as light as a feather.'

As though he carried nothing at all he sprang up the marble steps.

At the black-painted front door he paused. 'Blast. Jenkins is still at the church.'

Calista wriggled. 'You must put me down.'

'Not a chance, my Duchess. I've got you in my clutches at last.'

With one hand he managed to open the door, made it wide enough for them to enter with a kick of his foot.

Inside the vast, domed entrance hall Calista stared up at the ornate ceiling with its swirls of white.

This was her home.

For life.

Still holding her tight in his arms, Darius crossed the chequered floor.

Her heart thudded with happiness. 'Where are you taking me?'

'Where do you think?' His breath met hers as he leaned in for a kiss. 'We're alone.'

Darius swept Calista up the marble staircase of Albury Hall. 'You've played the mistress long enough. It's time for us to play husband and wife.'

Epilogue

*Heaven formed thee, gentle, fair, and full
of goodness,
And made thee all my portion here on
earth:
It gave thee to me, as a large amends
For fortune, friends, and all the world
beside.*

Nicholas Rowe: *The Fair Penitent* (1703)

Some years later

The applause nearly brought down the theatre roof.

'Bravo! Bravo!'

'Miss Fairmont is surely the greatest actress of her generation,' said a woman to another.

'To be sure.' The other woman's bonnet bobbed. 'No one else has ever played Shakespeare's Rosalind so well.'

On stage a dark-haired, slender figure bowed, sweeping her hand to the audience, her wide mouth fixed in a beaming smile as she accepted the call of the crowd.

Darius turned to Calista. 'No regrets?'

'None at all,' she replied softly, as they continued to applaud.

'You're not sorry you gave up acting for writing? I'd never have stopped you performing. You don't secretly wish it was you on the stage?'

'We have no secrets, Darius.'

The glance he gave her brushed over her skin, sending a flame through her body. That he could still create that sensation was something she'd never expected.

Her companion, friend and lover. Three in one. It was possible, after all, to find such a husband, who could be all those things.

'Columbine is marvellous,' she said. 'Better than I ever was.'

He laid a finger on her lips. 'Not so, my love.'

For a brief moment his fingertip caressed the soft flesh of her lower lip before he removed it. 'Perhaps the child you carry now will be the star of the next generation on stage, if we're lucky enough to have a girl this time.'

Calista raised a brow. 'You'd have your daughter be an actress, Your Grace?'

'Indeed. Or a playwright. Perhaps we'll call

her Aphra.' Darius grinned. 'If my daughter is anything like her mother, she'll follow that lady and do whatever she pleases.'

Calista laughed. 'Surely that's a characteristic of the Carlyle male. You're not content with your two sons?'

'I'm content with any family or fortune that comes, as long as my wife is beside me.' The Duke of Albury lifted Calista's hand to his lips. 'You're the star of my stage, Duchess.'

* * * * *

If you enjoyed Calista's story, don't miss Eliza Redgold's enchanting Historical Romance ENTICING BENEDICT COLE.

Historical Note

Actresses and the Aristocracy

Calista's story is inspired by the daring actresses of history who took to the stage and the men who loved them.

Traditionally, from the time women first took to the stage in the sixteenth century, royalty and the aristocracy took actresses as mistresses, but they rarely married them. Ever since women had first performed on the stage, when King Charles II was restored to the throne and reopened the playhouses after Cromwell closed them, the theatres of Covent Garden had been lures for love affairs. It was at the Royal Theatre, one of the first ever built in the Garden, that King Charles watched the actress Nell Gwynne perform and she soon became his mistress.

This became the norm in society, but during the first half of the nineteenth century a so-called 'epidemic' of actresses began to marry into the aristocracy.

You can find out more about these real-life actresses at: *http://regencyromanceworld.blogspot.com.au/2010/10/footlights-and-coronets-regency-romance_27.html*

Heroines and Seducers

The heroine of this story, Calista Fairmont, is named after Nicholas Rowe's heroine Calista in the play *The Fair Penitent*, which premiered in 1702 and was first published in 1703. Calista—which means 'fair' or 'beautiful'—is one of the first acting roles for women in a play that focused on a female heroine and gave women on the stage a starring role. The famous role of Lothario as a male seducer also comes from Rowe's play.

Women Playwrights

Calista's heroine, Aphra Behn (1640-1689) was the first English female playwright. Witty and scandalous, she was said to be a spy and was friends with many actresses of her day, including Nell Gwyn. Virginia Woolf believed that 'all women together ought to let flowers fall upon the tomb of Aphra Behn...for it was she who earned them the right to speak their minds.'

Behn's short story *The Fair Jilt*, the inspiration for Calista's play, is credited with giving the word 'jilt' a more positive connotation for women. Read some of Aphra's words on The Aphra Behn page at: *http://www.lit-arts.net/Behn/*

Stage Costumes through History

Women's clothing in Victorian times was amazing. Just as stunning have been women's stage costumes through time. 'Breeches parts'— when female actresses dressed as men—were often particularly popular with the audience after Restoration times. Check out the range of exquisite costumes actresses wore throughout history via the Victoria and Albert Museum in London: *http://www.vam.ac.uk/content/articles/r/reflecting-historical-periods-in-stage-costume/*

Harlequins and Columbines

An old stage tradition that became part of English pantomime plays was story-telling dances in which Harlequin, a magical character, played the leading role in order to impress his mistress, Columbine. The name Columbine comes from the Italian word for 'dove' and it is also a pretty English flower. You can find out more about the play-acting tradition of Harlequins and Columbines by visiting my website at: *www.elizaredgold.com*

Billiards, Ladies?

It was a surprise to me—and maybe will be to you, too—that women played billiards in the Victorian era. There was a great deal of female popularity for the sport, as both participants and spectators, as some wonderful old paintings reveal.

Victorian Nightgowns

Demure yet playful, this old-fashioned night-wear has a mystique all its own. If you're inspired to wear a nightgown like Calista's—or Mabel's!—visit: *http://www.victoriannightgowns.com/*

MILLS & BOON®

& HISTORICAL

AWAKEN THE ROMANCE OF THE PAST

A sneak peek at next month's titles...

In stores from 19th May 2016:

- **The Many Sins of Cris de Feaux** – Louise Allen
- **Scandal at the Midsummer Ball** – Marguerite Kaye & Bronwyn Scott
- **Marriage Made in Hope** – Sophia James
- **The Highland Laird's Bride** – Nicole Locke
- **An Unsuitable Duchess** – Laurie Benson
- **Her Cheyenne Warrior** – Lauri Robinson

Available at WHSmith, Tesco, Asda, Eason, Amazon and Apple

Just can't wait?
Buy our books online a month before they hit the shops!
visit www.millsandboon.co.uk

These books are also available in eBook format!

0516/04

MILLS & BOON®

The Irresistible Greeks Collection!

2 FREE BOOKS!

You'll find yourself swept off to the Mediterranean with this collection of seductive Greek heartthrobs. Order today and get two free books!

Order yours at
www.millsandboon.co.uk/irresistiblegreeks

516_IG

MILLS & BOON®

Mills & Boon have been at the heart of romance since 1908… and while the fashions may have changed, one thing remains the same: from pulse-pounding passion to the gentlest caress, we're always known how to bring romance alive.

Now, we're delighted to present you with these irresistible illustrations, inspired by the vintage glamour of our covers. So indulge your wildest dreams and unleash your imagination as we present the most iconic Mills & Boon moments of the last century.

Visit **www.millsandboon.co.uk/ArtofRomance** to order yours!

MILLS & BOON®

The Billionaires Collection!

2 FREE BOOKS!

This fabulous 6 book collection features stories from some of our talented writers. Feel the temperature rise with our ultra-sexy and powerful billionaires. Don't miss this great offer – buy the collection today to get two books free!

Order yours at
www.millsandboon.co.uk/billionaires

516_BR

MILLS & BOON®

Why shop at millsandboon.co.uk?

Each year, thousands of romance readers find their perfect read at millsandboon.co.uk. That's because we're passionate about bringing you the very best romantic fiction. Here are some of the advantages of shopping at www.millsandboon.co.uk:

* **Get new books first**—you'll be able to buy your favourite books one month before they hit the shops

* **Get exclusive discounts**—you'll also be able to buy our specially created monthly collections, with up to 50% off the RRP

* **Find your favourite authors**—latest news, interviews and new releases for all your favourite authors and series on our website, plus ideas for what to try next

* **Join in**—once you've bought your favourite books, don't forget to register with us to rate, review and join in the discussions

Visit **www.millsandboon.co.uk**
for all this and more today!

MILLS_WEB